Chapter One

Sweet Pea reclined inside of the steaming hot jacuzzi and lifted his champagne bottle full of Moet in toast.

"To these fine ass bitches, and to crack mutha-fuckin-cocaine!"

His boys shouted and whooped and hollered at his toast. They were all enjoying the good life. Dope had been good to them. Even in the midst of the country's severe cocaine drought, they were fairing better than most. The fact that Sweet Pea had stockpiled nearly a warehouse full of kilos during the good times, had paid off. They were one of the few crews in Ohio, and even the Midwest for that matter, who still had a steady supply of the white bitch. Sweet Pea's foresight, had allowed them to not only take over much territory and many clients, but also to charge those clients more than double what they would normally pay. In some areas, they were even getting three times the normal rate. Life was good.

Sweet Pea grabbed a hand full of ass that belonged to one of the strippers that was walking by the jacuzzi. He and his crew had rented a massive hotel suite, and were blowing money like it grew on trees. And to them it seemed as though it did. Profits from the coca leaf were virtually falling from the sky, and they couldn't spend it fast enough. And so, they found themselves once again hosting a party full

3

of strippers, lighting up cigars with hundred dollar bills, popping bottles of Moet, Grey Goose, and Hennessey, and pouring bottles of Dom P. into the jacuzzi. They were showing out, and spreading the word that they were the niggas to fuck with if you wanted dope. They were the crew to be down with, they were part of the Get Money Boys, and they wanted the world to know that they were indeed, getting money.

Drake and Two Chains were blasting through the stereo speakers, while the sweet smell of cush wafted through the air. The entire room was smokey, and one of the crew members had even changed out some of the regular light bulbs for red ones. They had transformed the normally buttoned down business suite, into a club-like den-of-sin. Get Money Crew members were fucking strippers in just about every room in the suite. While Chocolate, one of the strippers at the party, kept dipping her head below the surface of the hot jacuzzi waters giving Sweet Pea head. He leaned back in the jacuzzi and closed his eyes. He was definitely going to get with her later. She was one of the baddest strippers in the city, and he had been wanting to hit for a minute. Finally, he had her where he wanted her, and he was going to slay her something good before the night was over with.

Savion 'Sweet Pea' Jones was one of Columbus, Ohio's biggest drug dealers. He had been dealing drugs since the age of twelve, and had come up in the mean, hard, cold streets of Columbus. He had been a bastard child, fathered by one of his mother's johns. He never knew his father growing up, and never gave a second thought about it. The only thing he knew was the streets, and they were his first and only true love. It was the *only* love that his now deceased mother ever passed on to him. His love of the streets, and every aspect of street life. It was what made him into the cold, hard, son-of-a-bitch that he was today. And he thanked her every second of the day for making his life a living hell. It was that toughness, and lack of any real love, that turned his heart callous. And it was that lack of love that allowed him

4

to become one of the most brutal drug dealers on the streets of Columbus to date. And now, he was rich.

Chino climbed inside of the hot tub with another one of the strippers, and gave Sweet Pea a hi-five. He too, was enjoying life, and all of the good fortune that the drug game had brought his way.

"We living it up, baby!" Sweet Pea declared.

Chino lifted his own bottle of Moet. "Like we knew we would."

Chino was Sweet Pea's main man. He had been his ace since back in the day. They both grew up in the same neighborhood, and many nights, Sweet Pea found himself on the couch of Chino's mother's house. Chino was like the brother he never had.

Chino clasped a stripper's hand as she strolled by, and pulled her into the hot tub.

"Ahhh!" she shouted.

The majority of the strippers in the suite were in g-strings, while some still retained their bras, most had already gone topless. Several of the strippers were from Columbus' famed Dollhouse Strip Club, while others came from The Centerfold Club. The majority of them were from a new strip club called Chi-Chi's. It was the latter where all of the tatted up, big booty strippers came from. It was a hood strip club that catered to dope dealers and hood cats looking for juicy Nubian sized booties.

Trap peered across the room at her girl, Vendetta, and gave her a nod. The two of them were dressed in heels, with fish net stockings, and tight black leather clothing. It was time.

Vendetta reached into her purse and pulled out a small, fully automatic Mac-11 sub-machine gun. She also pulled out a silencer of equal length, and screwed it onto the tip of the barrel. Across the room, Trap did the same.

"What the fuck you doing?" one of the guys asked.

"I'm about to get the *real* party started," Trap said with a sinister smile. She lifted her weapon, squeezed the trigger, and put a bullet between his eyes. He dropped to the floor instantly.

It took several moments before anyone else in the party noticed anything. The loud music, smoky haze from all of the marijuana, and the drunken celebratory stupor that they found themselves in, lent little to the party goers sense of awareness. It was just how Trap and Vendetta had planned it.

Trap turned and worked her side of the room, while Vendetta worked her side. They quietly, and efficiently put bullets in the heads of each member of the Get Money Boys that they came across. It took several moments before some of the strippers realized what was happening and broke into panic stricken screams. By then, it was too late. Trap and Vendetta had eliminated most of the crew members, leaving only Sweet Pea, Chino, and Binky in the hot tub.

"Will you bitches shut the fuck up?" Vendetta shouted.

"What the fuck is going on?" Sweet Pea shouted. He rose from his seat in the jacuzzi, pushing away the head of the stripper who was sucking him down.

"Sit your five dollar ass down, before I make change!" Trap shouted. She trained her weapon on him.

Sweet Pea raised his hands, and re-seated himself. "What, is this a jack? You hoes want more money? Is that it? You ain't talking about nothing! Sweet Pea will give it to you, all you had to do was ask. Rocko!"

"Rocko is dead," Vendetta told him. "And so is Stone Cold, so is Demetrius, and so is Prentice, and the rest of your boys."

Sweet Pea peered around the room, taking in the scenery. Through the dim red lights and the smoky haze, he spotted several of his crew on the floor. Strippers were cowering in the corners whimpering.

"What the fuck is this?" Sweet Pea shouted.

"Somebody wants to have a word with you," Trap told him.

The door to the suite swung open, and Peaches and several of her

men strolled inside. Peaches held in her hand a nine millimeter
Beretta with a silencer attached to it.

"Peaches!" Sweet Pea shouted. "What the fuck is this? You done
crossed the line, baby girl. Naw, with this one here, *you done crossed
the line!*"

Peaches smiled, walked to the jacuzzi, and twirled her finger
inside of the warm water. She stared at the three strippers, and nodded
for them to get out. The three women shot out of the water like a
dolphins at a Sea World show. They raced to the corner where the
other women were gathered, and huddled with them.

"You on your period, Sweet Pea?" Peaches asked.

"What the fuck are you talking about?" Sweet Pea asked.

"I'm talking about all of this blood in the water," Peaches told
him.

Sweet Pea stared at the water, wondering what she was talking
about. Peaches pointed her weapon at Binky and squeezed the trigger.
A muffled puff sounded, and a hole appeared between Binky's eyes.
He slid into the water, filling the jacuzzi with the blood that was
pouring from the hole in his forehead.

"Fuck!" Chino shouted. He stood up out of the bloody water.

"Sit your bitch ass back down!" Vendetta shouted. She pointed
her weapon at Chino.

"You're going to kill me anyway!" Chino shouted.

"You don't know that," Peaches told him.

Chino shifted his gaze toward Binky, and then back at Peaches.
He nodded. "Yeah, you gonna kill me. You have to. You know this
shit ain't gonna ride."

"You fucked up, Peaches!" Sweet Pea shouted. "Get Money Boys
is gonna have your ass strung up on a telephone pole!"

Peaches shook her head and smiled. "Ain't nobody worried about
your little hood click."

Chino shook his head. "You just started a war. A war you know you can't win. The Get Money Boys is the deepest crew in Ohio. Not to mention the fact that Kharee ain't gonna like this shit."

"I'm counting on it," Peaches said. She lifted her weapon, and put a bullet in Chino's stomach.

"Got dammit!" Chino cried out. He clasped his bloody stomach. "Bitch! You sorry ass, bitch! I should have fucked you and left you in the dumpster!"

Peaches shrugged. "And now it's you, who's going to be found in a dumpster."

"Don't cross the line, Peaches!" Sweet Pea shouted, lifting his hand to stop her.

"Wait!" Chino shouted, also lifting his hand.

Peaches smiled, and squeezed the trigger on her weapon twice, putting two bullets into Chino's chest. He flew back against the wall, and then slid into the already bloody hot tub.

"Peaches, what the fuck are you doing?" Sweet Pea shouted. "What the fuck is going on, Baby Girl?"

"I'm not your baby girl," Peaches told him.

"Okay, what is this for?" Sweet Pea asked, swallowing hard. "What do you want? You want the Ave, you can have it. You can have it tonight. You want the action around the college, you can have that too."

"I just took it," Peaches told him.

"Peaches!" Sweet Pea shouted. "Don't start a damn war with Kharee, and Get Money! You know you can't win!"

Peaches shrugged. "I can try."

"Kharee will wipe you off the face of the Earth," Sweet Pea told her. "You don't have enough soldiers to handle Get Money, let alone Kharee. Let me smooth this over for you. We'll say it was all just a misunderstanding."

"The only misunderstanding, is that you don't understand what's about to happen," Peaches said with a smile. "I'm not only taking The

Ave, and everything around University, but everything else you own. All your traps, all your spots, all your corners, all your businesses, everything. And then, I'm taking out Big Meech, and taking all of his shit. And then Skinny, and all of his shit. And then Bug, and all of his shit. And then Poocus, and all of his shit. And then, After I have Columbus, I'm going to take the rest of Ohio."

Sweet Pea shook his head. "It'll never happen, Baby Girl. The Get Money Boys are gonna wipe you off the map. And Kharee is going to eat what's left of you."

"Too bad you won't be around to see it," Peaches told him.

"Fuck you!" Sweet Pea shouted.

"No, fuck you," Peaches told him.

She lifted her weapon and aimed it toward Sweet Pea. Before she could pull the trigger, she heard several muffled pops erupting to the right of her. She quickly turned to her right to find Vendetta's Mac-11 still smoking.

"Fuck that mutha fucka!" Vendetta said, still scowling at Sweet Pea's bullet riddled body. "He used me up when I was fifteen. He let his boys use me. I was drunk. Young, dumb, and drunk."

Vendetta squeezed the trigger once again, sending more bullets flying into Sweet Pea's body, causing it to jump.

Peaches nodded. She turned toward the strippers in the room. "All you hoes that work at my club, collect the ID's of the bitches who don't. All of you bitches who don't work for me, drop your driver's licenses on the floor. I want to know who all you hoes are, where you live, and how I can track your asses down. You snitch, you die, your babies die, your momma dies, your daddy dies, your brothers, your sisters, your cousins, your niggaz, and even ya muthafuckin gold fish if ya got one. I'm killing grannies, aunties, and the whole fucking family, understood? You wasn't here, and you didn't see shit."

Peaches turned and walked out of the suite.

"You bitches heard her!" Trap shouted. "Drop out! I want all

9

y'all ID's!"

Outside, Peaches climbed inside of her brand new white Range Rover. "To the crib."

Her driver nodded.

She took in the scenery as she left the motel parking lot. She was on her way. She had just gotten rid of one of her biggest obstacles to taking over the city. Sure, it would start a war with the Get Money Boys, but that was only if they found out who offed Sweet Pea. They would blame somebody else initially. Niggaz never thought that a female could be capable of being ruthless and handling shit. It was their stupid ass fault for being so chauvinistic. They would be caught up fighting and blaming each other, while she would be bumping their asses off and taking over the city. Columbus was her goal. She had to take all of Columbus, and take it quick. She had basically lied to The Commission and made them think that she already had all of the city under her control. And now, she had to make good on that lie. Columbus was the key. It was the key to getting big, and the key to being able to take the rest of the state. Taking Columbus would give her the soldiers she needed and the money she needed to battle Kharee, her biggest enemy. She knew that he was waiting in the wings to fuck her up, and to take her seat on The Commission. Darius had given her the heads up on the whole situation. The vote had been too close for comfort. Most of The Commission wanted to offer the Ohio seat to Kharee in the first place. It was only because of the Reigns family's backing that she got the nod instead. And so now, she couldn't fuck up. Not one teenie, tiny little fuck up. Or else, she'd be floating in the Ohio river. She knew that for sure.

Chapter Two

Peaches strolled across the marble floors of her two story foyer into her family room. She was back at her mansion in Dublin, Ohio, about to go over her next move with her girls, Vendetta and Trap, and her right hand man, One-Eyed Omar. The three of them were waiting for her at her kitchen/family room snack bar.

"Why you always eating up my shit, Omar?" Peaches asked.

Omar was seated on a bar stool, hunkered over a bowl of Frosted Flakes. "Get off my ass, Peaches."

"Damn, nigga!" Peaches said smiling. "Eat up your own shit. You act like we still at the trap and you still thirsty."

"Not thirsty," Omar said in his gruff, raspy voice. "Hungry, ma. Don't get the two twisted."

Omar was one of Peaches most loyal friends. They had been friends since the playground days while growing up in some of the poorest projects in Columbus. The long scar that ran down the side of his face, was something he got while being tortured by a rival drug dealer, who wanted him to set Peaches up. The dealer had run a Skill Saw down the side of his face, opening up one side of his head. The blade from the saw had ran down his face and across his left eye temporarily damaging his vision on that side, thus giving him his nickname, One-Eyed Omar. He was sometimes called Black Ass Omar as well, in reference to his dark complexion. Whichever name others chose to call him, one thing was certain, he was known to be a violent, sadistic killer.

"Whatever, boy!" Peaches said, waving him off. She strolled to her fridge, pulled out a can of soda, popped the top, and turned it up.

"Who work was that?" Omar asked, peering over at Vendetta.

"What are you talking about?" Vendetta asked.

"Sweet Pea," Omar said, still hunched over his bowl of cereal, slurping.

"Both of us," Vendetta said.

"Ahhh," Omar said smiling. "That's what I'm talking about. The two of you working together. I knew that you two working together could produce *explosive* results."

Trap rolled her eyes. "Not in a million years."

Omar laughed. "You gone get up on this magic stick one day, gurl."

"Not if you were the *last* nigga on Earth," Trap told him.

"Don't nobody want to fuck your old trash can dick!" Vendetta added.

"Both of y'alls!" Omar smiled.

"Will you stop fucking *slurping!*" Peaches told him. "You know that shit gets on my nerves!"

"I eats cereal like I eats pussy," Omar said, winking at Peaches. He peered up at Trap and Vendetta and stuck his tongue inside of his bowl of cereal and lapped up some milk. "I slurp that shit!"

"Not in a million years," Trap said shaking her head.

"Only in your *wildest* dreams," Vendetta told him.

Omar let out one of his trademark sinister laughs.

"So, where the fuck you been?" Peaches asked.

"Up north," Omar told her.

"Up North?" Peaches asked, placing her hand on her hip. She sat her soda can down on the counter in front of Omar. "What the fuck you doing up North, when I need your ass down here?"

Omar wiped his mouth on his sleeve, and sat up straight. "You don't need me. I taught you everything you need to know. 'Sides, you got Laverne and Shirley over here."

"Fuck you, black ass motherfucka!" Vendetta told him. She shoved the back of Omar's head.

"I got your Laverne and Shirley," Trap said, pointing between her legs.

"That's what I'm talking 'bout!" Omar smiled. "Give that shit up!"

Trap shot him the finger, and then seated herself on the couch. She leaned back, lifted the remote to the television, and turned it on.

"Can we fucking focus for one minute?" Peaches asked.

"Focus?" Omar said leaning back and frowning. "What the fuck you wanna focus on? You off'ed Sweet Pea, that shit is done. What's it to focus on? The time to focus was *before* you made that move, Sweetheart. Don't try to think shit through now."

"So what are you saying?" Peaches asked. "You saying it was a bad move?"

"What do you think?" Omar asked. He pointed out the window. "It's only a matter a time before muahfuckas start putting two and two together. Then, you gonna have them Get Money Niggaz beating down ya door, and you gonna have Kharee after ya ass."

"We agreed to off those mothafuckas!" Peaches shouted. "Now you growing soft on me? Don't go soft on me now, Omar!"

"That's not even in my vocabulary!" Omar told her. "Yeah, we agreed that's what needed to be done, but not now. Not yet. You wasn't big enough for that move yet, Peaches. You don't have the niggaz to make moves like that yet. You said you was gonna wait and give me some time. I need to get up with my manz and 'em, and my boys from New York, and my niggaz up state. Why'd you have to go and jump the gun?"

"It was a once in a lifetime chance to catch that fool slipping!"

"Once in a lifetime?" Omar raised an eyebrow. "Who you think you talking to? That nigga is slipping everyday of the week, and twice on Sunday. We could have gotten at that fool anytime."

"Not like this," Peaches countered. "This shit was perfect."

"Perfect?" Omar huffed.

"He wanted to party with some bitches, and he slipped up by reaching out to my people for some girls," Peaches explained. "He got caught with his pants down, and I mean that shit literally!"

Omar allowed himself a half smile. "And now? Now, you just put everybody on guard. They eying each other with suspicion. And Kharee, he ain't gonna go for that shit. Sweet Pea was one of his top money makers. And what about Marquez and them Get Money Niggaz? You think they gonna just let this shit ride?"

"They don't know shit!" Vendetta said, jumping into the conversation.

"Fuck them niggaz anyway," Trap added.

"Yeah?" Omar said, turning toward them. "And who's gonna take on them four hundred plus niggaz from Get Money? You, Cagney? You think you and Lacy over here gonna take out four hundred pissed off niggaz coming through the door at two in the morning?"

"Bring 'em on," Vendetta said with a smile.

Omar nodded. "Yeah, that's real brave of you, Sweetheart. Real brave."

"You scared?" Trap asked.

"Y'all using words that ain't even in my vocabulary," Omar told her.

"Nobody knows who hit Sweet Pea," Peaches told him. "They'll be blaming it on each other. And while they're looking one way, we'll be coming up on their ass from behind."

14

"That's all well and good," Omar said, rising from his seat at the bar. He walked to the refrigerator, where he opened the door and pulled out a beer. "But what happens when they *do* find out? You not big enough for this yet. The goal was to get big first. Big enough to handle the big fish. And then, you take out the little starving fish after their master Kharee is dead."

"Or, how about we take out all of the muthafuckas in Columbus, take over Columbus, and then take over Dayton, Cincinnati, Cleveland, Akron, Youngstown, Toledo, and the rest of this bitch. And then we use soldiers from all those spots, and then we wipe Kharee's ass off the face of the Earth!" Trap said forcefully.

"And he'll see you coming from a mile away," Omar explained. He jabbed at the air like a boxer. "You telegraphing your punches. You never want to do that. You never let 'em see it coming."

"It ain't like he don't know what's up," Peaches declared. "He wants me dead, and I need his ass to be very dead."

Omar nodded. "Exactly. You want to cut the head off the chicken. You cut the head off, and the rest of the body dies."

"I don't have that kind of time," Peaches said. She walked to the wall of windows and peered out into the backyard at her swimming pool.

Omar smiled. "Everything that's shiny ain't gold. I told you to leave that bullshit alone. You wasn't ready for it yet. But now, you had to run your ass down to Texas and play the big wig. You had to act like you was the big fish. And now, they expecting you to *be* the big fish."

"I can take this shit over," Peaches said softly. "All of it."

Omar drank from his beer, and then sat it down on the counter. He walked up behind his friend, pulled her close and kissed her on top of her head. "I know you can, ma. But the question is, do you have enough *time*? You put yourself in a tight situation. And now, you trying to hurry and do some shit that you fronted on, like it was a done deal. And when you hurry up, you make mistakes. And when you make mistakes in this business, people die."

Peaches elbowed Omar in his stomach.

"Umph," Omar cried out, and clasped his stomach. "What the fuck was that for?"

"For being so damn right all the time!" Peaches said angrily.

"I still say we kill these muthafuckas, and we take Columbus first!" Vendetta said.

Omar smiled and pointed at Vendetta and Trap. "Ya little Monster High dolls wanna terrorize the whole city."

"Fuck you, you black ass bitch!" Vendetta told him.

Trap laughed.

Omar shrugged. "The die has already been cast, ma. You already made the first move. You shot the opening salvo in this war."

"And now what?" Peaches asked.

Again, Omar shrugged. "And now, events have to take their course."

Peaches shook her head. "I don't let events control me. I control me. I make my own destiny."

"Then it is what it is," Omar said. "You have no choice now. You take Columbus. You take over Sweet Pea's shit, you get his men to bow down to you. You roll them in, and then you go after the next muthafucka."

"Which is?"

Omar thought about the big time dealers in Columbus for a few seconds, trying to think which one would be the most beneficial to take out next.

"Big Meech," Omar told her.

"Big Meech!" Trap shouted. "I thought you was gonna say Bug, or that bitch ass Poocus. Why Big Meech?"

"Because, he's the strongest," Omar told them. "You got enough men to take on Meech. And you can get him, and you can take over

16

his shit, and get his men to roll with you, then you're cooking with Crisco."

"What do you mean *you*?" Peaches asked. "You me *'we'* don't you?"

Omar let out a half smile.

Peaches shook her head frantically. "Uh-un! Don't you do this to me! You are *not* going to pull this bullshit on me! You are going to help me, you understand?"

"You don't need me," Omar told her. "You got Wonder woman, and Zena The Warrior Princess over there."

"Let me shoot him?" Trap asked. "Can I?"

Omar smiled and shook his head. "Baby gurl, you ain't cut like that."

"One day, Omar," Vendetta said nodding and staring at him. "One day..."

"One day, you're gonna give me some pussy," Omar told her in his raspy voice. "That's about all that's gonna happen one day."

Trap and Vendetta had to smile. Both knew that Omar was a true killer. He was scared of nothing, and no one. He had been shot multiple times, beaten and tortured by NYPD, survived a shootout with Detroit SWAT, and was one of the most feared men in all of Ohio. One Eyed Omar was a street legend in the Midwest, and on the East Coast as well. It was no secret that the only woman he ever truly loved had been gunned down by Detroit SWAT while they were in their teens. And he had never truly had a real girlfriend ever since. They both knew that his sexual advances were just that, sexual. No one could ever be Omar's woman, besides, both of them had men of their own. But still, it was thought that Omar *did* have another true love. She was standing in the window and staring out into her backyard. But neither he nor his unspoken love, ever spoke about their feelings for one another. They claimed one another as brother and sister, but everyone around them could clearly see how they felt about each other.

"Big Meech," Peaches said, nodding solemnly. She turned to her girls. "Trap, you want this one?"

"With pleasure," Trap said, with a sadistic grin.

Omar returned to the counter, where he lifted his beer and drank from it. "I guess it's farewell to Big Meech then."

The four of them broke into laughter.

Chapter Three

Kharee swung his golf club as hard as he could, sending the tiny white golf ball flying across the fairway. He always golfed when he was angry. And today, he was beyond pissed. His biggest drug mover in Columbus had been murdered in a motel suite, and not one single witness could be found. He knew that it was all bullshit. And he suspected that the Columbus Police Department was either covering it up, or directly involved. But either way, he thought it impossible that twenty niggas could be murdered in a motel suite, without a single witness, and without anyone hearing a single thing.

"Calm down," Bug told him.

"Fuck that!" Kharee told him.

It was *his* money at stake. Already, his enemies were moving in and eating up the territory that Sweet Pea had left behind. And his enemies didn't score from him, they scored from that bitch over in Dublin. That fucking street slut, that had fucked her way to the top. Who the fuck did she think she was, he wondered? Who the fuck was *she* to actually try to take over an entire city? An *entire fucking city*! And then the bitch had the nerve to think that she was going to run all of Ohio? She was a fucking mattress, a cum dumpster, a fucking dumb ass video chick with tattoos and gold teeth. Nothing more than a glorified hood rat, and she had the nerve to think that she was going to take *his* shit from him? She had the nerve to think that she was going to run Ohio? No, Kharee said, shaking his head. That bitch had another thing coming. And he knew that somehow, someway, she had a hand in Sweet Pea's death. Already, her people were picking over the bones of Sweet Pea's empire. They were moving in on his street corners, they were taking over the dealers that Sweet Pea supplied, they were taking over his clubs, his car washes, his dry cleaners, his hood stores, his restaurants, his bail bonds. They were already running his wife and kids and all of his loyal people out of town. She was worst than a fucking buzzard. She was the ultimate thirsty hoe, one without shame, without remorse, without any scruples. If she was willing to open up her pussy for every big time dope dealer to bust a nut in, then she was willing to do anything. On the cool, he thought the bitch a snitch and an informant. How the fuck every nigga you get with, gonna end up dead or in prison? She had to be a set up chick. The ones she couldn't set up for the kill, she set up so the feds could do her dirty work.

"Scandalous bitch!" Kharee shouted. He hated her more than anything else on the planet. And he wanted her dead. Not as soon as possible, he wanted her dead *yesterday*.

"Man, what's up?" Bug asked.

"What the fuck you mean, what's up?" Kharee asked. "Somebody blew Sweet Pea's dick off, and you acting like ain't shit happened!"

"Man, fuck Sweet Pea!" Bug said. "And congratulations to the muthafucka who killed that bitch!"

Kharee shook his head. He had forgotten that Bug and Sweet Pea were rivals. He supplied both men, and he was cool with both men, but that didn't mean that they were cool with each other. Perhaps he was even golfing with Sweet Pea's killer at that very moment. The possibility that Bug had actually bumped off Sweet Pea wasn't too far

20

fetched. If anyone was going to pull off a sneaky hit like that, it would have been Bug, or even Poocus. Big Meech wasn't subtle. He would have gone in with guns blazing, and been talking plenty of shit about doing it. So that ruled him out. But how could Bug have done it? However it was done, he knew that it involved bitches. And using bitches, was definitely Bug's M.O.

"What the fuck was all them niggas doing up in a room, with drank, and blow, and bud, and chilling in a fucking jacuzzi?" Kharee asked. "Twenty niggas, and no bitches? Sweet Pea was many things, but a punk wasn't one of them. He wasn't having no sausage festival."

Bug smiled. "The nigga might a been a punk. You know how them pretty ass yella niggas is. They go all ways."

"Naa," Kharee said, shaking his head. "Na, this was a set up. An old fashioned honey trap. There was some bitches in that room. I know that. The question is, why ain't none of them hoes come forward?"

Bug placed his ball on his tee. He moved in closer, and began to tee up. Kharee caught his iron in mid swing. "What the fuck?"

Kharee stared at bug with a fury on his face that would have made Jason from Friday The 13th run and hide.

"Sounds like a hit that an old school pimp nigga would pull off," Kharee said, gritting on Bug.

Bug started stuttering. He had a couple of men out on the golf course with them. But they were completely outnumbered by the twenty men that Kharee had on the golf course. This, and the fact that Kharee was built like the Incredible Hulk and could beat him to a pulp caused Bug to develop a slight lump in his throat.

"I didn't do it!" Bug protested. "I wish I would have, but I didn't kill that nigga. Why you tripping? Fuck Sweet Pea!"

"Sweet Pea made me a lot of money," Kharee told him.

"I don't make you a lot of money?" Bug asked.

Kharee released his golf club and nodded slowly. "Yeah, but,

21

loosing Sweet Pea was a big hit to my pocket. Are you gonna make up for the money I lost because somebody took it upon their self to off him?"

Bug lifted his eyebrows. "Kharee, you don't have any dope as it is! But once shit gets back rolling again, I'm down. I'm sure I'll be able to make up for some of it."

And Bug had just reminded him of his biggest problem. He was running out of supply, and running out of it fast. That deal with The Commission would have re-started his supply. But those ignorant ass fools chose to deal with that hot back bitch down in Columbus. But they were going to see what a mistake they made when they chose her over him. And they were going to see how stupid they were once she tried to move against him, and he sent her body to their next meeting in a fifty gallon drum.

He needed her spot on The Commission. He needed the reliable supply of drugs that membership brought. He also needed their political protection, he thought. But the one thing that he didn't need, was their soldiers. He had enough soldiers on his own. Plus, he had Marquez and those stupid ass Get Money Boys under his thumb as well. He would deal with The Commission if they stepped foot in Ohio, just like he was going to crush that little trick they chose to take over the state.

"You can make up for some of my loses right now," Kharee told him.

Bug took a step back. He was unsure of Kharee's meaning. Was a friendly golf outing about to turn into a kidnapping for ransom, he wondered?

"What are you talking about?" Bug asked.

"Why are you letting that bitch take over all of Sweet Pea's shit?" Kharee asked.

"You don't think Lil Momma had the nuts to pull off something like that?" Bug said with a derisive smile. He was an old school pimp

22

turned dope dealer. He had little respect for women. He thought them all weak, and easily influenced. "Sweet Pea thought with his dick, but he would've never let a broad get with him like that."

"You underestimate that hoe," Kharee told him. "Why is she picking up all the pieces?"

"Cause she's a chicken head, and that's what bitches like her do," Bug said, reverting to his old pimp voice. "They wait around, and scavenge, like hoes should. No, it was a lion who made that kill, not no buzzard ass bitch."

"You don't watch National Geographic much, do you?" Kharee asked.

"I know all I need to know about nature," Bug told him. "For one, I know that pimpin, is in my nature."

Kharee cracked a smile. Dumb ass, he thought. "What you apparently don't know, is that in the jungle, it's not the lion that makes the kill. It's the bitches. The lioness' make the kill, and then the lion comes in and eats."

"Like a true pimp should," Bug said nodding. "You let the bitches do the work."

"The moral to the story is, don't dismiss that hoe so quickly," Kharee said, peering off into the distance. "Scandalous ass bitches are killers too."

"She's a hoodrat," Bug said, waving his hand and dismissing her. "She let them weak ass niggas fall into that good pussy and fall weak. The first time a real nigga steps in and taps that, she's gone fall back into place."

"We don't want her to fall back into place," Kharee said. "And we don't want no real nigga to step in and take over. I want that bitch dead. I want her whole organization folded. I am the king of Ohio, and that bitch is in the way."

"In the way of what?" Bug asked.

Kharee shook his head. Bug was a dumb ass old school nigga,

and he would never understand The Commission, or what type of money was really at stake. He thought in terms of millions, and always would. He was a Cadillac nigga, not a private jet type of nigga. His idea of the good life, was running dope, owning his barber shop, his bail bonds, his barbecue shack, and all his other little nigga businesses in and around the hood. Like so many other hood niggas, he lacked vision.

"Let's just say I want her out of the way," Kharee continued. "And I want you to help me do it."

"You want to spank that hoe, then spank her," Bug told him. "You don't need nobody to help you with that."

Kharee knew that she would see him coming from a mile away. And he didn't need to start a bigger war than necessary right now. She was still considered Chesarae's girl, and Chesarae was still considered the top dog in that stupid ass Young and Holding Hustlers crew. And he didn't need a war with her, and with Young and Holding, along with Chesarae's boy's in Detroit, Dayton, and Youngstown. No, he needed it to appear to be a local hit, because of a local beef. Two muthafucka's from Columbus going at it over the turf of a dead dope dealer, that's what he wanted it to look like. It would also keep The Commission from coming in to the situation. They chose her, and for him to step in and try to knock her ass off, probably wouldn't sit well at this time. He had to play things smart for right now. And so, he would let Bug do his dirty work.

"I want you to pick up the pieces that Sweet Pea left behind," Kharee told him.

"I can't eat from that carcass," Bug declared.

"Why not?"

"With all the bad blood that me and Sweet Pea had?" Bug declared. "His boys would rather shoot me, than buy from me. Besides, them Get Money Boys is way outta line. I don't deal with youngsters like that."

Kharee waved his hand, and his men raced toward him in his golf cart. He turned to Bug.

"Make it happen," Kharee told him. "Pick up the pieces. Do whatever you have to do. Besides, that bitch is taking care of Sweet Pea's dudes. All you have to do, is take it from her."

"What do you have against this broad?" Bug asked. "She's just a little old broad who is holding down a spot for a nigga who ain't never getting out. She's nothing."

"Just do it!" Kharee told him.

Bug shrugged. "This chick is going to run home scared the first sign of trouble. You making a big fuss about nothing."

Kharee climbed inside of his golf cart.

"You spank this bitch real good, and I'll make it worth your while the next time you score."

"Bet!" Bug said with a smile.

"Bet!" Kharee told him. He tapped the seat of the driver, and his golf cart sped off. He leaned back in the seat of the cart, and a smile slowly spread across his face. He had just started a war in Columbus. He knew that The Commission wouldn't like that. Even better, if Bug managed to pull it off and kill the bitch, he would be offered the Ohio seat on The Commission without lifting a finger or getting his hands dirty. It would also prevent a war with Young and Holding, a wild ass group of young killers that he didn't want any part of. Yeah, he felt like the puppet master. He was pulling the strings of a bunch of idiots who hadn't the slightest idea about what he was making them do.

Chapter Four

Peaches and her girls stepped up into the infamous Club Ice and headed straight for their reserved spot in the VIP section. It was jumping off tonight, as Two Chainz was in town, and rumor had it, that Drake was going to make an appearance as well. Everybody who was anybody on the Columbus baller scene was in the house. Peaches slid into her private booth in the rear of the club.

"This shit is jumping!" Trap shouted over the loud music.

Vendetta nodded in agreement.

The three of them were dressed in all white, as were the rest of their entourage. It was a trend started by Peaches' ex boyfriend, Chesarae, back in the day. Every member of Young and Holding would wear white whenever they stepped out to the club, a concert, or some other event. Many of them kept the tradition going, even though Chesarae had long since been locked up, and the rest of the main members who started the crew were now doing their own thing.

"Girl, I know Tavion got his ass up in here somewhere," Vendetta said, peering around the crowded club for her boyfriend.

"And you know Ashaad is probably with him," Trap said, pursing her lips. "And his black ass ain't even tell me he was coming into town. But I know he here!"

"Listen to y'all!" Peaches said. "You two sound like some old ass married women! So what if they're here? We're here to have fun, and get our grove on."

"And get our drank on!" Trap said, pulling out a big bottle of Grey Goose.

"No you didn't!" Peaches told her.

"Yes the hell I did!" Trap said. "Girl, ain't nobody paying no arm and a leg for no damn Goose, when I can sneak that shit up in here in my purse. Thank you Michael Kors!"

The three of them shared a laugh.

"Girl, you just as ghetto fab as they come!" Vendetta said, laughing.

"Bitch, don't get boo on me," Trap told her. "You know how we do!"

Trap and Vendetta high fived.

"We need to get our drank on, so we can get Peaches drunk, so she can get laid tonight," Trap said smiling.

"Girl, please!" Peaches said recoiling. "I don't need no drunk ass nigga trying to get all up in my panties!"

"You need to get your groove back!" Trap told her.

"Right," Vendetta said, shaking her head in agreement. "You ain't had a nigga swerve up in that since who? Marquez went to the feds?"

"Now why'd you have to bring up Marquez?" Peaches asked, craning her neck.

"That was yo man!" Trap told her. "Y'all was all in love and shit after Chesarae got locked up."

"Girl, Marquez just caught me when I was vulnerable," Peaches protested.

"I can't tell," Vendetta said with a smile. "You was boo hooing and all fucked up when he got sentenced."

"Girl, please!" Peaches said, waving them off.

"Has he tried to get at you since he got out?" Trap asked.

Peaches shook her head. "Thank God, no! Don't nobody want to see his ass. He's fine right where he's at."

Trap and Vendetta exchanged looks.

"So, who you wanna hook up with tonight?" Vendetta asked.

"Nobody."

"Girl, pick somebody," Vendetta told her. "All these fine ass niggas up in here."

"We'll have Terence or one of the other men go and bring them over here," Trap said, peering over her shoulder at the body guards that were surrounding the table. They had brought five of them. Two of which were standing to their left, and two of which were standing to the right of them. The fifth was posted up at the entrance to the VIP section.

"No thank you," Peaches said, shaking her head.

"You need to get you some so you can relax," Trap told her.

"Who says I ain't had none?" Peaches asked.

Trap and Vendetta peered at one another.

"When?" Vendetta asked, lifting an eyebrow.

"Damn, you nosy!" Peaches told her.

"You know your ass ain't had no wiener!" Trap said laughing.

"I might have!" Peaches said.

"When?" Trap asked.

"You ain't been with me every day, all day!" Peaches told her.

"Girl, I've been with you every day since you got back!" Trap told her.

Peaches lifted an eyebrow and smiled.

"Bitch, quit lying!" Vendetta told her, shoving her shoulder.

"You ain't gave up no pooh nanny while you was in Texas!" Trap said, joining in.

"How do y'all know?" Peaches asked. "I could've met a nigga

who fucked my brains out."

"And you ain't tell us about it?" Vendetta asked, pursing her lips.

"I ain't gotta tell you everything!" Peaches frowned.

"Bitch, please!" Trap told her. "If you had some good dick, your ass would have flown back to Columbus, and not on no jet!"

"Good dick gives you wings!" Vendetta said laughing, as she mocked the Red Bull commercial. She and Trap hi-fived.

"And you would have brought it with you!" Trap told her.

"Well, maybe he couldn't come back with me," Peaches told them.

"Why not?" Vendetta asked.

"Because maybe he's a real man, with his own shit to handle!" Peaches told them. "Ever think about that?"

Vendetta shook her head, as she poured herself a drink. "You lying."

"How you just gone call me out like that?" Peaches asked with a smile. She shook her head. "Girl, that Texas dick..."

"Bitch, don't play with me," Trap told her.

"You met some nigga in Texas?" Vendetta asked, leaning in.

Peaches shifted her glance between the two of them rapidly for several moments, allowing the suspense to build.

"Spit it out!" Vendetta told her.

"He was fine, girl," Peaches told her.

Trap and Vendetta squealed like giddy school girls.

"And he was hung like a horse," Peaches continued. "And he didn't just put it down rough and raw, he put it down slow and steady. He had me straight busting nuts, one after the other for hours all throughout the night."

"Oooh, girl!" Trap shouted. "Why you ain't told us about him! What's his name?"

Peaches shook her head. "I don't want to say right now."

"Why not?" Vendetta asked. "Is he famous? He's somebody

famous, right?"

Peaches shook her head. "Not really. Not like y'all thinking."

"Why you hiding him in your pocket?" Trap asked. "Girl, what's up?"

"Yeah, what's the real deal?" Vendetta asked.

"It's complicated," Peaches told them.

"He's married?" Trap asked.

"He ain't married," Peaches said, dismissing the question outright.

"He ugly?" Vendetta asked.

"No, he ain't ugly!" Peaches told them.

"Them why you keeping Ol Tex a secret?" Vendetta asked.

"You'll find out," Peaches told them.

"You know I have no patience," Vendetta told her.

Peaches shrugged. "Well, you just gonna have to learn some."

Trap shook her head. "Bitch, give up the goods!"

Peaches laughed and shook her head.

"I see how you are," Vendetta said nodding. She peered around the room. "See, you gonna make me..."

Vendetta placed her hand on the side of Peaches' head and shoved her down into the booth beneath the table. Shots rang out before she could pull out her weapon. The two bodyguards to her right fell. Trap pulled out her Glock and peered around the room. Vendetta finally managed to get her weapon out as well. She could no longer spot the gun welding assailants, as the VIP room had now erupted into a mass of panic. More shots rang out, and the bodyguards to the left of them dropped their weapons and fell.

Beneath the table, Peaches pulled out her nine millimeter and began peering around. She knew that she had to move and get out of the club. Someone was shooting, and more importantly, someone was shooting at *her*. They had taken out her men, and there was no doubt in her mind that they were there to take her out. Who, was less important right now, than just surviving. She would figure out the 'who' part later. And that would give her the 'why'.

"Two!" Vendetta shouted. She pushed through the screaming, panicking crowd, and made her way into the next booth. To her surprise, the occupants in the adjacent booth had been hit. One was dead, and two were wounded. Also lying nearby, were two of the bodyguards they came with. She ducked down and crept through the crowd to get closer to the unknown shooters. It was a tricky task, because she kept losing sight of them within the fleeing crowd, and she wanted to use the cover of the crowd to her advantage.

"Stay down!" Trap shouted. She also climbed out of the booth and made her way through the panicking crowd. Whoever the shooters were, they couldn't shoot worth a damn, Trap thought. For one, they should have taken out their target first, and then worried about the bodyguards. These idiots were more worried about getting killed by the bodyguards, than taking out their primary target. That was 'if' Peaches was in fact, their target. Also, they had mowed down a considerable number of innocent club goers in the process. It was amateur hour for sure, and she was definitely going to use that to her advantage. Trap crept through the crowd, taking a roundabout path toward the gunmen.

Beneath the table, Peaches could hear rounds ricocheting off of the top of the table, and off of the concrete floor in front of her. They were definitely shooting in her direction, and she wasn't the one to be anyone's sitting duck. She peered through the legs of the fleeing crowd, trying to spot the legs that weren't fleeing, and that were facing in her direction. Most likely, they would belong to the shooter, or shooters.

Vendetta made her way through the crowd and finally came upon the shooter on the right. She lifted her weapon and put a bullet into his skull. He dropped instantly. And then she heard a popping sound to her right. The gunfire was followed by a searing sensation in her side. She peered down at her shirt, only to find that she had been hit. A second bullet struck her in her right arm, knocking her to the ground.

Beneath the table, Peaches aimed at the legs of the gunman shooting at her. He was obviously trying to get off a good shot, but the crowd kept getting in the way. In fact, they kept getting in her way as well. She took aim and waited for a pause in the crowd running by, and then squeezed the trigger on her piece. The gunman fell to the floor with a bullet in each of his shins. Peaches let loose, sending several bullets into the gunman's feet, and between his legs.

"That should hold you, you son of a bitch!" Peaches said angrily. She rose from the booth and peered around. She spotted Vendetta on the floor holding her side, and headed in her direction.

Trap made her way around the club. She spotted the bodyguard that had been posted near the entrance to the VIP section lying on the ground with blood pouring out of his ear. She knew that he was dead. She also spotted the likely culprit. He was crouching and creeping, trying to move in closer to where her girl Vendetta was. Trap pulled up on him, aimed, and placed a bullet in the back of his skull.

"Creep on that, bitch ass muthafucka!" she said, still dumping on him. She turned toward her girls. "Over here!"

Peaches lifted Vendetta off of the ground.

"I'm hit, girl!" Vendetta shouted.

"No shit!" Peaches said with a smile. "I thought that you was trying to take a nap on me."

Peaches placed Vendetta's arm around her shoulder, and headed toward the exit. She spotted Trap standing near the exit and quickly headed toward her.

"Punk ass muthafuckas!" Trap shouted.

Peaches peered down at her dead bodyguard and shook her head. "He just had a baby."

"Let's get the fuck outta here!" Trap shouted.

"They gonna pay," Vendetta said, clasping her side and shaking her head. "Better believe they ass is gonna pay."

The three of them headed out of the VIP section, and made their way through the panicking club. Trap was on point, with her weapon at the ready, as they headed for the club exit. The exit was jammed with a crowd of club goers trying to push through all at once.

"Move muthafuckas!" Trap shouted. She pointed her weapon toward the ceiling and started popping off rounds. The crowd screamed and dispersed. Most of them anyway. A few fell to the ground and covered their heads. The exit was clear.

Peaches, Trap, and Vendetta rushed through the door and into the parking lot. The bodyguard that was left with the cars was lying on the ground dead.

"Fuck!" Vendetta shouted.

"Check his pockets for the key!" Peaches told Trap.

"Fuck that!" Trap shouted. "They could have fucked with the cars."

Trap turned, headed into the street, and pointed her weapon at one of the cars filled with fleeing club goers. She put a bullet into the hood and aimed her weapon squarely at the driver, who immediately hit his brakes.

Trap raced to the driver's side, opened the door, and pulled him out of the car.

"Get the fuck on the ground!" she shouted. She peered into the vehicle. "What? You bitches need an invitation? Get the fuck outta the car! Anybody still inside of it, is *still* gonna be inside of it when homicide is putting tape around it and calling the coroner!"

The occupants quickly scrambled out of the vehicle. Peaches helped Vendetta into the passenger side of the late model Camry, and then hopped into the back seat herself. Trap climbed behind the wheel of the vehicle and sped off. Inside, the three of them peered at each other, and slowly, smiles crept across each of their faces. They had survived *another* one.

"This shit hurts!" Vendetta told them.

"Just be still," Peaches said. "You don't want that damn bullet to travel."

"Them bullets," Vendetta said, correcting her. "That punk ass nigga shot me twice."

Trap laughed. "And girl, that was such a cute outfit. I was gonna ask if I could borrow it."

"Girl, go to hell," Vendetta said, leaning back in the seat.

The three of them burst into laughter.

Chapter Five

Tavion pulled Vendetta close, and kissed her on the back of her neck. He was the love of her life, and had been for a long time. He and Vendetta had been together off and on since middle school, and had finally decided that they were meant to be together.

"Watch my arm, nigga!" Vendetta told him.

Her arm was in a cast and a sling, while her side was bandaged. She still felt a little bit of pain when she moved, but other than that she was fine. She had been out of the hospital for three days, and was enjoying some time in the park with her man, and his best friend, along with her girl Trap.

"I got you," Tavion said, pulling her closer and kissing her on her neck once again.

"Aw, he all lovey dovey with his Boo Thang," Trap said laughing. "He was scared his Boo Boo wasn't gonna make it."

"I know his ass was up in the club," Vendetta said, peering over her shoulder at Tavion. "Probably was all up in some bitch's face, while I was getting my ass shot off."

Tavion smiled, showing off his perfect pearly whites. His perfect

teeth were a contrast to his light bronze, but heavily tattooed skin.
Tavion was a pretty boy for sure. He wore his hair in long, silky
cornrows that hung down past his shoulders. He had highly
pronounced cheek bones, and gun slit eyes that slanted up, along with
long curly lashes that made him the envy of most women. Tavion also
had greenish brown eyes that drove women crazy. Women threw their
panties at him everywhere he went, and some of the time he accepted.
Vendetta knew that he strayed every once in a while, but at the end of
the day, he wasn't going to leave. She had two rules. Don't bring
nothing back that he hadn't left home with, and don't get caught.
Disease, kids, and disrespect were her three no-no's. Don't bring back
no VD, no babies, and don't be out there in a way that she get's
disrespected. If any of the above happened, he knew that she was
going to hold true to her threats to cut off his dick.

"See, why you trying to start stuff?" Ashaad told Trap. He pulled
her close. "Get outta other people's business."

"V is my business!" Trap shot back.

"I told you, I dipped as soon as I heard the shots," Tavion said,
pleading his case. "You think that if I knew it was you getting shot at,
that I would've dipped?"

Vendetta rolled her eyes at him.

Tavion nudged her with his shoulder. "I would have been in
there. Blasting them fools right next to my Boo."

"Yeah, right," Vendetta said sarcastically. "Who do you think
you're talking to?"

"And where were you at?" Trap asked Ashaad. The four of them
were seated on a set of park bleachers next to an empty basketball
court. Ashaad and Tavion were seated on row higher, while Vendetta
and Trap were seated between their legs. They were enjoying the mild
weather and beautiful Ohio sunshine. They were also celebrating
Vendetta getting out of the hospital.

"I was outside in the parking lot when the shooting started,"

Ashaad told her.

"Doing what?" Trap asked. "Talking to some bitch?"

"Na, ma," Ashaad said smiling, and shaking his head. "I was blowing a nice fat spliff."

Trap shook her head. Ashaad's first love was marijuana. She often told him that if a fire broke out and he could only save one thing, he would choose his blunts over her. He never disputed the assertion.

"You and that damn weed!" Vendetta told him, shaking her head. She shoved Ashaad on the back of his head. "Old big head ass."

"Watch the waves, Lil Mama," Ashaad said, in his always calm demeanor. Nothing seemed to faze him, and nothing seemed to be able to kill his perpetual buzz. Ashaad kept a magnetic smiled sprawled across his handsome, dark chocolate, dimpled face.

"So what's the deal with the niggas?" Tavion asked.

"What niggas?" Trap said, turning toward him.

"Then club shooters," Tavion answered. "What's up with them?"

"What do you mean?" Vendetta asked.

"What was that shit about?" Tavion asked. "Was that them Get Money Niggaz?"

Trap shrugged. She didn't know. Peaches was on it, she knew that for sure. But no one was certain at this point.

"What was that shit about?" Ashaad asked.

Tavion and Ashaad exchanged knowing glances. Neither was stupid, and both had ears to the street. They were both big time hustlers, and they knew everything that happened throughout the state. Especially in Columbus, and especially when it involved a big shootout at a popular club like that. They also knew about Sweet Pea getting whacked, and they knew Peaches very well. They both had their suspicions about Sweet Pea's killers. They suspected that they were sitting between their legs at that very moment.

"I don't know," Trap said, shrugging once again.

"So, you telling me, that somebody was trying to blow your damn heads off, and you have no idea who or why?" Ashaad asked. Again, he exchanged glances with his boy.

"Damn, what do you want me to say?" Trap asked. "I don't know who the muthafuckas was."

"Okay, so who do you *think* they were?" Tavion asked.

Trap and Vendetta exchanged glances and shrugged.

"Why do you think they were shooting at you?" Ashaad asked.

"I don't know," Vendetta said. "Maybe a bitch took they parking space or something. Damn, what is this, the Spanish Inquisition or something?"

"Cause this is some bullshit, and you know it's some bullshit," Tavion told her. "You know why somebody would want to shoot at your ass. What the fuck you been doing lately?"

"I ain't been doing shit!" Vendetta protested.

"Yeah," Tavion nodded. "And that's why you got two bullets in ya ass."

"Muahfuckas be getting shot all the time, that don't mean they did nothing!" Trap told them.

"Yeah, but I suspect you two know why some niggaz was trying to blow your heads off," Tavion shot back.

"And so close to Sweet Pea getting killed," Ashaad added. "Know anything about that?"

"I know what you know!" Trap said.

Ashaad leaned back and stared at her. Trap shifted her gaze away from him momentarily, and then decided to playing the staring game. She dramatically shifted her gaze back to him and stared him in the eye.

"You can look me in the eye," Trap told him. "That shit don't prove nothing!"

"I know when ya lying," Ashaad told her.

"Oh, so you a lie detector now?" Trap asked.

"I know when my girl got something up her sleeve," Ashaad said smiling. He tickled Trap under her arm. "And I know when she hiding something."

"Stop it!" Trap said laughing and squirming away.

"Why y'all do Sweet Pea?" Tavion asked, leaning back on the bleachers.

"Who said *we* did it?" Vendetta asked.

"Who else did it?" Ashaad asked. "A room full of hoes. And then, all the hoes up and disappeared. Police can't find no witnesses? That shit sound like your M.O."

"I ain't have nothing to do with that shit," Vendetta said, turning away.

"Why Peaches make a move like that?" Tavion asked. "She trying to make big girl moves, and that shit gonna get a nigga killed."

"Yeah, ya'll know them Get Money niggaz ain't gonna sit by and take that shit," Ashaad added.

"Then, they gone think Young and Holding had something to do with it," Tavion told them. "That stupid ass shit a get niggaz killed. Baby Girl need to be happy doing what she doing. Just taking what my nigga Chez left her, and roll with that."

"Well, first of all, if it was Peaches, she ain't worried about no Get Money niggaz, and she don't need nobody to fight her battles for her," Vendetta told them. "So you don't have to worry about that."

"Oh, she Super Woman, huh?" Ashaad asked. "She got a cape and a phone booth somewhere stashed?"

"Like she can fight all them damn niggaz," Tavion added. "Thousands of them niggaz, and she can handle it by herself, huh?"

"Who said that she did it?" Trap asked.

"And then, y'all forgetting about Kharee!" Ashaad told them. "You think that nigga is gonna take that shit lightly? That nigga Sweet Pea was making that nigga all kinds a money. He ain't fixin to be pleased with that shit. Does Baby Girl think before she acts?"

"Does she understand the concept of war?" Kharee asked. "*A big ass war?* Can't nothing good come outta that shit."

"Man, ya'll jumping down my girl throat, and jumping to conclusions and shit," Vendetta told them. "Like y'all just know she done it."

"Who else gonna make a move like that?" Ashaad asked.

"*Kharee!*" Trap said. "Ever think that he wasn't happy with Sweet Pea? Maybe Sweet Pea could have owed him some money or something? Ever think about *that*?"

"And what about Big Meech?" Vendetta asked. "Big Meech could have deaded that nigga. What about Pocus, or Bug? It could have been anybody. Hell, it could have been LaQuan, or even Tavion's ass, for that matter!"

Tavion laughed. "Yeah, that's what y'all *want* people to think. That's what y'all was banking on. But there was just one problem with ya little scheme. Ain't nobody but Peaches gobbling up his territory."

"Yeah, ain't nobody else move on his shit the day after the nigga got killed," Ashaad added with a smile.

Tavion shook his head. "I know she's your girl, but don't let her get you fucked off."

"And everybody else in the process," Ashaad added.

Again, Vendetta and Trap exchanged glances.

"I have one big important question," Tavion asked. "Why? What the fuck is she after? She's comfortable. I know she's got some mil tickets stashed. She ain't hurting, so why risk everything? What's she after?"

"You still *assuming* that she had something to do with it," Vendetta told Tavion.

He gave her a crazy look. "Don't play with me, V. We been down for way too long to play games. What's ya girl after?"

Trap and Vendetta stared at each other for a few seconds, before reaching a silent agreement.

"*Assuming* that she *did* want to expand, what's the problem with that?" Trap asked.

"Why?" Ashaad asked.

Again, the girls stared at one another.

"Maybe she needs to," Vendetta told them.

"Why?" Tavion asked. "Why would she *need* to? What would make a person need to kill somebody and take over their shit?"

"What's so special about Sweet Pea's shit?" Ashaad asked.

"Was her and Sweet Pea beefing or something?" Tavion asked.

"Who said there was anything special about Sweet Pea's territory?" Vendetta asked. She knew that she was letting the cat out of the bag.

"Why did she bump him for it?" Ashaad asked.

Trap closed her eyes and exhaled. "Who said that she's done?"

Tavion bolted upright and he and Ashaad stared at one another.

"What? What the fuck are you saying?" Tavion asked.

"You heard me," Trap said.

Ashaad shook his head.

"Tell me that you're fucking kidding me!" Tavion said excitedly. "Tell me that you're fucking playing!"

Trap's silence told him what he needed to know.

"Has Peaches lost her *fucking* mind?" Tavion shouted. "What the fuck is wrong with her? What the *fuck* is going on?"

"Time to put the cards on the table," Ashaad told them.

"She made a new connect," Vendetta told them. "Some major mofos. They think that she controls most of Ohio, and they are going to help her take over the rest of the state."

Tavion through his head back in laughter, while Ashaad shook his head and peered down toward the bleachers laughing as well.

"Control Ohio?" Tavion asked. "Baby Girl don't even control all of *Columbus!*"

Vendetta elbowed Tavion's leg. "That's the problem, fool! They *think* she does. She cut a major deal with these people, and they don't

43

play. If they find out that she doesn't control what they think she does, she's dead."

"Damn!" Tavion said, shaking his head. "How the fuck did she get herself into this mess? Why come she didn't just say no thank you! What's wrong with the truth every now and then? I know I ain't no truthful motherfucka all the time, but *damn*. Every once in a while a nigga let it drip from his lips."

"And this was one of those times when she should have," Ashaad added.

"Okay, well, it's done," Trap added. "We past that point. Now, we gotta fix it."

"Why come she just don't tell them she ain't interested?" Tavion asked.

"Because, they already let her in," Vendetta explained. "She's knows too much. They'll kill her ass for sure. And probably me and Trap along with her."

Tavion rolled his eyes at her. "You sure know how to get yourself into some bullshit!"

"I ain't ask you to do nothing, Tavion!" Vendetta shot back.

"Yeah, like I'mma just sit back and let you get killed?" Tavion told her. "You *still* ain't learned? All that hot shit you be talking, running around thinking you bad and shit! What you do, affects me too! It brings me into shit! You still haven't learned that lesson!"

"I ain't asked you to do shit for me!" Vendetta shouted. "I don't need your help, your protection, your approval, or anything else! I'm a grown ass woman!"

"That's real sweet, V! And real smooth, and real fucking logical! You know damn well, that I can't sit back and let you bump your hard ass fucking head, and do nothing! *Dammit!*"

"What we gotta do?" Ashaad asked. He had a crew. They were in Youngstown, not Columbus, but they were real killers, and he could have them there in hours.

"Nothing, right now," Trap told him. "Just chill."

"So, you have to pretty much take over most of Ohio, in order for this new connect to not kill y'all asses for being full of shit?" Tavion asked.

Vendetta rolled her eyes at him.

"Have y'all forgotten about the person who really controls most of Ohio?" Ashaad asked.

"Fuck Kharee!" Vendetta said forcefully.

Tavion shook his head.

"Y'all have to take over Columbus first," Tavion explained. "Which means you now have to kill Big Meech, Bug, and Poocus. Which also means that by the time y'all get through all of them, y'all will probably be at war with Melvin, and all them fucking Get Money Boyz, and probably even be going at it with Kharee. How in the hell did Peaches ever think that she could do something like that?"

Trap nodded slowly, now seeing things more clearly now. "Okay, she bit off more than she can chew. But that shit is done. We need to handle the shit now."

"Who's next?" Tavion asked, leaning back once again.

"Poocus would be the logical choice," Vendetta said.

Tavion nodded. "He's the weakest one. I see what she's doing now. She knocking the low hanging fruit off the tree first, and gobbling up they shit. If she can get they people to roll with her, then she gets bigger and bigger as she rolls along."

Ashaad nodded. "Not a bad plan."

"That's the only way this shit can work," Tavion declared. "But, after she knocks off Poocus, then Bug and Big Meech is gonna be on they guard. And muthafuckas is gonna know for sure that shit ain't random. And when she gobbles up Poocus' shit too, all eyes are gonna turn to her. They gonna know what she's doing."

"So, what does that mean?" Trap asked.

"It means, that she's gonna need some help to take out Bug, the next nigga in line," Tavion told her. "That means, she's gonna need a nigga to get at Bug. Somebody who he ain't expecting, in a way he ain't expecting it. And then, Big Meech is going to really fortify. That fool will be untouchable. It'll be a major war for Columbus then."

"And then, your new connect can step in and help," Ashaad told them.

Trap shook her head. "No, because they think that we already control Columbus. They won't step in, until it's time to wrap up all of Ohio."

"Against Kharee," Ashaad said nodding. "But by then, it'll be too late, because that nigga will already be warring with y'all in a major way. And just controlling most of Columbus, ain't gonna be good enough to take on that nigga. I can put my boys with your boys, and Tavion's boys, and we *still* won't have enough to shake a stick at."

"What about Jakeem and Terrell?" Vendetta asked. "What about LaQuan? What about JerMarcus? And don't forget about Hassan."

Tavion shook his head and waved his hand in the air. "Yeah, all the rest of them is cool, but you can forget about Hassan. If he brings all of them Detroit niggaz down here, that shit will just muddy the waters. Niggaz a be fighting them instead."

"Besides, Hassan ain't been too cool of late," Ashaad declared.

"Let me sleep on this shit for a minute," Tavion told them. "Slow creep on ya next move, while I think about some shit."

Trap and Vendetta nodded.

"At least let us get with everybody, and start getting big on the cool," Ashaad added. "That way when it pops off, at least we'll all be ready, and all be on the same page."

"That got damn Peaches!" Tavion said, shaking his head. "If she wasn't my nigga's girl, I'd a been done quit fucking with her ass."

"Don't say that," Vendetta told him.

"Man, I'm serious," Tavion told them. "I know she's ya girl, but damn. Y'all done hitched y'all asses to a crazy star. Not a fallen star,

46

but a crazy one. She'll get a muthafucka fucked off!"

Chapter Six

Ruth Chris was one of Peaches' favorite spots. She loved the barbecued shrimp and the stuffed chicken breast. She also loved the tender filet steaks that the restaurant had mastered. Ruth Chris was one of her favorite spots to hit up when she was in Columbus. And the fact that the majority of the patrons who were dining, were often conducting business deals of their own, insured that they were too worried about their own business, to be all up in hers. She could wheel and deal, and not worry about people trying to listen in on her conversation. Besides the food, this was the primary reason she liked to do business inside of the restaurant.

Peaches ordered her drink. She loved mixed drinks, especially the sweet tropical stuff. Anything with rum, orange juice, pineapple juice, and coconut, she was down for. She ordered a Painkiller with extra honey and extra nutmeg, and peered out of the restaurant window. She could see her dinner guest pulling up in his red Rolls Royce Ghost at that very moment.

Hassan stepped out of his Rolls and checked out the scene. He was originally from Detroit, although he had lived in Columbus for many years, before returning home to build up his own empire and crew. And although he knew just about everyone in Columbus, he still kept his guard up. Columbus was beefing with Detroit again, and even though most cats in Columbus viewed him as being one of them, he still refused to get caught slipping. He believed in rather being safe than sorry.

Hassan ran his hand down his Armani trousers and striped Armani polo shirt, checked his diamond studded Piaget, smoothed his waves, and pulled off his Armani sunglasses. He hooked his sunglasses onto the front of his shirt, and then headed inside. He knew that he looked good, because he always dressed to impress. His Armani cologne even had him smelling like a million bucks. And make no mistake, Hassan was a millionaire.

Peaches rose from her seat at the table when Hassan walked inside of the restaurant. He hurried over to where she was standing, opened his arms, and the two of them embraced tightly.

"Hey, baby girl!" Hassan said, hugging her tightly and rocking her from side to side. "You looking good!"

"You too!" Peaches said, smiling from ear to ear.

Hassan leaned back and checked her out. "You still fine as hell!"

Peaches waved him off. "Boy, go on! You're still crazy as hell."

Hassan waved toward her seat. "Please, have a seat."

Peaches reseated herself, and Hassan pushed in her chair. He then walked around the table and seated himself across from her.

"So, how you been?" Hassan asked.

Peaches shrugged. "Making it. You know how it is. The question is, how have *you* been?"

This time it was Hassan's turn to shrug. "Laying low. Taking it day by day."

"Laying low?" Peaches asked, lifting an eyebrow. "In a bright red

Rolls Royce? That's what you call laying low?"

Hassan smiled. "I'm in Detroit, Motown, Motor City, Detroit Tigers, Detroit Pistons, Detroit Lions, Detroit Red Wings. We got enough niggas with paper to allow me to blend in. Besides, I have some legit shit as well. I ain't one hundred percent criminal."

Peaches threw her head back in laughter. "Boy you crazy."

"Don't smile like that," Hassan told her. "It brings back too many memories."

"What kind of memories?" Peaches asked.

Hassan leaned back in his seat. "Memories of me staring at you, wishing that you were mine."

Peaches turned away. She didn't know what to say. It was rare that she was at a loss for words.

"So, speaking of memory lane," Hassan continued. "How is my nigga doing? When's the last time you heard from Chesarae?"

Peaches shrugged, and faced him again. "It's been a minute."

"Why? You write him don't you?"

"We stopped doing that a minute ago."

Hassan folded his arms and rested his fingers against his chin. "Why is that?"

"You know how that shit is," Peaches said. "Niggas go through emotional ups and downs. They trip. They think that life stops once they get locked down. They try to control you from inside, not understanding that putting their prison theories into real life practice, ain't as easy as it seems. Plenty of arguing, and not a lot of talking. After a while, you get tired of yelling at each other on the phone, and then having to wait fifteen minutes so that they can call back and you can finish arguing."

Hassan laughed. "Man, don't do it like that."

"Do it like what?"

"You know the saying, the Feds broke us up? You can't let that be you. You two are stronger than that."

"Apparently not," Peaches told him. "The way I was thinking, was that we could just work that shit out later. But then, I would always go back to wondering when later would be. Hell, Chesarae got thirty years in the feds. So, when is later? Thirty years from now? And then, I would always say that I would holler at him and try to straighten shit out, but then something else would come up."

"Don't give up on him," Hassan told her. "You know he's going through a bunch of shit right now. It's tough. Dealing with prison bullshit is tough. And he needs you now more than ever. Don't cut him loose when he needs you the most."

"I didn't cut him loose," Peaches told him. "We were both just tired of arguing."

"He's just missing you," Hassan told her. "The arguing is just a manifestation of his frustrations. Being snatched away from your woman, your family, your friends, and everyone and everything that you love, is tough. He misses you more than life itself, baby girl. You were my nigga's whole world."

"Hmmph!" Peaches huffed. "I thought Young and Holding was his whole world. I thought the *game* was his life. I felt like I came in fourth behind his niggaz, his bitches, and the dope game."

Hassan stared at her and shook his head. "I don't know why you feel like that. That man cherished the ground you walked on."

"He kept me locked in the house like a ghetto China doll while he went out and hoed around," Peaches shot back. "And then, when he got caught up, and I had to go to court and support his ass throughout the trial, I got to see that trash that he was sticking his dick in. Skank ass hoes all up in the courtroom claiming him as they man, and talking shit to me, and trying to run up on me and check me and shit."

"Man, I know you ain't sweating no hoes," Hassan said smiling. "If he was fucking with them, that's all they was. Just boppers. *You* are the wife. The money was coming back to you. Them hoes got dick, and a condom flushed down they toilet, you got the Bentley, the house, the dope, the connects, and the money. So, who was the queen?"

Peaches nodded. "I ain't tripping on no old shit."

"Then sit your ass down, and write my nigga," Hassan told her. "Make it right. You know I'm right about this."

Peaches nodded. "I will."

"So, let's get down to some business," Hassan said, leaning back once again. He rubbed his hands together. "You holding?"

Peaches nodded. "A little. I ain't hurting."

"Can you hook ya boy up?"

"For you?" Peaches smiled. "I'll do anything."

"You say that now," Hassan told her. "You should have gave me ya number back in the day. You'd a been Mrs. Hassan right now."

"Boy go on!" Peaches told him.

Hassan laughed.

"What you need?" Peaches asked, peering around the restaurant. No one was listening.

Hassan held up ten fingers. Peaches recoiled.

"Ten birds?"

"Naaa!" Hassan said shaking his head. "Why you tripping?"

Peaches laughed. "I was about to say. You might need to trade in that Rolls or something."

"Ten hundred," Hassan said in a low voice.

He wanted a thousand keys. Which also made her recoil. It was much more than Hassan had ever ordered before. It raised the hairs on the back of her neck. She instantly put her guard back up.

If it was one thing that Chesarae left her, it was his knowledge of the game. Niggas didn't jump in weight that fast. Not unless they were ordering for themselves and other niggas of equal status, which usually didn't happen. Everyone at this level, had their own connect. So that was not a real probability. And the only other reason a nigga ordered way above his weight class was if he was going to beat his connect. And the fact that this even crossed her mind disturbed her greatly. She and Hassan hadn't seen each other in a while, and they had grown apart. After Chesarae got knocked by the feds, his entire crew, and all of his boys from Young and Holding, an organization that he founded, fell away and started doing their own thing. Out of all of them, Hassan was the one who was closest to Chesarae, and he was also the smartest, and the most conniving. Chesarae had told her who would betray her, and he also warned her that she would be surprised by a couple of the people who would double cross her. He never mentioned Hassan, but he gave her enough hints that she now was able to put things together. She was shocked. But even more so, she was hurt.

"Damn, that's a lot, baby boy," Peaches said, swallowing hard.

Hassan shrugged. "I'm trying to make some moves."

"*Some damn big ones*," Peaches told him.

"I figure with the way things are right now, with dope being tight, I can score big and take over most of that shit," Hassan explained. "I'll be one of the few, if not the *only*, nigga in Detroit with dope. I can take over the city, and most of the state for that matter. That's if you can come through for me."

Peaches nodded. "That's a lot. I might be able to get you. But it's gotta be cash, up front."

"Why?" Hassan asked. "We usually go fifty fifty. Half up front, half later."

"Yeah, that was when it was flowing," Peaches told him. "Now, I got a new connect, and they don't take American Express. They want it cash, and they want it up front. And I ain't got it to float you like that. So if you want it, and if I can get it, it'll have to be cash and carry, baby."

Hassan thought about it for a few moments. He would have to move some money around, or perhaps dip into his savings, but taking over the Detroit dope scene would be worth it. Especially if Peaches came through. A thousand keys, and then another thousand right afterward, and he would be in. If he could push a thousand keys a week through Michigan, then he would be set.

"Okay, I can do that," he told her.

A lump formed in Peaches throat. He wanted a front, because he was going to beat her, she thought. And now that she asked for all cash up front, and he had agreed to it, that meant that he was going to try to kill her and beat her for *all* of it. Her heart was broken.

"You got the people to push that much weight?" she asked.

Hassan nodded.

"Why don't you loan me some of them?" Peaches asked, with a half smile.

"What?" Hassan lifted an inquisitive eyebrow. "What are you talking about?"

"Shit, if you got it like that, then maybe we should think even bigger," Peaches told him. "You want all of Michigan and I need all of Ohio. Why not work together."

"In what way?"

"You need dope to take over your state, and I need niggas to take over mine," Peaches explained. "I got the dope, and together, we'll have enough niggaz. Between me, you, and the rest of Young and Holding, we can do it."

Hassan laughed. "Young and Holding. Ain't no more Young and Holding. We were kids, hustling ounces and riding around lifted, and burning out, and fighting, and putting that crazy shit on the internet. We ain't young and dumb kids no more, Peach."

"I know that," Peaches told him. "But between you, me, JerMarcus, LaQuan, Ashaad, Jakeem, Terrell, Omar, and Tavion, we can do it. If we all put our crews together, we can do it."

"Do what?" Hassan asked. "Take over Ohio? You mean, go against Kharee?"

Peaches leaned in, reached out and clasped Hassan's hands. "We can do it!"

"Go to war with Kharee?" Hassan asked. "What would be the purpose of that? I mean, what's in it for me? What am I supposed to tell my Detroit niggas? Why would they get into an Ohio beef?"

"For dope," Peaches told him. "For riches. If I can take Kharee, Ohio is mines. I control it, I set the prices, and..."

"And then you'll have to spend all your time and money consolidating this shit hole," Hassan said peering around. He leaned back and stared at her, pulling his hands away. "I'd rather just buy the dope from you. Why would I get into that and send my people to get killed, when we can just buy the dope and take over Michigan, and not have to spill a single drop of blood. Niggas are going to come to *us*, and beg to be down with *me*, because I'll be the only one with dope. I don't need to get my hands dirty to accomplish my objective."

"And what objective is that?" Peaches asked.

"To take over this shit," Hassan said, allowing an evil grin to spread across his face. I'm going to be the biggest dope dealer in the Midwest."

"Ohio's in the Midwest," Peaches said with a slight smile.

Hassan shrugged. He rose from the table, walked to where Peaches was sitting, leaned forward and kissed her on her cheek. "It was good seeing you, ma."

"I'll call you and tell you where we'll meet to make the delivery," Peaches told him.

"What? We ain't going to do it at the warehouse where we usually do it?"

Peaches leaned back. "I prefer to do things differently now. You know, new connect, new product, new ways of doing things. I'll call you."

Hassan held out his hands. "Suit yourself."

He turned and walked out of the restaurant. Peaches lifted her drink and took a long swig. She could feel a little bit of liquid welling

56

up in her eyes. At that moment, she knew that the day would come, when she would have to kill Hassan.

Chapter Seven

That Joaquin was a pretty boy was undisputed. He was one of the biggest play boys in Columbus. He was half Dominican, and half Black, had naturally curly hair, big green eyes, and most of all, had a mack game that was out of this world. He could charm a female out of her panties in minutes. He had the gift of gab, and million watt smile, and plenty of cash flow. He was a baller in his own right, in addition to being the brother of the most notorious chick in the game. Peaches was his big sister.

Joaquin whipped his convertible Jag into the detail shop and pulled around the back. He climbed out, tossed one of the workers his keys and winked at him.

"Hand wash, and don't use the buffer on my paint job," Joaquin told him. "I don't want buffer scratches in my shit."

"Fuck you, bitch!" the guy told him, tossing his keys back to him.

"Where's your daddy?" Joaquin asked.

"I got your daddy right here," he told Joaquin, while pulling on his dick.

"You got pussy, nigga!" Joaquin told him.

"Well, let me give you one," the guy told him. "I'll give you a pussy right in the middle of your forehead."

He reached beneath his shirt.

"Ladies, cut it out!"

Both men turned toward the back door of the detail shop. Melvin was standing in the open doorway.

"Can we get down to business, or do you two want a room together?" Melvin asked. "I hope that one day you two just fuck and get it over with."

Melvin and several others made their way out of the building and down the steps. He and Joaquin exchanged a quick embrace.

"What's up, my nigga?" Joaquin asked.

"What's up?" Melvin asked.

"Chilling, chilling," Joaquin told them. "What up, my dude?"

Kellen nodded. "What's up?"

"Just trying to get it," Joaquin told them.

"Where's that fine ass sister of yours?" Kellen asked.

"Gone on wit all of that," Joaquin replied.

"I'm just saying," Kellen continued. "You know she fine as a mother fucker."

"I always said, she give me a chance, she wouldn't be fucking with no punk ass Young and Holdin niggaz," Melvin said, slapping hands with Kellen. "She'd be straight up Get Money."

"Why we gotta be some punk ass niggaz?" Joaquin asked. He didn't like the way the conversation was going. He was Young and Holding, while Melvin and his boys were Get Money Boys. But they still did business together, and they still got their dope from his sister, which is why he was at the detail shop. He was ready to leave. They next time, he would tell Peaches to have them meet up somewhere besides one of Melvin's businesses.

"Aw, nigga," Kellen said, waving him off. "Don't get ya panties all in a bunch."

"Fuck you," Joaquin told him.

"Where my shit at?" Melvin asked.

"I got it," Joaquin said.

"I hope it ain't bunk," Melvin told him. "I heard she got a new connect."

"Shit, where else is it gonna come from?" Joaquin asked. "Ain't nobody else got no dope, so who gone complain?"

"Still," Melvin said. "Dope might be short right now, but when shit get to jumping off again, I don't want muahfuckas to jump ship saying that my shit is bunk."

"Have I ever sold you some bullshit?" Joaquin asked with a smile.

"You ain't never sold us shit," Kellen said, smiling back. "Nigga, this yo sister's shit. Don't be trying to act like you balling. Nigga, you work for *her*. She wears the drawers in yo family."

Melvin and his boys started snickering.

Joaquin walked to the rear of his convertible Jag and popped the trunk. Inside of the trunk was a black Nike gym bag. Joaquin unzipped the gym bag and opened it. It was filled with kilos of cocaine.

Melvin peered around the area, and then lifted one of the bricks and examined it.

"It's good, nigga," Joaquin told him.

"All thirty of them are here?" Melvin asked.

Joaquin nodded.

Melvin placed the key back inside of the bag, and then lifted the bag from the trunk. He put the strap over his shoulder and turned and began to walk away.

"Yo, yo, yo, hold the fuck up!" Joaquin told him. "Where the money at?"

Melvin turned back to Kellen. "Give this nigga what we got for him."

Joaquin turned to Kellen, and watched as Kellen pulled a Forty

Caliber Glock from beneath his shirt.

"Whoah!" Joaquin said, lifting his hands. "What the fuck?"

"Nigga, you know what this is!" Kellen told him.

"Man, why y'all tripping?" Joaquin protested. "Go on with this bullshit, Melvin!"

"Nigga, tell that bitch ass sister of yours I said thanks," Melvin said laughing. "I should a got that hoe a long time ago!"

"Man, why ya'll tripping?" Joaquin asked.

"Cause, you Young and Holding fags ain't gonna do nothing about it!" Kellen told him. "We get money, nigga! And sometimes we get it by taking punk ass nigga's shit. Break yo self!"

"Man, don't do this!" Joaquin told him.

Kellen cocked his Glock, chambering a round. "I said break yo self, hoe ass nigga!"

Joaquin pulled out his wallet, and Kellen snatched it. He pulled out all of Joaquin's money, and tossed the wallet back at his feet.

"Rabbit ears, nigga!" Kellen shouted.

Joaquin turned his pockets inside out.

"Jewels, nigga!" Kellen shouted.

Joaquin shook his head. He pulled off his rings, his watch, and his chain, and handed it to Kellen.

"You think I'm blind, nigga?" Kellen asked. "You think I can't see them big old pretty diamonds in your ears?"

Joaquin huffed. One by one, he pulled off his diamond earrings and handed them to his jackers.

"I would have you suck my dick too," Kellen told him. "But you might enjoy that shit too much!"

Melvin and the rest of his crew broke into laughter.

"But if I catch you again, it's on," Kellen told him. "I'mma fuck you like we was in prison, soft ass muthafucka! Tell that sister of yours, I'mma fuck her too!"

Melvin nodded toward Joaquin's Jag. "Get the fuck outta here!"

Joaquin backed away toward his car, with his hands still in the air. Once he got to his vehicle, he slowly climbed inside, and then backed out of the detail shop, and pulled into the street. Once down the street, he pulled over and ran to a pay phone.

"Hello?"

"Peaches! It's Joaquin!"

"Hey, what's up, baby?"

"Them niggas jacked me!"

"What? Who?"

"Melvin and them!" Joaquin said excitedly. "They was with that bullshit! Talking about they get money, an Young and Holding ain't shit!"

"Are you all right? Are you hurt? Did they shoot you?"

"Na, I'm fine! They let me go."

"*They let you go*?"

"Yeah. They did that shit, and they let me go."

Peaches exhaled. She knew exactly what was going on. They let him go, because they wanted to send a message. Killing him, would have sent a message that they were ruthless. But it would have also sent a message to the streets saying that they *had* to kill him. But by letting him go, it said that he wasn't shit, and that Peaches wasn't shit, and that they didn't give a fuck if she knew who did it. It was the ultimate disrespect.

"Where are you?" Peaches asked.

"Down the street from Melvin's detail shop!"

"Get the fuck away from there!" Peaches told him. "Just go. Hurry up and get back in your car and get the fuck on. Go get another cell phone, and call me later. Get off the street. I'll get up with you later."

"All right. Peace."

"Peace."

Joaquin hung up the pay phone, hurried back to his car, climbed inside and pulled off. Melvin and his Get Money Boys had just started a war. A major war. Not only was his sister not going to take it, but his homeboy's weren't going to take that shit either. Young and Holding had fell off big time since Chesarae went to prison. Everybody was doing their own thing. But now, something like this, was bound to get everyone's blood running again. It was not just a sign of disrespect to his sister, but to the entire set. If there was one thing that could bring everyone back together, it was this. Being violated and disrespected by the Get Money Boys was a no no. Ohio's two biggest drug clicks were now on a collision course toward war. And being that the two organizations hadn't gone to war in years, this one was bound to be a big one. Things in Ohio were about to get bloody. Real bloody.

Chapter Eight

Trap's specialty was explosives. She was had been a genius in chemistry class all throughout high school, and it was that love of chemistry that taught her how to mix and match and work with different molecules on all different levels. In any other situation, she would have been a scientist, or a geologist. But like so many others born in her circumstance, the streets took her under. She used her mad skills with a beaker to elevate her whip game to legendary status. She could cook crack cocaine with the best of them. Ecstasy she could cook up blind fold. She had even created a name for herself on the Meth scene. White boys would pay her big bucks to cook up their supply. And then she went to juvenile.

Trap came out of juvenile with a love of computers. It was that love of computers that grew into an unquenchable search for knowledge. She used Google and Wikipedia to research and devour all kinds of information. She was a virtual ghetto almanac. It was during one of her many searches that she came across the infamous *Anarchist Cook Book*. And it was that book that led her to discover other books of a similar nature. Soon, her love for computers and technology, combined with her love for chemistry, and she was not only cooking up killer batches of dope, but killer batches of explosives as well. Soon, one thing led to another, and she found herself quickly becoming an expert in homemade explosive devices. And then, her girl Peaches came up once her man Chesarae got knocked by the Feds. The rest was history.

Trap always had a violent streak. She always loved the streets, and all of the gritty shit that life in the street involved. Chilling up in the trap house was how she got her nickname. She was known to always be up in a trap house hustling. And when Peaches needed her to use her hustle skills and knowledge of weapons to help her consolidate her hold on Chesarae's empire, she was only too willing. Sure, she could blow a mother fuckers head off without hesitation, but to her, the real art in killing, came from not being around when the mother fucker bit the dust. And in order to make that happen, she had to utilize her skills in explosives. Trap had long progressed beyond the homemade grenades, and the home built pipe bombs. She had learned rocketry from the internet, and from amateur rocket launching contest. Her skills in chemistry gave her the knowledge to improve upon the store bought fuel that the amateur rocketeers used. And her knowledge in computers, explosives, and electronics, allowed her to construct shaped charge warheads inside of the rockets, and to reconstruct the toys until she had them able to reach uncanny speeds. And then, she put those rockets into tubes, added electronic triggers to the tubes, as well as scopes to aim with, and created her first generation of home built rocket launchers. She was now on her third generation. And on top of that, she had now advanced beyond rudimentary detonation methods for her other types of explosives. She was now a master at crafting electronic triggers, tied to wireless remote detonation devices. And that was what she was using today. Pipe bombs, wired to cell phone detonators. All she had to do, was dial up the cell phones in order to trigger the bombs. Her years of toying with explosives had taught her that the simplest devices, were the best and most reliable ones.

Trap adjusted the long dark wig she was wearing, and peered around the room through her dark sunglasses. She knew the detail shop well. She knew the trinkets that the shop sold to patrons who were waiting inside while their cars were cleaned. She knew the waiting areas, the public restroom area, and the design of the building itself. She knew where to place her explosive toys for maximum effect, and that was what she was doing. She had left one in the trash can inside of the ladies restroom. She had placed a device that she had crafted to look like a Coke can, on top of the soda machine. She had placed another device that she built inside of a large can of creamer, next to the coffee machine in the lounge. She had placed a third device inside of a briefcase that she left beneath a seat in the front of the detail shop. And last but certainly not least, the largest and most powerful of the explosives, was inside the trunk of a stolen car that she had one of the guys drop off earlier to get a hand wash and full detail job. And now that she had placed all of her devices, it was almost time to go. She waited patiently as her own whip was being finished up by one of Melvin's men. The fools didn't understand what was about to hit them.

"Your car is finished, ma'am," the clerk behind the counter told her.

Trap rose, walked to the counter, and grabbed her keys. She paid in cash for her car wash. It was the best twenty dollars she had spent in a long while. She had always wanted to hit this shop, and finally, she was getting her chance. Melvin and his fucking Get Money Boys needed a spanking a long time ago, and taking out this car wash, was one of the best spankings they could get. Melvin's little detail shop did more than just make cars shiny again, it was one of his biggest fronts for pushing his dope and washing his drug money. Taking it out, would be a nice little blow to his pockets.

"Thank you," Trap said, smiling. She strutted out of the shop, with her Manolos clicking with each of her steps. She climbed inside of her stolen Benz, dropped the top, and pulled out of the shop. Down the street, she pulled over, climbed out of the convertible Mercedes, and pulled her iPhone out of her purse. Smiling, she dialed the numbers to the cell phones wired to the explosives that were spread throughout the shop. Each phone had the same number, and all of the phones received the call simultaneously, and each one triggered its respective explosive instantly.

The fireball that went up could be seen for miles. In fact, the set of explosions combined to create one large explosion, that rocked the ground beneath her feet. It was beautiful to her. The orange and blue hues of the fireballs sucking up more and more oxygen as the explosion expanded skyward was a sight to see. It was like the Fourth of July to her. She viewed each of her explosions as being unique, each of them was her baby, and each of them made her want to orgasm.

Trap inhaled deeply, trying to catch a whiff of one of the explosive compounds that she used in her creations. She loved the smell of Pentolite, TNT, and even gunpowder. It was like smelling a beautiful flower to her. Unfortunately, she was too far away to catch a whiff today. She had to make due with the smell of the rising smoke from the burning cars and buildings.

Trap turned back to her Benz, and climbed back inside. She had to take the car over to East Columbus and ditch it for her own wheels, before making her way back to Dublin. Her part of the today's mission was done. She could sit back, relax, and enjoy the ride. But most of all, she relished the thought of finally being able to get out of those tight ass heels that she was wearing.

*****

Vendetta loved guns. She got her love of guns from her crazy uncle who served in the Marines. He had been in Grenada, Panama, and the first Gulf War, and he had been a die hard devil dog until his sanity slipped away from him. But before that happened, he taught his favorite niece how to use a wide variety of weapons. Taking her to the gun range during the weekends, and taking her camping and teaching her survival skills during the summer had become an obsession for him. It was to the point where Vendetta knew more than most Marines about survival tactics, and could survive in the woods under the most extreme conditions for weeks or even months, if not indefinitely. Under any other circumstances, Vendetta would be in the Marine Corp. But the life she lived had been far from normal.

Vendetta saw her father murdered by a Chinese shop keeper when she was six. It was a memory that would stay with her forever. In fact, it was that six year old child's vow to get even that earned her the name change. She was born Vernetta, but at the age of sixteen, she found that Chinese shop keeper, and using her knowledge of weapons she took out him and his entire family. She had kept her grudge for ten years, thus earning her the name Vendetta. And it was a name that stuck.

Vendetta had a reputation for getting even. You fucked with her, it wasn't a matter of 'if', but of 'when'. She was going to get back at you, that was written in stone. If it took days, weeks, months, or as in the case of her father's murderer, years, she was going to do it. And it was going to be violent, and in most cases, bloody.

Vendetta enjoyed doing what she did. She loved Peaches, and thought of her and Trap as the sisters she never had. And using what she knew in order to bring money and success to herself and her girls

69

was a given. Helping Peaches consolidate her hold on Chesarae's territory gave her an outlet for her frustrations, as well as an ability to get money on her own. She didn't have to lay on her back to get it, and she didn't have to put up with some dope boy's bullshit either. She could love on her own terms, and she could get the money that she needed to support her mother on her own. Rehab was expensive. Especially the really good ones. And so, she needed to earn in order to support herself and her mother's stints in rehab, as well as provide her mother with a place to stay while she was out of the various treatment facilities. The VA took care of her uncle for the most part. Between her uncles military retirement, the VA, and his Social Security Disability, he was fine as far as money went. It was just a matter of maintaining a safe home for him to stay in. And so, she did what she did not only for herself, but for the two people in her life that she loved the most. Her mother, and her uncle. It was an enormous burden for a young woman in her early twenties, but it was not beyond her abilities to handle. Her uncle had made her strong and self sufficient, her mother's addiction had made her mature at an extremely young age, while the death of her father had steeled her to deal with a world that was not always kind to Black people. She was ready to take on whatever came her way, and whatever task she was assigned. And today's task, was a walk in the park.

Peaches needed a message to be sent to Melvin, and by extension, to the rest of the streets. She needed everyone to know that she wasn't weak, and that she could hit back. Taking over Chesarae's territories and maintaining them hadn't earned her enough respect. And apparently people in Columbus had short memories. She needed to remind them not to fuck with her. And so Melvin was about to get a double punch. Vendetta was going to handle the detail shop, while she was going to take out Melvin's used car lot. It was another one of Melvin's drug spots, and one of his principal means of washing his drug money. Taking out his cars, and bringing attention to the shop, would shut it down for a while, and cost Melvin plenty of bread. He would have to patch up the bullet holes in a lot of his inventory, as well as repaint the cars and replace the shot out windows and bullet riddled interior parts. Dashboards, seats, engine blocks; all of it could cost a pretty penny if she did her job right. And she always did her job right.

Vendetta rolled up on the shop, pulled her mask over her face, and climbed out of the stolen vehicle she was in. She reached back into the car and pulled out an AR-15 assault rifle, an AA-12 semi automatic shotgun, and her trademark Mac-10's. She looked like a masked Albanian terrorist about to attack a village in the Balkans. First things first, she lifted her assault rifle and sprayed the windows of the sales office, causing everyone inside to duck and flee. She needed panic to ensue, so that she could be free to wreak havoc on the cars.

Vendetta sprayed the windows, and all of the buildings, and even took out a few of Melvin's soldiers who were guarding the drugs that he kept on the lot. It would have been the perfect opportunity to jack all of his supplies, but she wasn't here for that. Today, it was all about sending a powerful message to the streets of Ohio.

Vendetta ejected the empty 100 round drum clip on the AR-15, and inserted a second one. The fully automatic assault rifle spit out rounds at a frightening pace. The remainder of Melvin's men inside had nothing to compete with it, so they stayed on the ground ducking down. A pistol against a fully automatic assault rifle would be fruitless, and would also mean a very bad day for whoever was stupid enough to raise up off of the ground to try and return fire. Besides, they didn't know how many people were outside shooting at them. All they heard was a constant ripping through the air of assault rifle fire. It was ear splitting, and terrifying.

Vendetta turned her second clip on the cars in the lot, peppering them full of holes. Most of them were SUV's, and all of them were late model vehicles that Melvin had purchased from various

71

automotive auctions for resale at his lot. She was going to cost him tens of thousands, if not hundreds of thousands in repairs and damages. The AR-15 was spitting out bullets so fast that a thin haze of smoke begin to surround her and fill the area. Soon, she dropped that empty clip, and inserted a third.

Vendetta walked through the lot taking out tires, windows, rims, and just about every piece of exterior she came across. She was determined to leave no vehicle untouched. Soon, her weapon emptied once again, and this time, she slung it over her shoulder instead of loading a fourth clip. She then pulled her semi-automatic Russian made AA-12 shotgun from around her shoulder, and begin to aim at the front of the cars, and put slugs through the engine blocks. Replacing engines blocks was going to cost him big. It was what she was counting on to run the totals up into the hundreds of thousands of dollars.

The AA-12 shotgun used a clip with a large rotating drum at the bottom. Hers held thirty rounds. She loaded the first fifteen rounds of each clip with slugs, and the last fifteen rounds with Double O buck shot. The slugs were for the engine blocks, and the buckshot was to do more damage to the exterior and interior of the cars. It also allowed her to keep the people inside of the shop honest. She turned and sent a few blast of buckshot toward the sales office, just to remind them to stay on the ground.

Vendetta reloaded clip after clip, and continued to make her way through the car lot, and then back to her waiting vehicle. She had destroyed several cars outright, and many were smoking, while several of them were even burning. It was time to go. She would need a shower after putting in so much work. The power of the AA-12 shotgun had made her orgasm several times.

Vendetta tossed her assault rifle into her car, followed by her semi-automatic shotgun. She then pulled her two Mac-10's from around her shoulders, and let them rip toward the office and some of the cars just for good measure. The Macs were her trademark, and she always finished up a job with them whenever possible. The distinctive prattle of the two 9mm assault pistols pierced the air, and then she was off. Vendetta climbed into her vehicle, pulled out of the lot, and sped off down the street. In her rear view mirror she could see the shop in smoldering ruins. A wide grin slowly spread across her face. It was another job well done.

Chapter Nine

"Hey, Boo!" Peaches said, lifting her cell phone to her ear. She was rolling down the boulevard in her Aqua Blue convertible Porsche Boxster S, enjoying the music and the wind in her hair. "Hold on, let me cut the music down."

Peaches hit the toggle switch on her steering wheel mounted volume controls lowering the sound pouring out of her speakers.

"How have you been?" Darius asked.

"Good," Peaches said. "Just missing you. You missing me?"

"I want you here so bad I'm hurting."

Peaches laughed. "I can imagine what part of you is hurting."

"Not my balls," Darius told her. "Why it's always got to be about sex with you? I knew you just wanted me for my body."

Again, Peaches laughed. Talking to him made her feel good. He took her mind off of her troubles, which were many. She wished that she were back in Texas with him, and some small part of her wished that she had taken his advice and turned down the seat on The Commission. She wasn't ready for it, and now, she was paying a price in stress and stupid moves for not being completely ready for it. She was no where near taking over all of Ohio, and hadn't even taken all of Columbus yet. Her greed had gotten the better of her. She wanted it all, and now she was desperate to put herself into position so that she could eventually take it all. But that stress, was for another day. Now, she had her Boo on the phone.

"You're crazy!" Peaches told him.

"I'm crazy in love with you," Darius replied. "So, when are you bringing that fine ass back to Texas to hang out with me?"

"I thought it wasn't about sex?" Peaches asked. "I know them balls is hurting. You need some relief, huh?"

"Naw," Darius told her. "You know how many chicas try to get at me on a daily?"

"Don't make me fly down there and cut your dick off," Peaches told him.

Now it was Darius' turn to laugh. He knew that she was serious, and that she would probably try to do it.

"You know I'm saving this for you!" Darius told her.

"Yeah, you better be! Don't play with me."

"So, when you flying down?"

"Why?"

"Because I wanna see you," Darius told her. "I want us to hang out."

"I just left!"

"You been gone two weeks."

"Why you counting my days?" Peaches asked with a smile. It made her feel good to know that he knew exactly how many days she had been gone. "You all up in my space, nigga!"

Darius laughed once again. "Get yo ass on that plane!"

"I can't."

"Why not?"

"Have you forgotten that I'm on The Commission now?" Peaches asked. "I just can't hop on a plane and fly into your brother's territory!"

"He ain't gonna say nothing!"

"Oh yeah? It's called an act of war to show up unannounced in somebody's house when you weren't invited."

"I'm inviting you."

"Well, you don't run Texas."

"He won't know you're here," Darius told her.

"If he doesn't, then he's not as good as everyone thinks he is," Peaches told him. "He'll know the minute I step off the plane. He hasn't survived this long by being stupid."

"Okay, then meet me somewhere else," Darius suggested. "How about Vegas? We'll gamble, we'll hit the clubs on the strip, we'll just go out and have fun."

"Vegas?" Peaches asked. "Are you serious? You're trying to get me killed?"

"Okay, how about Mexico? Or Canada? Or Jamaica?"

"I wish I could," Peaches said, sounding dejected. "But I have a lot of work to do here."

"See, I told you."

"You and I both knew what I was in for," Peaches told him. "Ohio ain't gonna just lay down by itself."

"You're not becoming one of them, are you?"

"I'm the same person I was when you met me. Or should I say, *pursued* me."

Darius laughed. "I wasn't the only one doing the pursuing."

"Yeah, you was."

"No, I wasn't. You wanted some of this Texas stud when you first laid eyes on me."

"Boy please!"

"What are you doing up there?"

"Handling business."

"All day, every day?"

"What are you getting at?"

"Ain't no niggas in the picture, right?"

Peaches laughed. "No. You don't have to worry about that. All the niggas up here want to choke the shit out of me."

"Sound's like something you'd like," Darius told her. "You are freaky like that."

Peaches laughed. "I like to be slapped on the ass. But choking me until I die... I think I'll pass."

"You need me?" Darius asked.

Peaches closed her eyes briefly. She sat at the traffic light biting her top lip. She wanted to scream *yes*. She *did* need him. If only to come to Ohio and hold her, to comfort her, to give her some of that confidence that he inspired whenever they were together. But still, she knew that she couldn't bring him into her predicament. She couldn't put him in danger because of *her* lies, and because of *her* war. These were battles that she was going to have to fight alone.

"No."

"You didn't say that like you meant it."

"No!" Peaches said more forcefully. "I don't need you to come up here. I'm a big girl, and I can handle my own shit. I've handled it thus far, right?"

"I'll give you that," Darius told her. "But just know that if you ever need me, I'm only a phone call away. Everybody needs somebody, every once in a while. Ain't no shame in accepting help."

"Thank you. And I'll keep that in mind."

"You don't have to be hard core with me, Peaches," Darius told her. "I'm not them niggaz, and I'm not the streets of Ohio, and I'm not any of those people who have hurt you in the past. You can open up to me. You can be vulnerable with me. You can *need* me."

Peaches exhaled. "I gotcha."

"I miss you," Darius said softly.

"I miss you too," Peaches whispered.

"Stop being a stranger, and call me more often."

"I will," Peaches told him. "I just been so busy trying to get things together."

"I'm only a phone call away," Darius reminded her.

"Thanks."

"Talk to you later, Babe."

"Later."

Peaches disconnected the call, and stared at her phone for several minutes. She wished that she could meet Darius in Jamaica. Lying on a beautiful white sand beach all day, and making love in a gorgeous, luxurious suite all night, would be a dream come true. She would get there one day, she thought. She would get there. She was determined to make that dream come true. But right now, she needed to handle her business so that she *could* get there. She needed to push forward in her quest to take Columbus.

The sound of sirens snapped Peaches out of her thoughts. She peered in her rear view mirror, and sure enough, Columbus' finest were behind her with their lights flashing. She was getting pulled over.

Peaches navigated her Porsche toward the side of the road, and pulled off her sunglasses. She watched her rear view, waiting for the patrol officer to approach, but instead, he remained inside of his patrol car. She knew that she hadn't been speeding, and she had been obeying all traffic laws, so she was curious as to why he had pulled her over. The first thing that crossed her mind, was that she was being set up. And she was. But it wasn't by a rival dope dealer, it was by her worst nightmare. A female patrol officer turned detective, who had taken a vested interest in her since she was young. She had tried to get Peaches off the streets, tried to get her help, and even had allowed Peaches to crash at her house for a while. She was a dedicated cop, one who really cared about young Black girls lives, and who didn't just walk the walk, but talked the talk. She was a real asset to the Columbus community, and under any other circumstances could have

79

saved Peaches, like she had saved so many other young girls. But these weren't average circumstances, and Peaches didn't want to be saved.

Detective Sheila Ward pulled up in her unmarked patrol car, climbed out, and headed to where Peaches was parked. Detective Ward was a no nonsense sister who had graduated from Spelman College in Atlanta, and who had majored in social work. She could have landed a cushy job anywhere in the country, but chose to return to Columbus, and chose to put on a uniform and hit the streets. She wanted to help young sisters get out of the traps that the drug life and poverty had set up for them. And she had done much of what she had set out to do. She was a legend in the community, respected by judges, representatives, prosecutors, and more importantly, by the streets and the young girls she was trying to help. She was part big sister, part mother, part counselor, part minister, and part cop. She played all of those roles and many more. And it was in the role as community police officer that she had met Peaches so many years ago. Peaches had been her biggest effort, and her biggest failure, because she thought that she had the most potential of all the girls that she had come across. And although Peaches was now grown, she still hadn't given up on her. She still thought that something inside of her could be redeemed. But it was a redemption that would have to come on the other side of a prison sentence. She knew that Peaches had been guilty of some heinous crimes, and she wanted Peaches to pay for those crimes. She also wanted Peaches to turn her life around and to come out of the situation as a better person. She was willing to help her, and walk with her through her journey through the system. But she *was* going to send her through the system, there was no doubt about that. Peaches needed to go to prison first.

"You've been busy lately," Detective Ward said, approaching Peaches' car.

Peaches smacked her lips. "Man, Ms. Ward, why you sweating

me?"

"It's my job," Detective Ward replied. "Why you kill Sweet Pea?"

"I ain't kill no Sweet Pea!" Peaches protested.

"Yeah? You think I don't recognize your M.O. That shit had you and your little partners in crime written all over it."

"I ain't did nothing," Peaches reiterated. "Why you even gonna come at me like that?"

"Not doing it, and getting away with it, are two different things," Detective Ward told her. "Sooner or later, somebody's gonna talk. What's done in the dark, will always come to the light, you better believe that. And when it does, you in for a hard lesson."

"We ain't did shit!" Peaches told her. "Why you don't go and sweat them niggas across town. How you just gone put me in something like that?"

"Why you do it?"

"I ain't did nothing!"

"And then blowing up Melvin's car wash?" Detective Ward asked, lifting an eyebrow. "That shit had ya girl Trap's thumbprint all over it. And then shooting up his car lot?"

Peaches shook her head. "Don't know what you talking 'bout."

"Why you beefing with Melvin?" Detective Ward asked.

"Ain't nobody tripping with no Melvin?" Peaches told her.

"Is Young and Holding beefing with the Get Money Boys?"

"I couldn't tell you," Peaches said, turning away from the detective. "You gone have to ask one of them."

"Oh, so you ain't claiming Young and Holding no more?" Detective Ward asked with a smile. "What your boyfriend Chesarae gonna say about that?"

"Uh, Chesarae ain't my boyfriend, and whatever he say about it, he just gonna say. Ain't none of what you talking about, got anything to do with me."

Detective Ward pursed her lips. "Un-hun, I'll bet."

"It don't!" Peaches said, turning back toward her. "Why you sweating me?"

"Cause you are stepping deeper and deeper into some shit you won't be able to get out of!" Detective Ward told her. "I don't want to see you go down forever, over some street bullshit. Girl, you're too bright for this. Chesarae is gone. You're free. You ain't got nothing left to prove. Go to college, get your life together, get away from this lifestyle. It's not too late."

Tears flowed down Peaches' cheeks. "Why you tripping with me?"

"I ain't tripping," Detective Ward told her. "I still see a beautiful young lady, who can make something out of her life. Years ago, you let them tell you that you were less than what you actually were. They took a beautiful young lady, someone who had a beautiful smile, and had her get grilled out. They took a young lady with beautiful flawless skin, and had her put tattoos all over her body. They took a young lady with a wonderfully inquisitive mind, and convinced her that school wasn't the way out. My question is, why are you still letting the streets dictate to you who you can be?"

Peaches sniffled and wiped away her tears. "I ain't doing nothing."

"You can lie to most others, but you can't lie to me," Detective Ward told her. "And more importantly, you can't lie to yourself."

"I ain't!"

"Peaches, I love you like a little sister, and like a daughter even," Detective Ward told her. "But when I catch you, I'm going to put the cuffs on you, and you are going away to prison. How long you go away, is going to be up to you. Is it going to be for a long time, or a little? That's the question you have to ask yourself. You can stop doing what you're doing, and you can go to college, and you can make a life for yourself. You're still young, you don't have any kids, you're not tied down. *Now* is your time to get your life together. Don't get found dead in a ditch like your little friend Tanya, and like so many other young girls that you grew up with."

Peaches continued to wipe away her tears.

"You are being investigated for the murder of Sweet Pea and his men, and for shooting up Melvin's car lot. I'm just going to keep it real with you. The prosecutors aren't playing. If you are guilty of that shit in the hotel, then you are in a lot of trouble. And you won't be able to run from it, or hide from it, or cry your way out of it. You already got away with plenty of shit in the past, because you pulled your innocent little girl routine, and your abused dope dealer girlfriend routine, and your I'm just a scared little juvenile routine. You're running out of routines, Sweetheart. And the State of Ohio is running out of patience. And a life sentence upstate is not what you want. So you think about that, you hear me?"

"Yes ma'am," Peaches said sniffling.

"Get out of here," Detective Ward told her. She turned, and waved at the patrolman sitting inside of his patrol car, giving him the all clear. The patrolman turned off his flashing lights, and pulled away.

Detective Ward watched as Peaches pulled off in her Porsche. She knew that Peaches was guilty. And she knew that she was going to put the cuffs on her and walk her into jail for a really long time. She just prayed that she wouldn't have to use her gun and put her down permanently.

Chapter Ten

Peaches had never been to Louisville before today. She had ventured into Kentucky a few times, and had even gone as far as Lexington, but had never set foot in Louisville. She had always wanted to visit the famous Louisville Slugger factory, and had always wanted to experience the world famous Kentucky Derby. Today, she was going to check one of those things off of her list. She was going to meet with a fellow commission member at Churchill Downs. Although the derby was not taking place at the moment, being able to see the place where it did actually take place was thrilling to her. Or at least it would have been. Today was not about tourism, it was about something else. The Commission wanted to meet with her, and their request for a meeting hadn't exactly been a polite one. She had been summoned.

Many thoughts were racing through Peaches' mind at that moment. Were they on to her? Had they found out about her deception? How much did they know? Was this going to be her end? Why here? Why in Kentucky? Why not meet her in Ohio? And why was she meeting with Chacho Hernandez when Kentucky wasn't even his state? She had many questions, and few answers. And all of the answers that she came up with on her own hadn't been good ones. She was sure that today's meeting wasn't going to be about roses and sunshine. They were upset with her, and they wanted to send her a message. What frightened her more than anything, was that she knew the type of messages that The Commission sent. Usually, the recipient of those messages was found floating face down in a nearby river. Was this her turn?

Trap walked just in front of her, with a couple of her men. Vendetta walked just to the rear, with even more of her soldiers. Omar was next to her, and that gave her a little bit of comfort. She had her peeps with her, and maybe that would give her a fighting chance to make it out of the situation alive. After that, perhaps they could all scramble and get lost somewhere. Where, she did not know, but there had to exist some place on Earth where The Commission couldn't get to her. She would have to figure out where that place was, once she made it out of this situation first. The key to making it out, she thought, was to look professional.

She had rented several brand new Cadillac XTS limousines to transport her and her crew to the meeting. She had everyone dress in their best, most professional business suits, and she had everyone looking sharp and fierce. Her girls had on dark colored DKNY pants suits with Louis Vuitton heels, while her bodyguards were decked out in dark colored Armani suits. She needed to look like she controlled a state, and like she was truly a member of The Commission. Perhaps she could bluff her way out of the situation if she looked the part and talked the part. She needed them to give her more time.

Peaches spotted several Latino men standing around the entrance of the race track, and she knew who they worked for. They were wearing dark, custom tailored Brioni suits and dark sunglasses. They looked out of place at the track. In fact, they looked out of place in

86

Louisville. Dozens of well dressed, well groomed Latino men in seven thousand dollar business suits was not a common sight around town. And the fact that they were wearing ear pieces added to their mystique. She could also tell that they were all armed, by the way their arms rested outside of their suits. Shoulder holsters and custom cut suits could hide a lot, but not the way a person had to hold their arm because of the weapon beneath it.

"Hola, Senora," one of the men told her, as she approached. She brought fifteen people with her in total, and they were all quickly surrounded. She quickly deduced that Chacho had brought an army. "Please, Senora, follow me."

The lead bodyguard waved his hand for her to follow. Trap, Omar, Vendetta and the rest of her crew tried to follow, but Chacho's men stepped in between them and her, holding up their hands and stopping them cold.

"Your people will be comfortable here," the lead bodyguard told her. More of Chacho's men seemed to appear out of nowhere, and her men were surrounded by even more men. Her stomach dropped. She searched through the crowd to see if she could spot Trap and Vendetta. She just wanted to see them, to gaze into their eyes for what may be the last time. She had a horrible feeling about the entire situation.

"Come, follow me," the bodyguard told her. He nodded for her to follow.

Peaches swallowed hard, turned, and followed the bodyguard and several other men into the racetrack. They headed up a long set of steps leading to the upper seating levels of the grand stand. She emerged from the stairs to spot even more Latino men seated in the middle of the grandstands watching the track. She recognize Chacho Hernandez instantly. He was seated in the center of the men, and was clearly in charge.

Chacho was fairly young, in his early thirties, well groomed, fit, and dressed to kill. He was adorned in a seven thousand dollar custom tailored suit by Kiton, and was staring into a set of binoculars examining something on the far side of the track. Chaco sported a new haircut, she noticed, it was more tapered on the sides, and spiky on the top, giving him a younger, more hip look. She was led into his presence.

"Have a seat, chica," Chacho told her, without lowering his binoculars.

"I'm good," Peaches told him. She knew that she had to play the game. She had already fucked up, because she hadn't brought enough men, whereas he had at least two hundred or more men at the park. He had shown her that he was in charge, and he actually looked like a member of The Commission. He had the money and the resources to roll super deep. And she looked like it was amateur hour at the Apollo. They were supposed to be equals on The Commission, but this meeting didn't feel like it. In fact, it didn't feel like a meeting at all. A meeting was when two people of equal stature met to discuss something. This felt like a student being called to the principal's office. She had to reassert herself. She had to stand strong, and tall, and bluff her way through the situation. The Commission had to think that she was stronger than she actually was. If they believed for one second that she wasn't already running most of Ohio, then someone would be fishing her body out of the Mississippi River next week.

"Suit yourself," Chacho told her. He lowered his binoculars and peered at her. "What's the deal with Ohio, chica?"

"What do you mean?" Peaches asked.

"We're hearing things," Chacho told her. "And they're not good things."

"We all hear things that we don't want to hear sometimes," Peaches told him.

Chacho lifted his binoculars and peered at a group of men tending a horse on the other side of the track. He then lowered the binoculars and handed them to Peaches.

"Take a look," Chacho told her. "See that white thoroughbred on the other side of the field?"

Peaches exhaled. She turned toward the field and lifted the binoculars to her eyes. "Yeah, so?"

"That's my baby," Chacho told her. "I paid over a million dollars for that bitch."

Peaches lowered the binoculars and nodded. "Waist of money."

"I got it to waste," Chacho said with a smile. "How about you? You got a million dollars to throw away on a damn horse?"

Peaches swallowed hard. "Maybe. You called me all the way to Kentucky to talk about my bank account?"

Chacho shook his head. "Naw, I called you to Kentucky to talk about horses. What better place to take about horses than bluegrass country? What better place to talk about betting, than the Kentucky Derby?"

"Horses?" Peaches said, lifting her eyebrow. "I'm not a betting woman."

"Neither are we," Chacho told her. "But we did bet on you."

"I'm not a horse," Peaches told him.

"We're all horse, mamacita," Chacho told her. "And this in just one big fucking horse race. And where we finish, depends on how strong we are, and how well we work together with the rest of our team. And if the horse is not as strong as she seemed to be, her ass is put out to pasture, and a new horse is brought into the race. And horses that are put out to pasture, don't do nothing but eat and shit, and those useless muthafuckers are the first ones to hit the glue factory, you got me?"

"Is that a threat?" Peaches asked coldly.

"I don't threaten nobody," Chacho said shaking his head. "I just state the facts."

"What do you want from me?" Peaches asked.

Chacho leaned back and smiled. "You got people wondering if

they've backed the wrong horse, lil mama. Did we back the wrong horse?"

"That's not for me to decide," Peaches told him.

"You're right, it's not," Chacho told her. "And the people who do decide, are wondering if Kharee is the thoroughbred, and you're just an old paint, that should have been turned to glue a long time ago."

Peaches shrugged.

Chacho pulled out a pack of cigarettes, tapped the bottom of the pack, tore open the top, and pulled one out. He stuck the menthol in his mouth, and one of his men quickly lit it. Chacho inhaled, and blew smoke into the air.

"What the fuck am I supposed to tell them?" he mused.

"Tell 'em what the fuck you want to tell them," Peaches told him. "If you think that you chose the wrong person to sit on the seat for Ohio, then that's on you. But Kharee ain't taking it from me. And neither are you."

Chacho smiled. It was what he wanted to her. He had questioned her fire, questioned whether she was hard core enough to take over and run a state like Ohio. And the rumors that had been getting back to The Commission had them questioning their choice.

"You think that Kharee can't take Ohio from you if we helped him?" Chacho asked.

"You want to try?" Peaches asked, bluffing.

Chacho nodded. "What's this we hear about all of this noise you're kicking up? Your under bosses are rebelling?"

Peaches had been caught off guard. "What the fuck are you talking about?"

"We hear that you killed one of your under bosses," Chacho told her. "In a very messy and very public way. You leave that many bodies in a hotel room, Sweetheart, and the police aren't just going to go away. We don't need that kind of attention. You don't need it. You're not strong enough and your police and political protection isn't

90

strong enough to deal with it."

An enormous relief came over Peaches. The Commission thought that Sweet Pea was one of her under bosses, and that she had to whack him for getting out of line. She could feel herself exhaling, as the tension bled from her body.

"I'm moving forward and consolidating," Peaches told him. "That's what you wanted. I was told to consolidate my hold on the entire state. I have to make sure that my house is tight as well. I need loyalty amongst my people, as I bring the state into line."

Chacho nodded slowly. "Don't stir up a hornet's nest. Don't make too much noise. And most of all, don't get busted. You're new. You get busted, a lot of people are going to pull the trigger on you to shut you up before you can do a deal with the Feds and start running your mouth."

"I'm not a snitch," Peaches said.

"We have a way of making sure of that," Chacho said coldly.

"Is that all you want?" Peaches asked.

"You know what my horse's name is?"

"What?" Peaches asked, peering across the field toward the horse again.

"Lucky Bitch," Chacho told her.

Peaches shifted her gaze back toward him.

"But I'm going to have to change her name," Chacho told her. "The Association won't allow a horse with profanity in her name. Besides, we can't have two lucky bitches running around here now, can we?"

Chacho's men broke into laughter.

"Watch yourself," Peaches warned.

"No," Chacho said, shaking his head. "You watch yourself. This meeting was a courtesy. Most of The Commission wanted you dead. Lucky for you, the fucking Reigns family cried their little eyes out to save you. You should watch yourself, chica. I think Princess wants some of that pussy."

Again, Chacho's men broke into laughter.

"If we have to meet again, I won't be as charming," Chacho told her. "And the next time, Kharee will be standing next to me. I'll give him the pleasure of putting a bullet between those pretty little eyes of yours."

"I'll remember that," Peaches told him. "I'll remember everything about our little meeting today."

"Please do," Chacho told her. "I want you to. Because if you forget anything that was said today, it could be fatal. Hurry your shit up, and do it right. Stop fucking around."

"Are we done here?" Peaches asked.

Chacho nodded toward the exit dismissively, telling her to get the fuck out of his face. Peaches felt two inches tall. She was just starting out in the game at this level, and Chacho was a major member on The Commission. He had a major family, tons of money, and virtually unlimited resources. He talked to her like she was shit, and he had brought hundreds of soldiers into a neighboring territory. The message was very clear. She was playing in a much bigger pond than she was used to. In fact, she was no longer playing in just a pond. She was now swimming in a giant ocean, and it was filled with great white sharks. She needed to take Ohio, and she needed to do it quickly. She was nothing but prey, swimming amongst a bunch of big ass predators. She needed to get big.

Peaches turned toward the exit and began to walk away. Chacho whistled. She turned back toward him.

"A word of advice, chica," Chacho told her. "And this is between me and you."

"What's that?" Peaches asked.

"As long as Kharee is alive, The Commission has an alternate that they can turn to. No Kharee, then there's nobody to hold over your head." Chacho told her. "And that advice is free of charge."

Peaches nodded. She got the message loud and clear. As long as Kharee was alive, he remained a possible replacement. And The Commission would continue to hold him over her head. She had to get rid of Kharee, and she had to get rid of him as soon as possible. And that meant, that she would have to hurry up and get big enough to take him on. She was now even more desperate to hurry up and take all of Columbus. Chacho had been very clear about that as well. The clock was ticking, and her time was winding down, and winding down fast.

Chapter Eleven

Trap poured herself a shot of Patron and tossed back the stiff drink. "Okay, we're back home now, P. You ready to talk about it now?"

Peaches paced nervously back and forth across the marble floors of her Dublin, Ohio mansion. She was shaking nervously.

"Girl, what's the deal?" Vendetta asked.

Omar pulled the bottle of Patron from Trap's hand, poured himself a shot, and tossed it back. "They serious, huh?"

Peaches paused her pacing and nodded.

"Big boys sent you a serious message?" Omar continued.

"You're damn right," Peaches said, nervously.

"Okay, so talk to us!" Trap said forcefully. "Why you holding it in?"

"You know we your girls," Vendetta told her. "We got your back no matter what."

Peaches shook her head. "I'm sorry. I'm sorry for getting y'all into this."

"Into what?" Vendetta asked.

"Into all of this bullshit," Peaches told them.

"What bullshit?" Trap asked. "P, what's going on?"

"They made it loud and clear, and plain and simple," Peaches told them. "I don't have much time. I don't take Ohio, I'm dead. It's just that simple. And they ain't gonna leave you two alone either."

"Who said we wanted to be left alone?" Trap asked. "Girl, we are all in this together. We go down, we go down together."

"And we go down fighting!" Vendetta added.

"So, what are we waiting for?" Omar asked.

The three women turned toward him.

"You need to take Ohio, then what the fuck are we waiting for?" Omar said, tossing back another shot.

"We can't take Ohio, without taking Cleveland," Peaches explained. "We can't take Cleveland, without taking Cincinnati. We can't take Cincinnati without Dayton. And without Youngstown, we can't take Dayton. And we can't take Youngstown, if we don't even control all of fucking Columbus!"

"Then fucking take Columbus!" Omar shouted. "Sitting around bitching about it ain't gonna do nothing. You need to take this bitch, then quit pussy footing around, and take this bitch."

"Oh, now you down?" Trap asked.

"Since you already stepped in it, you might as well jump into the shit with both feet," Omar told her.

"That means we need to take out Big Meech, Poocus, and Bug," Trap explained. "We take out one, the other two will see us coming from a mile away. And so will Kharee."

"You act like it's a fucking secret that Kharee don't like you!" Omar said angrily. "Why the fuck are you tiptoeing? That nigga wants you dead, and you want him dead, so why the fuck are you walking on eggs? You control one third of Columbus, now that you've taken over Sweet Peas's shit. Big Meech, Poocus, and Bug control the other two thirds. You're stronger than any *two* of them. So why are you picking *one* of them to fight? Pick *two*, and let the dice roll where they may."

"I'll still end up fighting all three," Peaches told him. "Plus Kharee will send his boys into the mix. Plus those fucking Get Money Boys. That's too many!"

"And if you do nothing?" Omar asked.

"Then I'm dead," Peaches said, throwing her hands up in frustration.

"Right," Omar said nodding. "You're damned if you do, damned if you don't. So what have you got to lose?"

Peaches turned and walked to her giant clerestory window that overlooked her backyard. Omar was right. What did she have to lose? The answer was obvious. Nothing. She had nothing to lose.

"Well, let's get this shit popping," Vendetta said.

"Ain't shit to think about," Omar told her. "We go out, we go out fighting. We go out there, and we make war, ma. And if we die, then we make sure that muthafuckas will never forget that we was here. You make them remember your name forever."

Peaches let out a half smile. "I never thought that it would come to this."

"It is what it is," Trap told her.

"I'm sorry," Peaches said, sniffling.

"What?" Vendetta asked, turning up her palms. "What the fuck are you talking about?"

"I didn't mean to do this to y'all," Peaches told them. "I didn't mean to get y'all into this."

"Cut that shit out, P!" Trap told her. "We in this shit. We was in this shit from the very beginning. You ain't brought us into shit. We knew what we was doing when we signed up for this shit."

Vendetta walked up to Peaches and hugged her. "Girl, you know we down like four flat tires."

Omar poured himself another drink. "You know I got you, ma."

Peaches wiped away hers tears and begin to nod. Resignation slowly begin to set in. She knew that she was going to bite off more than she cold chew. She knew that they were all about to die.

"Don't trip," Omar said, tossing back another shot. "It ain't all bad. Who knows, maybe one of us might make it. We got soldiers, ma. Don't forget that. We ain't just got niggas rolling with us for pay, we got niggas who are down with us for real. Niggas who been down since the playground days back in the hood. That's loyalty. And ten loyal dedicated muthafuckas can take on a hundred paid niggas any day a the week. We small, but we fierce."

Peaches let out a half smile.

"And if we don't make it, then fuck it," Omar said. "We got further than any of us ever thought we would. We got to hit Vegas, hit the islands, roll big cars, cop big cribs, fuck bad bitches, smoke big spliffs. The streets said we was supposed to be dead at the age of eighteen. So fuck it. We been living on borrow time any muthafuckin way."

"Pick two," Trap said with a smile.

"I know who I want to kill," Vendetta said, providing her own smile.

"I know what muthafucka I wanna put a bullet in," Omar said, letting out a half smile.

Peaches joined in with a smile of her own. "We really gonna do this?"

Omar lifted his shot glass in a toast. "I have only one regret."

Peaches was taken aback. One eyed Omar was a man of no regrets, she thought. He did what he did, and lived like he lived. For him to say he regretted something took her by surprise.

"And what's that?" Vendetta asked.

"That I didn't get to have you and Trap at the same muthafuckin time," Omar said laughing.

"Nigga please!" Trap said. "Not in this lifetime, the next one, the one after that, or any other one!"

"Black ass, muthafucka!" Vendetta said, shoving the side of Omar's head.

"Let's do this," Omar said, tossing back his drink.

"Let's do it," Peaches said softly. She knew that she was about to commit herself and the lives of her friends to a war that they couldn't win. She hugged them all.

*****

Trap sat inside of the black Escalade watching the front of the bail bonds. She knew that Bug liked to personally collect his money from his various establishments around the city. He was old school to his heart, and his old school habits would never change. He viewed his old school ways as the reason for his success and longevity, and as the reason why he never did any major time upstate. Unfortunately for him, his habits were what betrayed him on this occasion.

It was no secret that Bug also like to use the bail bond office to entertain various female acquaintances. It was where he met most of them. Young girls whose boyfriends had gotten caught up by the police, who were desperate for help, and who were in their most vulnerable state. Bug and his boys used their situations to take advantage of them, to offer them discounts for sexual favors, or to provide the bonds even if they didn't have all of the money. And it was these same girls, and many more, who came back to the bail bonds time after time looking for money in exchange for sex. The thought of Bug's old wrinkled ass climbing on top of some young desperate girl disgusted Trap to no end. He was her first choice to kill. And the fact that he had approached her on several occasions in the past and offered her money in exchange for sex made it even more personal. To her, he was a predator who had to die.

Bug pulled up to the bail bond office and climbed out of his own black Escalade. He peered around, fixed his dress shirt, and then headed inside. A white XTS Cadillac pulled up seconds later, and several girls climbed out. They were quickly escorted inside of the bail bonds. He was going to party hardy tonight, Trap thought. Or at least he *thought* he was. She lifted her two way communicator and spoke into it.

"Viagra is in the bottle," Trap said smiling. Viagra was her code word for Bug's old ass. She wanted to call him Chester, as in Chester the Molester, but she and Vendetta settled on Viagra for his disgusting old ass.

"Roger," Vendetta replied. "How many pills in the bottle?"

Trap thought about the number of soldiers she saw go into the building with Bug. She thought about how many men he had brought with him in his Escalade, how many were already waiting for him when he arrived. She added those numbers up with the number of men he used to bring over the four young girls in the XTS.

"Fifteen pills, plus Viagra, plus the four recipients," Trap told her.

"Roger," Vendetta told her. "Shift change beginning in now."

"Gotcha," Trap acknowledged. They knew the time that the Columbus Police Department changed shifts. That meant that the patrol cars in their area would be heading back to the station, while the next shift would just be grabbing their coffee and getting ready to go out. If anything needed to go down, it was best to do it during the shift change, to make sure that you stood a chance of getting away. It was time.

"I'm going," Trap continued.

"Good luck," Vendetta told her.

"Same to you, Boo," Trap told her.

Trap climbed out of the Escalade, and walked toward the bail bonds. She winked at some of her soldiers who were posted in an Acura sitting down the block. They started up the car, and began creeping toward the bail bond. Trap walked inside.

"Hi, I need to speak to someone about getting a bond," Trap told the guy working behind the counter."

She surveyed the establishment. There were three guys working the front, while another was seated in the front waiting area flipping through a Source magazine. She spotted another posted up near a door leading to the back room, which was no doubt where Bug was entertaining his female guests. That made five out of fifteen.

"Do you know how much the bond is?" the worker asked.

"A fifteen thousand dollar bond," Trap said. "Does that mean I need fifteen thousand dollars? I don't have no fifteen thousand dollars!"

The guys laughed. "Naw, you need fifteen hundred. So, has he already been arraigned?"

Trap nodded.

The guy walked up to his computer. "What's his name? Do you have his date of birth, and all of his other information?"

Trap nodded. "Yeah, I wrote it down. It's..." She began searching her bag. "Damn! It's on an envelope! I must have left it in the car. Hold on, I'll be right back!"

Trap turned and rushed out of the bail bonds, leaving her bag on the counter. She climbed inside of her Escalade, lifted a remote, and aimed it toward her purse inside of the bail bond office. And then she ducked.

The explosion ripped through the bail bond office blowing the roof off of the structure. Windows from the nearby buildings and cars shattered, including those on the driver's side of her Escalade.

"Dammit!" Vendetta shouted into the walkie-talkie. "Bitch, don't you know how to use just a little bit of that shit! You ain't got to blow up the whole fucking block!"

Trap raised up, climbed out of the Escalade, and then walked over to where the Acura was parked. She was handed an AK-47, which she cocked, and then turned toward what was left of the bail bond office. She could see Vendetta and some of her men making their way through what was once the rear section of the building. She began her walk through the front part.

"Damn, bitch!" Vendetta shouted with a smile. She waved her hand, clearing away some of the smoke from the burning fires.

Trap heard moaning and labored breathing. She walked to where it was coming from. One of Bug's men was trying desperately to get up. Trap pointed her AK and put a bullet through his back, causing him to fall instantly. She watched for a few seconds to make sure that he was no longer breathing. Once she was sure that he was dead, she continued on. Soon, she stepped over a three foot pile of bricks, which used to be the brick wall separating some rooms. She joined Vendetta and her men, who were searching through the ruble, killing off survivors. They came across one of the young girls who didn't make it. Trap and Vendetta exchanged glances. They hated that she died, and that she had gotten caught up, but her death, meant that Bug wouldn't be taking advantage of any more young girls. Her death, was also tempered by the fact that the other three were found alive. They were battered, bruised, bleeding, but alive. Soon, they came across their reason for being there, they came across Bug himself.

Bug was bleeding. His pants were pulled down to his ankles, which meant that he was probably getting head from one of the girls before the explosion ripped through the building. To their surprise, he was also still breathing. Vendetta took her boot, wedged it beneath him, and rolled him over. Blood ran down his face, and his breathing was labored, but he was still able to focus.

"You bitches ain't did shit," Bug told them. "You think you did something, you ain't did shit! At the end of the day, I'm still gonna be a pimp, and y'all still gonna be hoes! And at the end of the day, Kharee is gonna see all a y'all!"

Trap and Vendetta exchanged glances. Both of them lifted their weapons, and both aimed at Bug. Almost simultaneously, they both squeezed their triggers, putting numerous rounds into Bug. They didn't have to respond to him. And both felt that they wouldn't even give him the dignity of their words. And both felt good about doing what they had just done. They had just took out a predator who had slept with girls as young as thirteen and fourteen. And even if there weren't a war going on to take the streets of Columbus, they both felt that killing him had been justified.

*****

Blades and Fades was Columbus's hottest barber shot. It had twenty barber chairs, seventy five percent of which were always in operation. The establishment prided itself on short waiting times, as well as having the baddest barbers in all of Columbus. It was here where a lot of ballers got their hair cut. At least those who didn't pay their favorite barbers to come to the house and hook them up weekly. Normally, big timers didn't venture out to the shop unless they wanted to show off. Perhaps a new Benz, or Bentley, or some other new toy. Or, unless they owned the establishment and could walk in and get the next chair without having to wait, which was the case in this instance. Poocus, a former barber turned dope dealer, was the owner of Blades and Fades, and could walk right in and climb into the next chair without nary a protest from anyone else. Everyone in Ohio knew who he was, and no one in Columbus was going to challenge him. Especially in a joint that he owned. And so, today, Poocus showed up to Blades an Fades in his shiny new Beluga Caviar colored Bentley Continental GT, hopped out, and walked into his barbershop. The barbers and patrons all greeted him with much adulation, and like any other egotistical dope dealer, he basked in their compliments, while waiting for his favorite barber to do a rush job on his current patron in order to clear the chair for him.

Poocus climbed into his barber's chair, and pointed outside toward his Bentley, that he had parked in the front of the shop. "See that right there! Two hundred thousand! Off the showroom floor!"

Ooohhhs, and Ahhhs, went through the shop. One particular sycophant, was an older barber, and former crackhead name Lucas who went out of his way to walk to the window and stare at Poocus' new toy.

"Man, that thing is something fierce!" Lucas told him. "You say it cost two hundred thousand dollars? That's more than most people's house!"

Poocus leaned back in the chair beaming with a smile that could have lit up Times Square. His barber placed his hair cloth around his neck to insure that the hair didn't get on his clothes. He took his duster, sprinkled some powder on it, and then brushed around the sides of Poocus' head. He turned and pulled his clippers out of the ultraviolet sanitizing station, spraying them with sanitizing oil, and then turned them on. The clippers snapped alive, and then continued to emanate a soft buzzing sound.

A couple of guys walked into the shop and posted up in the waiting area close to the door of the shop. They flipped through several magazines before choosing a couple to browse.

"When did you get back from L.A.?" the barber asked, making conversation with his client.

"I been back," Poocus told him. "I went out there and hooked up with my homie who wanted to pitch me on a film project. He's looking for some financing, and I told him that I'd take a look at it and see if it was something I'd be interested in pursuing."

"So, you getting into making movies now, Big Dog?" Lucas asked from across the room.

"Yeah, I think it's time for me to get some of that Hollywood money," Poocus said loud enough for everyone in the shop to hear him. "It's time to spread my hustle."

Laughter went through the shop.

Poocus stared at the gentleman seated in the barber chair at the station next to him. "You look familiar. Where I know you from?"

"I'm from 8 Mile," Omar said in his scruff and raspy voice. "Ever been to D-town?"

"Oh, you one of them Detroit niggas!" Poocus said loudly. "Yeah, yeah, I used to swing through there all the time. Ain't no pussy like Detroit pussy. I used to swing through and bang up all the hoes up there. As a matter a fact, I still got a few boppers up that way."

"Oh yeah?" Omar said smiling. "What part?"

"All over," Poocus bragged. "West Bloomfield, Amberleigh, you know, I like them classy bitches."

Laughter shot throughout the barbershop.

"I'm telling you, you look familiar like a muthafucka!" Poocus continued. "Where you get that scar from?"

Omar smiled. "Dope deal gone bad. I got caught up, niggas tortured me. Ran a Skill Saw down the side of my face, trying to carve out my brains or something. The docs told me that it was a miracle that I didn't bleed out. An even bigger miracle that they was able to save my eye. They had to put a metal plate into my skull to hold it together."

"Damn, so you a tough one, huh?" Poocus asked. "Usually them 8 mile niggas is all hype. Eminem got muthafuckas thinking that bitch is the hardest place on Earth. But them 8 Mile niggas ain't holding nothing. Most a them niggas is soft as a muthafucka."

Laughter shot throughout the shop.

"So what brings you to my town, Detroit?" Poocus asked.

"You," Omar told him.

"Me?" Poocus asked. "What the fuck you want with me?"

"Nothing," Omar smiled. "I just need your bitch ass to stop inhaling and exhaling."

Omar rose and tossed off the barber's hair cloth, revealing a sawed off pistol grip shotgun. He aimed, just as Poocus was trying to get up out of his chair.

"What the fuck?" Poocus shouted.

The blast from Omar's shotgun sat him back down, and blood spurted from his mouth and nose. His men sitting in the waiting room rose, and went for their weapons, but Omar's men leaped from their barber chairs and sprayed them with small semi automatic weapons. The bodyguards fell instantly. More of Poocus' men ran into the shop, only to be dropped instantly by more automatic gunfire from Omar's crew. Omar walked to where Poocus was sitting, and place his small 12 gauge shotgun beneath his chin.

"Damn, homie, life is a bitch," Omar told him. "One minute you pulling up in a brand new Bentley, and the next minute you sitting in a chair squirting out blood. Didn't think your day was gonna end up like this, did you?"

Poocus gritted, and closed his eyes. Blood poured down his heaving chest with each of his labored breaths. Soon, he stopped breathing on his own.

Omar pulled his shotgun away, and turned to his men. "Make sure ain't no more of these bitch ass niggas outside."

Some of his men raced out of the back door, while others carefully pulled open the front door of the shop, and made their way outside. One of them turned back to him.

"It's all clear."

A smile ran across Omar's face. "Call baby girl, and tell her that it's all good. And get these bodies outta here. Some of you niggas mop up this blood. Ain't nothing happened here today, y'all got that. Ain't no bodies, so it ain't no crime. Anybody want to get smart, or get a conscience, I know where you live, and I know how to get at your people. Don't make me have to come for you."

Omar turned, placed his shotgun on his shoulder, and walked out of the shop. Two major pieces had been taken off the chest board in a single day. And now, it was their enemies turn to move. He just hoped that they weren't about to be overwhelmed by a bunch of pawns, and that they could stay at least two moves ahead.

Chapter Twelve

Peaches walked through her Dublin Ohio mansion, and headed into her master bedroom. It had been a long day, and she was tired. Bone tired. Her fatigue came more from mental stress than actual physical activity. She had replayed her moves, and today's events, over and over in her head. She had created dozens upon dozens of possible scenarios, and thought of move and counter moves, to guard against each possibility. She had taken out two of her biggest rivals in the city, and tomorrow she would begin the process of wiping out all of their underlings who didn't swear allegiance to her. And the ones that did, would be ordered to attack the ones that didn't. She would also have to make moves against Bug's wife and kids, as well as Poocus' wife, who were the heirs to their legitimate businesses. Businesses that they used to move their products, businesses that were key sites that helped to control key neighborhoods. Taking them over was critical to gaining control of the neighborhoods drug trade, and getting the street level niggas to score from her. It would also bring in fresh recruits, and deprive Big Meech and Kharee of recruiting grounds, as well as take some potential recruits away from those Get Money Boys. She had so much to do, and all of had to be done while

at war with Kharee and Big Meech, who were no doubt freaking out
and calling up men to deal with her moves. The good thing about it,
was that the two of them hated each other, just as much as they hated
her. They would each go to war with her, but not coordinate and join
forces. Kharee would be desperate to keep her from taking over all of
Columbus, while Big Meech would be desperate to simply survive.
He would be the more dangerous of the two, because it was his
livelihood, and life, on the line. And so, she was determined to focus
her energies on getting rid of him first. He was the key. Getting rid of
Meech would give her all of Columbus, and give her the manpower
and the money she needed to start knocking off other cities. But she
would have to win the war first. And taking on Get Money, Big
Meech, and Kharee at the same time, would be an impossible task.
They just had way too many niggas at their disposal. For every one
nigga she could put in the street, Meech could put one, Kharee could
put three or four, and Get Money could put six. It was literally ten
against one. Getting Poocus' soldiers and Bug's soldiers, would break
it down to five against one, and so she was desperate to get them to lay
it down and join her. That would be the key to being able to continue
to fight. She could feel another headache coming on. Thinking about
this all day, had given her a couple of migraines. She turned toward
her nightstand, only to discover that she had used up all of the Liquid
Advil that she kept next to her bedside.
        Peaches climbed out of her warm comfortable bed, adjusted her
pajamas, slid her feet into her slippers, and headed down the hall and
into her kitchen. She kept an extra bottle in one of her kitchen
cabinets, and she definitely had to pop two of the green gel tabs before
her headache worsened. She opened up her cabinet, located her spare
bottle, and poured two of the gels caps into her hand. And now, she
needed something the drink. Peaches headed to her massive 48"
stainless steel Sub Zero refrigerator and pulled open the door. She had
some soda in the fridge, as well as a pitcher of Appletini Crystal Light,

which was her favorite. She pulled out the pitcher, and headed back to another cabinet for a cup. And then, her doorbell rang.

Peaches sat the pitcher down on her granite counter top and headed to her front door. Her housekeeper had gone home hours ago, so answering the door was a task that was relegated to her. What was unusual however, was that she was not expecting any guest at this hour, and no one from her security gate had called to inform her that someone had arrived. Even when it was Trap or V, they usually called and gave her a heads up. This piqued her curiosity to the point where she made a quick stop at the hall chest in her foyer, slid out a drawer, and pulled out one of the spare handguns that she kept hidden around her house. She pulled back the slide and cocked it, chambering a round. And then she continued to her door.

Peaches opened her front door, her heart jumped out of her chest and she dropped her weapon.

"*Oh my God!*" she screamed. "*What the fuck are you doing here?*"

"Hello, Ms. Espinoza." Chesarae stood at her front door with a wide smile.

Peaches peered around outside, thinking that the U.S. Marshals were hot on his trail and about to raid her house. And then she had to reach out and touch him to make sure that he was real.

"*Chesarae!*" she gasped. "What are you doing here?"

"Is that how you greet your man?" Chesarae asked, still smiling.

"No, I'm sorry," Peaches said shaking her head, and trying to clear her thoughts. "What are you doing here?"

"I'm here to see you."

"That's not what I mean!" Peaches told him. "Stop playing with me, you know what I mean. What are you doing *here*? Why are you out of prison?"

"Damn. No, I'm happy to see you. No, I'm so glad you're home. No hugs, no kisses, no tears of joy. Just, what the fuck are you doing

111

here?"

"You know I'm happy to see you," Peaches said. "But how did you get out? You had thirty years in the Feds!"

"They changed the crack law," Chesarae said smiling broadly. "I went from 100 to 1, to 10 to 1. I filed my paperwork, got time served, and the judge ordered my immediate release."

Peaches shook her head. "I can't believe this."

"Is that good or bad?" Chesarae asked. "Are you just going to leave me out here?"

Peaches stepped to the side, opening her door wider. Chesarae stepped inside and peered around.

"Whew!" he declared, taking in her home. "You sure have done well for yourself, Baby Girl."

Peaches raked her hands through her hair, sending it back over her shoulders. "Okay let's cut out the bullshit. You're serious? This is for real? You're home?"

Chesarae turned up his palms. "I'm here, aren't I?"

Peaches shook her head. The day that she had prayed for had finally come true. Crying herself to sleep all of those nights, begging God to send her man back to her, all of the court dates, the trials, the visits, the fighting, the bullshit that she had been through, and now this? Chesarae just appeared at her doorstep like some magical fucking unicorn, and everything that she knew, her new world, had just been thrown out of the window. The man standing before her, had been the love of her life. Before he went to prison, he had been her everything.

"Okay, so, what are you doing here?" she asked again. "How... How did you even know where I lived? How did you even get in here, and then past my security?"

"Are you fucking kidding me?" Chesarae asked. "How did I get past security? Like I'm some fucking drifter, or interloper, or some fucking homeless bum on the street?"

112

Peaches placed her hand on her forehead. "I'm sorry. That didn't come out right. Chesarae, you can't just show up all of a sudden and expect me not to be fucked up. This is too much for a person to digest in seconds. You went from being in prison for thirty years, to standing on my doorstep."

"I wanted to surprise you," Chesarae told her. "I told the guys..."

"Wait a minute," Peaches said stopping him. "You told the guys? Those are my men..."

"They're my men!" Chesarae said cutting her off.

"They're mine!" Peaches shot back.

"Look, I'm not here for that," Chesarea told her. "I'm not here for another pissing contest, and I'm not here to argue with you over who controls what. You did good for yourself, Peach. And, I'm not here looking to step in, or take over, or ask you for anything."

"Okay, so why are you here?"

"I'm here to see you, Peach." Chesarae walked closer to her. Her pulled her close. "I came to talk to you. We need to talk about a lot of things."

Chesarae kissed her on her forehead. "You look good."

Peaches placed her arms on his. "You look good too."

She could feel herself melting.

Chesarae was half black, half pacific islander. His father was a from Senegal, a French speaking West African nation, who worked for Peugeot, a French car company. He met Chesarae's mother, a French Tahitian woman, on a business trip to the Pacific. The two of them fell in love and were married, and one year later Chesarae was born. One year after that, Kiantae, showed up. And five years after that, the family relocated to Detroit, where his father took a job at General Motors.

Chesarae had his mother's features. Thick wavy hair, which he wore cut short in a fade. He had high, well pronounced cheek bones, and narrow, slanted, gray eyes, and a small perky nose that also came from his mother's side of the family. He inherited his father's full lips, that reminded her of small tangerine slices, and he also had his mother's cocoa butter skin tone. Chesarae also spoke with a slight Pacific Islander accent, mixed with a slight French accent. And last but not least, the Feds had been good to him. He had apparently spent his time in federal prison working out constantly. He had muscles on top of muscles rippling across his body. Peaches wanted to lick every single tattoo he had, and he was covered in them. He had *Nothing To Lose* tattooed across his neck in cursive, with a smoking AK-47 assault rifle beneath it. He had a black rose tattooed on the other side of his neck, that matched the black rose that she had tattooed across her pussy. He had six tattooed tear drops running down his cheek from the corner of his left eye, and *Young Gangsta* tattooed on his knuckles. All over his body, his tattoos showed that he lived for the streets. His muscles made all of his tattoos even sexier to her.

Peaches swallowed hard, and dug deep inside of herself to find enough willpower to pull away from him.

"Okay, so, what did you want to talk about?" Peaches said, clearing her throat.

Chesarae dropped his arms. "I thought we both wanted to talk about us."

Peaches could feel herself growing weaker and weaker ever second she spent in his presence. He not only smelled good, but his arms and chest were bulging out of his tight white thermal shirt.

"Okay, I'm listening," she said softly.

"What happened between us?" he asked.

Peaches shrugged. "A lot. So much that I can't even begin to think of it all."

"If you can't remember it, how important was it?"

"It was pretty damn important," Peaches told him. "Sitting in that courtroom, and having all those bitches show up talking about you was *they* man. And then seeing bitches leaving from the holding facility while I was arriving, and I know who they was visiting!"

Chesarae waved his hand. "That's small shit. Them bitches didn't matter. That shit was just recreation. *You was the wifey!* You was! You got the money, the houses, the cars, everything! Them hoes got nothing!"

"It *did* matter!" Peaches shouted. "It mattered to me. You left me with all that shit, granted. But the one thing you didn't leave me with, was *respect*! That shit hurt, Chesarae! That was some disrespectful, painful ass shit that you put me through! Having bitches laughing at me, pointing at me, whispering about me, like I was fucking Celie from *The Color Purple* or some shit! It wasn't just about *things*, Chesarae! Why can't you understand that? It was never about stuff! It was about being your wife, and about being respected! I would have preferred that, over a dozen fucking houses! I would have been down with you if you didn't have shit! Remember that? Whether we in a Bentley, or on the fucking number ten bus! I'm a ride or die bitch, nigga! And you disrespected that shit! You violated the code!"

"Can I talk now?" Chesarae asked.

"What?"

"You talking about small shit," Chesarae told her. "You worried about none muthafuckin factors. Bitches who don't even fit into the equation! You was supposed to be down for me, no matter what! *You* violated the code! You stopped writing, and you started a bunch of bullshit ass arguments just so your conscience would be clear, and you could go on and do your damn thing!"

"Do my damn thing?" Peaches stepped into his face. "Nigga, is you crazy? Do my damn thing? Everything I ever did, was for us! *Everything*! All of the struggles that I went through out in this bitch, alone I might add, I went through for us! You worried about if another nigga was jumping up and down in my pussy, now who's worried about the small shit? Yeah, that's what I thought! When it's you jumping up and down in a bitch, it's just rec. But when it comes to me,

115

it's a major muthafuckin violation. I got tired of arguing with you, Chesarae! Arguing about nothing. That place had you going crazy! Crazy for no reason. I wasn't doing shit! I wasn't creeping, I wasn't dating, I wasn't doing shit! But for some reason, you couldn't believe that!"

"It had me going crazy because I loved you, got dammit!" Chesarae shouted. "I loved you more than anything in this world! You were my life, my breath, my air, my everything! And they took you away from me. So yeah, I was fucked up. All I could think about was you. All I could think about was holding you, kissing you, having you in my arms."

"*Then why didn't you say it?*" Peaches screamed. "Instead of accusing me of being in someone else's arms, all you had to say was that you wanted me in yours!"

"I didn't know how," he told her. He sniffled. "How do you pray for something, knowing that you got thirty years? Do you know the battle that I fought with myself? Thirty years? I would have been selfish trying to keep you, not letting you go on with your life and finding someone to be happy with. But my heart wouldn't let go. And then on top of that, them punk ass niggas, them bitch ass guards, dealing with all of that shit day in, day out, yeah, I was fucked up."

Peaches sniffled and wiped away her tears. "What do you want from me, Chesarae?"

Chesarae shook his head and looked down. "I don't know."

"This is much longer than a one night conversation," Peaches told him.

Chesarae nodded. "At least we got the yelling out of the way."

Peaches laughed. "Yeah, I guess we did."

"So, what comes next?"

Peaches shrugged. "You tell me."

"I'm going to put my life back together, one step at a time," Chesarae told her. "I guess I just wanted to check on a key piece of

116

that puzzle."

"I'm here," Peaches said softly. "And anything you need, just say it and it's yours."

"I need a place to crash," Chesarae told her.

Peaches motioned toward the couch.

"Oh, you gonna put me on the couch?" Chesarae asked. "That's how you gonna do me? You gonna walk around here, with all of that fat ass you got, and you gonna keep a hungry lion on the couch. A lion who ain't had no pussy in years. Chesarae pulled off his shirt and tossed it onto the couch, showcasing his rippling muscles and heavily tattooed body. He had abs for days.

Peaches closed her eyes and bit down on her lip. She could feel the liquids inside of her body flowing. He was finer than a *muthafucka*, she thought.

"You gonna miss out of years of frustration?" Chesarae asked with a smile.

Peaches knew that Chesarae was packing, and that he could beat up some pussy like a heavy weight champ. And for him to not have had no pussy in years, just made her cream even more. She knew that he would destroy the first pussy that he got to. She could feel him driving her insides all night long.

"I'll bring you a blanket," She gulped and said weakly.

Chesarae laid back on her sofa. "I'm a get up with the rest of the fellas tomorrow."

"About?" Peaches asked.

"Shit, I'm back!" Chesarae said with a smile.

"Yeah, but you've been gone for years," Peaches told him. "Ches, a lot of things have changed since you left. Things ain't the same no more. Just take your time and check things out first, before you start trying to holler at everybody."

"What are you talking about? It is what it is. But I know my homeboys love for me ain't changed."

117

Peaches shook her head. "Ches, you can't come out here thinking that everything is still the same. Baby, you went away, we didn't. Time kept moving forward. Everybody is doing their own thing now."

Chesarae smiled. "What are you talking about? My niggaz are still holding it down. Shit, them youngsters was coming up in the joint representing."

Peaches let out a slight laugh. "Babe, Young and Holding is not the same. Yeah, you have some youngsters still representing, but it's not like it was. JerMarcus and Ashaad are back in Youngstown. And the only reason I see Ashaad is because of Trap. LaQuan is here, and so is Tavion. But Jakeem, and Terrell, are back in Dayton. Omar is here. I don't know where Tysaund is. Hell, I haven't even seen Kiantae in years."

"My brother hasn't swung by and checked on you in years?" Chesarae asked. "Are you serious?"

"Everybody is doing their own thing," Peaches told him. "Everybody has their own crews."

"And Marquez?" Chesarae asked.

Peaches shook her head. "Haven't seen him since he got out."

Marquez was an awkward subject between them. Marquez had been her man before he went to the feds the first time, and that was when she got with Chesarae. And then Chesarae went to the feds and Marquez got out, and the two of them hooked back up briefly. And then Marquez went to the feds a second time. But even when Marquez went the first time, and she got with Chesarae, Marquez still was considered one of the crew. And there had been no hard feelings between he and Chesarae. At least on the surface.

"And what about my nigga Hassan?" Chesarae asked with a smile.

Peaches lowered her head.

"What?" Chesarae asked.

"I don't know about Hassan," she said softly.

"What do you mean?" Chesarae asked, smiling broadly. "Hassan is my nigga! I'm a go to Detroit and see that fool as soon as I get a chance."

Peaches shook her head. "Don't."

"Why not?"

"Hassan has changed, Ches. Things are not the same. He's different now. Way different."

"Peach, you're tripping," he said, waving her off. "Hassan is my ride or die nigga."

"Yeah, and if you go and see him, you will die," Peaches said flatly.

Chesarae sat up. "Peach, what the fuck are you talking about?"

"Hassan will kill you if you go to Detroit," Peaches told him. "He's not the same. *Nothing* is the same. You think that Hassan is your boy, but Hassan was your boy, because he envied you. But he never liked being in your shadow. He always wanted what you had. And now that he's back in Detroit, he's come up, and the only thing you'll do by showing up, is remind him of what he once was, which was your flunky."

"Hassan wasn't my flunky," Chesarae protested. "We was boys."

"Maybe you seen it like that, but everyone else could clearly see it. You kept me in the house, but you didn't pull out my eyes, Chesarae. I could see it clearly. Hassan was, and always will be, jealous of you. And I'm telling you, if you show up in Detroit, he will kill you."

"I'm from Detroit," he told her. "And Hassan, and nobody else is gonna keep me from going home."

"Don't go there, and don't go to Dayton. Marquez has been saying some things since he got out as well. The people who you thought were your friends, are not your friends. Open your eyes, Chesarae."

"I'm putting my life back together, Peach," he told her.

"Young and Holding is dead!" she said forcefully. "Let it go. We're not kids anymore."

"I know that. And that's why I need to holler at everybody. The feds gave me time to think. Time to sit back and examine things, and see things clearly. Yeah, we were all young and dumb, and doing crazy ass shit. And I realized while I was locked up, that we could have been so much more. We had connections and niggas from every city in Ohio, and even homeboys in Detroit and Chicago. We could have taken over this shit. We could have controlled all of this shit, and really put it down and made some major paper."

"What are you saying, Chesarae?" Peaches asked.

"I'm saying, that I'm getting the homies back together, and all of their separate crews, and Young and Holding is back into effect. But this time, we're going to do this shit right. This time, we are going to take over all of Ohio."

"And what about Kharee?" Peaches asked.

Chesarae waved his hand dismissing the thought. "What about him? That nigga ain't shit. He's a peon."

"Not anymore!" Peaches said forcefully. "That's what I'm telling you. Things have changed! Niggas have come up, and other niggas have fallen. It's a completely different ball game now!"

"Two things I know for sure," Chesarae told her. "I need to borrow your shower for one. And two, can't nobody fuck with Young and Holding."

Chesarae pulled off his Mek jeans, and stripped down to his boxers. He headed down the hall, searching for the master bath. "I'm telling you, babe. I got a plan. This shit is gonna be big. We gonna take over all of this bitch, and we gonna see money like we ain't never seen it before."

Chesarae disappeared into her master suite, and Peaches leaned against her wall, folded her arms and closed her eyes. The man she loved more than life itself had just showed up at her doorstep, throwing her life into chaos. Chesarae was her heart, her life, her love, her everything. And now, he was back. Under any other circumstances it would have been the happiest day of her life. But these were not normal circumstances. The love of her life had just shown up out of nowhere with a plan, and a determination to take over the State of Ohio. A state that she needed to take over herself. He was stuck in the old days, with an old mindset. He knew nothing about The Commission, or about the way things worked. He was a local baller trying to think big, while she was a big baller trying to move into even bigger circles. And that's what frightened her more than anything. The fact that her dreams, and his dreams, were diametrically opposed. They both wanted the same state, but for different reasons. She wanted to be a member of an international drug consortium, while he wanted to take it and control it for himself. She knew Chesarae, and she knew that he wouldn't fit within The Commission. He was hotheaded, as well as hardheaded. And he had never met a rule that he didn't break. And The Commission had rules. And so now, she had a choice to make. Rolling with The Commission and her new love, Darius, or taking Ohio for herself, and rekindling her romance with her soul mate, Chesarae. And if she chose Chesarae, then The Commission would strip her of her seat and give it to Kharee. Which in turn would mean that they would back him when the time came and he needed to wipe out the last bit of resistance in Ohio. And that would put her back at the starting point. The Commission coming to kill her.

Could it all really be that simple, she wondered. Her life, or Chesarae's? Peaches wiped away the tears falling from her eyes. The thought of having to kill the only man that she ever truly loved, was ripping her apart on the inside. Could she? Would she? It would be like stabbing herself in the chest and carving out her own heart. Chesarae had certainly thrown a monkey wrench in her plans, and now she had a decision to make. She stared at the gun she had dropped by her front door, and then peered toward her master suite where she could hear her love taking a shower. She could feel her heart fall to her feet. Could she kill Chesarae? Could she?

Chapter Thirteen

Peaches hit the gear shifter on her Porsches' Tiptronic transmission, downshifting, and accelerating her two seat convertible to mind blowing speeds. She needed the wind in her hair, she needed to feel the cool crisp air against her face. Dropping the top and hitting the highway was what she did to clear her mind when life started to overwhelm her. So much had transpired in her life of late, and so much had yet to transpire. Her situation with The Commission had been greatly exacerbated by the unexpected arrival of her former boyfriend. Chesarae showing up on her doorstep the previous night had completely thrown her for a loop. And the fact that he was adamant about getting his boys back together and jumping back into the Ohio drug scene, had really complicated things. The love of her life was moving in a direction that would make him an obstacle to the things that she had to do. Her hubby was on a path to becoming her enemy.

Peaches hit the gear shifter once again, sending her Porsche into a higher gear, and then lifted her foot off of the accelerator. She allowed her sports car to slow to a safer 90 miles per hour, and then took the ramp from Interstate 71 onto Interstate 270. It was time to head back toward Dublin. She knew that she could drive as fast as her car would allow, and yet, she still would not be able to outrun her problems. She had to face them. She had to return home and face Chesarae.

The blue tooth connection on her Porsche rang loudly, signaling that she had an incoming call. She hit the answer button on her steering wheel.

"Hello?"

"Hey, what's up?"

"Who is this?" Peaches asked.

"It's Melvin."

"*Melvin?*" she repeated, recoiling slightly. "What the fuck you want?"

"I need to holler at you."

"About what?" Peaches asked. "What kinda words do we have for each other?"

"I need to square you for that issue."

"*What?*"

"I need to make good on that issue," Melvin repeated. "Say, we need to squash this shit before it gets out of hand. Me and you are better than this. We do good business, and I want to keep it that way."

"You gotta be fucking kidding me, right?" Peaches asked laughing. "You smoking crack now, Melvin?"

"Say, Peach, I didn't have nothing to do with that shit," Melvin told her. "That was Kellen with that bullshit."

"Naw, that was you too!" Peaches told him. "Why didn't you stop that shit?"

"I stopped them niggas from killing him!" Melvin told her. "Hell, just trying to get them to let him make it was a big enough deal. Hell, they could have killed *me*!"

"Melvin, you are so full of shit!"

"Man, I got your paper," Melvin told her.

Peaches thought about telling him to keep it. She didn't trust him. She had did major damage to his car lot, so why he was trying to pay her, was a mystery. Still, she could definitely use the money. She had sent every penny she had to Dante in Texas for a shipment of dope, and she had nothing left. She was living off of her credit cards.

"What makes you think that I'm going to trust you?" she asked. "You think I'm crazy?"

"Naw," Melvin told her. "Look, I can bring it to you myself. And I'll bring it any place you want me to, and I'll come alone. I want to squash this bullshit. If it don't make money, then it don't make sense, ya feel me?"

"I use to think we was on the same page," Peaches told him. "But that was before you pulled this bullshit. Meet me at the storage."

"Alright," Melvin told her. "What time?"

Peaches peered down at the clock on her navigation/stereo system. "I can be there in twenty minutes."

"Twenty minutes," Melvin repeated. "All right. Bet."

"Bet." Peaches disconnected the call. She changed lanes, and headed toward Muirfield, where she owned a U Haul Storage franchise. She was going to see what Melvin was talking about. If she could get Melvin out of the picture, then that would take some of the Get Money Boys out of the war, and that would be a big help to her. The fact that Melvin was about to pay her $450,000 thousands for the 30 keys he jacked would be the icing on the cake. The big enchilada, would be to get his ass out of the fight. Slowly, a smile began to spread across her face. Her odds of survival had just crept up from none, to a little bit. And she would take that any day of the week.

*****

Peaches pulled up to her storage facility. It was a modern, U Haul, air conditioned, self storage facility. It not only leased storage space, but also U Haul trucks. It also sold packaging supplies such as boxes, packing tape, locks, ropes, bubble wrap, and everything that a person would need to move or store their belongings. The franchise had been one of her best investments. She used it to wash her dope money, to employ her soldiers, and even as short term storage for her drugs. Her storage franchise had been a gold mine.

"Your guest is already here," the store manager told her, as she climbed out of her Porche. "He's waiting inside of my office."

"Thanks, Rico," Peaches told him. "He alone?"

Rico nodded.

"Be careful," Peaches said, peering around the area. "Have the guys break out the assault rifles and get ready just in case. I don't trust his ass. He might have some boys around just waiting for me to arrive."

"I called in some extra muscle," Rico told her. "I got twenty guys here already."

"Good," Peaches nodded. She headed for the office.

Melvin was seated in front of the desk when she walked in. He had the black Nike duffel bag that the dope had been in, sitting on the floor next to him.

"What's up, Peach?" Melvin said, nodding.

Peaches walked around the desk and took a seat. "What's up?"

Melvin leaned down and grabbed the Nike bag. He lifted it and set it on the desk. "Four hundred and fifty stacks."

Peaches rose, unzipped the gym bag, and peered inside. Bundles of cash were inside. She lifted several stacks and flipped through them. All hundreds.

"It's all there," Melvin told her.

"Why the fuck did we have to go through all a this?" Peaches asked.

"They was all already tripping when I got outside," Melvin told her. "I tried to break that shit up, but it had already gone too far."

"Why you didn't call me right away?" Peaches asked.

"I really didn't know what to do," Melvin told her. "Shit, I was heated at them niggaz, and I knew that you would be heated. I just figured I would let shit calm down first, and then get at you. I knew that me and you could work shit out."

"I ain't got no beef with you," Peaches told him.

"I ain't got no beef with you," Melvin told her. "So, are we good on this shit?"

"Peaches nodded. "We good."

"When I need to re-up..."

"Call me," Peaches said, cutting him off. She knew that he was worried about being able to get his hands on more dope. And the way she figured it, as long as she could keep him in check using dope, then he wouldn't be so quick to roll with his boys in Get Money and go to war against her. "From now on, we'll meet somewhere else."

"I'm cool with that," Melvin said, shrugging his shoulders. I just wanted to make sure we squashed this shit before it got outta hand, you know? Get Money don't need to be going to war with Young and Holding. Too many people a get killed over some bullshit."

Peaches nodded. She was curious as to why he would even bring Young and Holding into the equation though. She got her answer shortly.

"So what's this I hear about Chesarae being out?" Melvin asked.

Peaches was taken aback. "What do you mean?"

"I hear that Chesarae is out," Melvin told her.

"Where you hear that at?" Peaches asked. As far as she knew, he had only been out a day.

"Shit, the streets is buzzing," Melvin told her.

Peaches nodded. "Yeah, he out."

"Damn!" Melvin said, placing his first up to his mouth. "How that happen?"

"They changed the crack law," Peaches told him.

"Damn, so they cut that nigga loose!" Melvin said excitedly. "That's cooler than a muthafucka! You know, we didn't always see eye to eye and shit. After we grew older we went with different crews and shit, but that's cool. I'm happy that nigga out. We need some real niggas out here in this bitch. Them fake ass niggas and bitch ass niggas was getting deep. Tell that nigga I said what's up. I would ask if he need anything, but I know you got him. You held that nigga down, huh?"

Peaches was growing more and more disturbed by the conversation. *She held it down?* So all the shit she had done, all the shit she had built, she had just been holding it down? And so now that Big Daddy was home, she was supposed to go back in the kitchen and start cooking dinner while he took over again? *Is that what this nigga was saying?* Was Chesarae being home the reason why he had called her to make peace? Was it about being scared of Chesarae and Young and Holding, or about respecting her and her business sense? She was growing more and more heated with each passing moment. *She had built this shit*, not Chesarae! *She* was in charge, and was going to remain in charge! She had recruited soldiers, grew her own organization, had taken out most of her main competitors, and was trying to take over the entire state, and yet these niggas viewed her as just *holding it down*? She could feel heat emanating from her head down throughout the rest of her body. She wanted to grab her pistol and put a bullet in Melvin's forehead. She needed to get out of there.

"I'll tell him you said what's up," Peaches told him. She grabbed the bag off of the desk and stormed out of the office. She walked through the facility outside to her Porsche, where she threw the gym bag into the passenger seat and climbed inside.

"Son of a bitch!" she shouted, as she banged her steering wheel. Peaches started her car, back out, and then raced down the road. Never mind that she had nearly half a million dollars sitting in the passenger seat next to her, she needed some more air. She needed to think. She needed to kill some muthafuckas and show them who they really needed to fear. Fuck Chesarae! She was the one they needed to worry about. She was the black widow.

128

Chapter Fourteen

Tavion kicked his boots up on the coffee table and leaned back on the sofa.

"What the fuck are you doing, nigga?" Vendetta asked, strolling into the room.

"What?" Tavion asked, turning up his palms.

"Get your fucking boots off my table!" Vendetta told him. "And get your sweaty ass up off my couch! What the fuck you think this is?"

"Damn, I'm tired. You had a nigga working his ass off around here all fucking day."

"Good!" Vendetta told him. "A little hard work is good for your ass. You probably ain't never did a hard days work in ya life."

"I ain't no muthafuckin gardener."

"You are if you gonna be laying up around here!" Vendetta told him. She sat her hedge clippers down on her kitchen bar. "Besides, mommy gonna hook you up with a little something special later on."

"Damn, I gotta mow the lawn to get some loving?" Tavion asked with a smile.

"No work, no punanny," Vendetta said with a smile.

"Come here, girl," Tavion told her.

Vendetta walked to the sofa, and Tavion pulled her down on top on him.

129

"Stop it!" Vendetta said, trying to get back up. "I said *later*. You ain't took no shower, and I ain't either."

"That's when it's good. That nasty, sweaty, stanky love!"

Vendetta laughed. "I don't think so. Get up off my coach and go hit the shower."

Tavion let her arm go and Vendetta rose.

"Speaking of work," Tavion said, sitting up. "Your girl got some?"

"In a minute."

"A minute? What's a minute?"

"Give her a day or two, and then she'll be strong. Why? What'cha need?"

"Shit, ten, twenty."

"Ten or twenty?"

"Twenty."

Vendetta nodded. "I'm make sure you get some when it comes in."

"So, this new connect of hers. It must be the real deal."

"Real as a muthafucka."

"And how that other shit coming along?"

"We'll know in a minute."

"I hollered at LaQuan, Terrell, and Jakeem. Ashaad hollered at Jermarcus. Shit, everybody is down."

Vendetta leaped into Tavion's lap. "For real! Are you serious?"

Tavion nodded. "Everybody gonna get down. You know we wasn't gonna let Chesarae's girl be out there by herself like that. We gotta get big. The way I see it, if we get big enough, that should counter Get Money. And if she can get Sweet Pea's niggas, Bug's niggas, and Poocus' niggas to roll with her, that should give her enough to battle Kharee and Big Meech. We can do it. The question is, what is Hassan gonna do? Remember, you got Hassan sitting in Detroit with all them niggas, and you got other ballers like Lay Low, and Big Hustler who could get involved. She just gotta watch them, and make sure they don't hook up with Kharee."

Vendetta nodded. "She knows what she's doing."

"I hope so." Tavion wrapped his arms around Vendetta. "I don't want to lose you behind no bullshit."

"You ain't."

Tavion shook his head. "I sure hope that whatever she's doing, is worth it. Worth it for you."

Vendetta nodded. "It'll be worth it for all of us. C'mon, let's hit the shower."

"Together?"

Vendetta nodded. She rose, extended her hand, and pulled Tavion up off of the sofa.

"Last one in the shower has to stand in the back!" Tavion shouted. He took off toward the master bathroom.

"Ooohhh!" Vendetta shouted. "I hate it when you do that shit! I better be able to get some hot water!"

She stormed off toward the bathroom as well.

*****

Peaches pulled into the drive-through of a nearby Chic Fil A.

The speaker crackled and came alive. "May I help you?"

"Yeah, let me have a number one with no pickles, and some Polynesian Sauce."

"And to drink, ma'am?"

"Let me have a lemonade."

"Thank you, pull forward and we'll have your total at the window."

Peaches pulled forward in her Porsche. Unfortunately for her, it was lunch time, and the drive-through was packed. She had six cars in line ahead of her."

"This some bullshit," she said, shaking her head.

A van pulled up behind Peaches. It was a older dark blue Ford Econoline work van. The paint was old and faded, and the van appeared to be scratched and dented and well worn. It was a typical workman van that could have belonged to any plumber, or mason, or electrician.

Under any other circumstances, she wouldn't have paid the van any attention, but what caught her suspicion was the fact that the occupants that she could see were young and Black. That would have been innocent enough, accept for the fact that they drove right past the ordering menu as they pulled in close up on her. She reached into her waist band and pulled out her 9mmSig Sauer semi-automatic pistol and cocked it. Sure enough, the rear van door opened, and out hopped another young Black male. This one reached back inside and was handed an AK-47.

Peaches' turned, and opened fire. She wasn't about to waste any time. She dropped him instantly. A second gunman hopped out, and she exchanged fire with him as well. The driver of the van raced forward, ramming the rear of her Porsche.

"Got dammit!" Peaches shouted. She could only imagine what the damage to her car was like. They had just wrecked her baby.

Peaches rose up from her seat, and fired at the driver and passenger. Blood shot onto the windshield, telling her that she caught the passenger. The driver had managed to duck just in time. Peaches turned back toward the open rear door of the van, only to catch another gunman jumping out. She fired rapidly in his direction. She was desperate to keep them from getting out and being able to open up on her with one of the AK-47's they were trying to put into action.

The cars in front of her panicked and fled, giving her enough room to maneuver. She turned, shifted her car into gear, and then raced forward. The drive-through was still blocked by vehicles, and the Chic Fil A building blocked her exit to the left. Her only option was to take her low slung Porsche over the curb to her right and try to get the hell out of the death trap that had been set for her.

Peaches frantically turned her steering wheel and hit the gas. The Porsche pushed it's way over the high curb, ripping off it's lower front valance and the low side skirts attached to the vehicle. Sparks flew off of the concrete curb as the bottom of the sports car scraped against it.

"Dammit!" Peaches screamed.

The Porsche made it over the curb, and she turned her steering wheel, and hit the gas. The Porsche spun slightly, and then caught its grip on the street and raced off. She could hear the AK-47's opening up behind her. She could also see the van jumping the curb and racing after her.

Peaches turned right, and hit the access road, almost ramming into another vehicle in the process. She needed to hit the highway. She didn't know how bad the damage was to her vehicle, but she did know that it was moving, and that was all that mattered. If it could keep moving, and do what it normally did, then she would be okay. She just didn't want to have to stop and face off against a bunch of AK-47's, when all she had was a pistol, and two more clips. That gave her thirty two rounds. One AK by itself held thirty. And the rate of fire that it spit out those thirty rounds would make it a very bad day for her. In fact, it would probably make it her last day.

Peaches came up on the entrance to the highway, and hit the gas.

"C'mon, baby!" She pleaded with her Porsche. "C'mon, baby! I need you to fly! I need you to get me outta here!"

She peered over her shoulder, and the van was still coming. She hit Highway 33 and floored it. The Porsche responded. The needle on the speedometer rapidly climbed past , fifty, then sixty, then seventy, and soon, past one hundred. The old Econoline van was no match for her. She peered over her should and watched as the van slowly faded into the distance. She had gotten away with another one.

Peaches made the sign of the cross, kissed her finger, and peered up toward the sky. She wasn't church going, but she was a believer. She thanked The Almighty for getting her through another one.

Was it Melvin's boys, she wondered? Or had it been Big Meech's people? It could have been some of Kharee's men, or Bug's crew, or Poocus's crew, or Sweet Pea's boys. It could have been a combination of all of the above. She had made enemies. Numerous enemies. Finding out who had just tried to off her, would be next to impossible. But what she did know, was that she had to take some enemies off of the table. She had to meet with Sweet Pea's under bosses, Poocus' under bosses, and Bug's under bosses, and she had to try to cut a deal with them and win them over. She had to. It was the only way she would be able to survive.

133

Peaches needed to find an exit, and turn around. Highway 33 was taking her out toward Marysville, and she needed to get back to Dublin. She needed to get home to safety. She need to hit the shower, relax, unwind, and calm her nerves. She was now trembling uncontrollably. Falling into Chesarae's arms would be good for her. Or at least seeing him, and knowing that he was there with her, would bring her a measure of peace as well.

Peaches found her exit, took the turn around, and pointed her torn up Porsche in the direction of home.

Chapter Fifteen

Peaches strolled into her living room to find Chesarae dressed, and ready to go.

"Hey, you got some wheels I can borrow, Peach?" Chesarae asked.

Peaches hurried to where he was standing, wrapped her arms around him and rested her head on his chest.

"What's the matter?" he asked.

"Just hold me," Peaches said softly.

"What's the matter?" he asked again. "Girl, you're shaking like a leaf. What happened?"

She shook her head. "Just hold me for a minute."

Chesarae wrapped his arms around her and held her tight. He kissed her on the top of her head.

Omar walked into the room. "What the fuck happened to your car?"

The sight of Chesarae standing in Peaches' living room caused his mouth to fall open. Peaches' wrecked Porsche, Chesarae standing in the living room, tears forming in the corner of Peaches' eyes; it was all too much for his mind to process.

"Ches?" Omar continued. He approached carefully, taking in the situation. His face looked as if he were staring at a ghost. "What the fuck?"

Peaches released Chesarae, who turned to Omar and smiled.

"What the fuck is going on?" Omar shouted. He opened his arms and he and Chesarae embraced tightly. "What are you doing here?"

"Chilling," Chesarae told him.

Omar rested his hands on Chesarae's shoulders, examining him. "My nigga, what the hell are you doing here? How in the fuck did you get out?"

"They kicked me out," Chesarae said with a smile. "Said I was too fly to be locked up."

"Get the fuck outta here!" Omar shouted.

Chesarae laughed even harder. "They changed the crack law, baby!"

"They sure in the fuck did," Omar said nodding. "I forgot about that shit. They gave you action?"

"Plenty of action," Chesarae told him. He spread his arms out and spun around. "I'm here, ain't I?"

"You sure in the fuck are," Omar said, hugging him again. "My nigga, my nigga! It's so good to have you back. Damn, I happy you outta that cage! We gotta celebrate!"

Omar walked into the kitchen, opened the wine refrigerator and pulled out a bottle of Moet.

"I thought you was talking about hitting the club," Chesarae told him.

"We can do that too!" Omar said, popping open the bottle of champagne.

"I can hit the club once," Chesarae told him. "But after that, it's time to get to work. I've been on vacation long enough."

"I hear you, my nigga," Omar told him. He poured Chesarae a glass, and then poured another one for Peaches. He handed them their glasses, and then poured himself one. He lifted his glass in toast. "To real niggas! And to the realest of the real. To my nigga Chesarae, and to his freedom!"

The three of them lifted their glasses and then tossed back their drinks. Peaches drank for more than just a toast. She needed it in order to calm her nerves.

"When did you get out?" Omar asked.

"Yesterday," Chesarae told him.

"Damn, you fresh out!" Omar said. "You ain't had time to cut no corners and check shit out."

Chesarae shook his head. "Not yet. I was just about to get some wheels from Peach and head to Detroit."

"Word?" Omar asked.

"Why you going up there?" Peaches asked.

"To see my folks," Chesarae told her. "You know, I *would* like to see my parents."

"I know that," Peaches told him. "But you know you ain't just going up there to see your parents. You gonna hit the streets too."

"Okay, so what's wrong with visiting the place where I grew up?" Chesarae asked.

"It ain't the same," Peaches told him.

"Damn, you acting like I've been gone for twenty years or something!" Chesarae told her. "You act like Earth is an alien planet or some shit. Peach, I know my way around. I know what spots to avoid. I ain't lame."

"Hard head makes a soft ass, my grandmother used to say." Peaches said, shaking her head.

"What you tripping on, girl?" Omar asked.

Peaches smacked her lips. "Mr. Know-it-all don't realize that shit done changed. He thinks that everyone is his friend, and that it's all sunshine and bubble gum."

"I don't think that," Chesarae said with a smile. "But I ain't tripping on no niggas. You so worried about Hassan and Marquez, and a bunch of he say, she say drama. Man, ain't nobody tripping with each other."

"Hassan ain't the same, Ches!" Peaches shouted.

Chesarae stared at Omar. Omar shrugged.

"Hassan is gone be Hassan," Omar said. "He funny acting, like he always been. He got his ways, and he have his days."

"She think this nigga got beef," Chesarae said. It was more of a question than a statement.

"Ain't no telling with that nigga," Omar said.

"You serious, dog?" Chesarae said, turning up his palms. "This Hassan we talking about."

"I know who we talking about," Omar said, allowing himself a half grin. "That nigga always was hard to read, and he always was funny acting. Shit, you never know. I ain't saying don't go home. Shit, you can always go home. And I ain't saying this nigga gonna have beef with you. But he ain't been too cool with everybody else of late. He on his own time, and he smelling himself now. He got all them Detroit niggas following him, and buying dope from him, and he think he's the muthafuckin king of the city. But that's just how that nigga is. I don't know if he's got beef with you though. Shit, call that nigga. Let him know you out, and see what kinda reaction you get."

"I can't believe this shit," Chesarae said, shaking his head. "I gotta call ahead to go back to my hometown?"

"Just see where his head is at," Peaches said. "Talk to him on the phone before you just pop up trying to see him. Just be smart, Chesarae."

"She's just worried about you," Omar said. "I don't see why."

Peaches rolled her eyes at Omar.

"If it makes you feel better, I'll roll up North with my nigga," Omar told her. He placed his arm around Chesarae's shoulder. "You know I got his back."

"You don't think I need you here?" Peaches asked, lifting an eyebrow.

"I'll be back in a flash," Omar told her.

"I'mma shoot up there for a couple a days," Chesarae told her. "Two at most."

"You can take my Range," Peaches said. She reached into her pocket and pulled out her keys. She removed the key to her Range Rover and tossed it to him.

"What happened to your Porsche?" Omar asked.

"What happened to it is obvious," Peaches told him. "Who did it? Now that's an entirely different question, and one I don't have an answer for."

Chesarae walked to the front door, opened it, and peered outside. He turned back toward Peaches. "You want to tell me what's going on?"

"That's more than a five minute conversation," Peaches told him.

"I got time," Chesarae told her.

"I thought you were leaving?" Peaches asked.

"Don't play with me," Chesarae replied flatly.

"I got caught slipping at a drive-through," Peaches explained.

"Slipping at a drive-through?" Chesarae repeated. "What the fuck does that mean? Why is somebody trying to blow your *got damned head off*? What the fuck are you into?"

"It's the dope game, Chesarae!" Peaches screamed. "I told you, shit has changed! It's the jungle out there, and muthafuckas is trying to take what you got! And there's a big fucking drought out there right now!"

"So you telling me this was a jack move?" Chesarae asked, lifting an eyebrow. He wasn't convinced.

"I'm telling you that I don't know what the fuck it was," Peaches told him. "Look, I'm checking into it. I'll let you know what's up when you get back."

"I ain't leaving until I get some answers," Chesarae told her.

"Look, go see your parents," Peaches told him. "Go hug your moms and pops, and let them see you. I'll be all right. I ain't going nowhere while you're gone. I'm stuck at home anyway, so everything a be cool."

"You sure?" Chesarae asked.

Peaches nodded.

"I'mma get to the bottom of this shit when I get back," Chesarae declared.

Peaches nodded. She walked Omar to the door, and watched as he and Chesarae made their way to her Range Rover and climbed inside. She waved to them from the door. Once they were out of sight, she closed the door, and headed for her master bathroom. She needed a nice, hot, relaxing massage inside of her jacuzzi tub. And then, she would get out and finish that bottle of Moet that Omar opened. She needed to get drunk.

139

Chapter Sixteen

Joaquin pulled up in his Jag and blew his horn several times. He stared impatiently at his sister's front door, waiting for her to emerge. Like most youngsters he was extremely impatient. His youth, combined with the fact that he was on baller status, and was used to being waited on hand over fist, caused him to have even less patience than most guys his age. Besides, he knew how his sister was. Like most women, *right away*, meant five or ten minutes later. There had to be a couple of trips to different mirrors, one last trip to the bathroom, a quick check of the house to make sure that everything was turned off, etc... This, despite the fact that she had rushed him all morning to come and pick her up, and despite the fact that he had just gotten off of the phone with her, where she promised that she was ready to go.

"Come on, girl!" Joaquin shouted toward the front door. He had things to do. He had connects to meet after he got his share, and then he had a couple of fine ass women to hook up with later. Driving his big sister around town was not something that he looked forward to. Not only was she taking up his valuable time, she also served to cramp his style. He hated being known as Peaches' little brother, and had worked hard to establish himself as a baller in his own right.

Peaches stepped out of her house, locked the door, and headed for her brother's car. She opened the door and climbed inside.

"Hold your horses, boy!" Peaches told him.

"You acting like I got all day!" Joaquin shot back. "I got shit to do."

"What do you have to do?" Peaches asked, pursing her lips. "Not a got damn thang! Especially if you wanna get this shit. Don't play with me. Your ass a be sitting around looking funny and talking about how you ain't making no money if we don't take care a this shit."

Joaquin shifted his car into gear, and pulled off.

"When you gonna get another whip?" he asked.

"Soon. Maybe today. I might have you drive me to a dealership."

Joaquin rolled his eyes at her. "You tripping."

Peaches shoved the side of his head. "Quit acting like you don't want to hang around with your big sister, boy!"

A smile slowly crept across Joaquin's face. He loved his sister more than life itself. She had always been there for him, and she had always taken care of him. Growing up, she had been more like a best friend and a second mother, than just a big sister.

"What kinda whip you thinking about knocking off?" he asked.

Peaches stared out of the window and shrugged. "I don't know. Maybe one of these. Or that new Jag that just came out."

"That F Type!"

Peaches nodded and smiled. "Yeah, I think that's the one. It's small, right?"

Joaquin nodded. "A little two seat convertible?"

Peaches nodded. "Yeah, that's the one. That bitch is clean, right?"

"Hell yeah that bitch is clean!"

"Drop the top, and roll in that bitch," Peaches said smiling. "Can you picture me rolling?"

"You ain't fly enough for that," Joaquin said with a smile.

"Nigga please!" Peaches said laughing and dismissing his statement. "I'm flier than any of them bitches you be fucking with!"

Joaquin laughed. "Yeah right! I got some bitches that a make you sick to your stomach. Make your ass look like Puppy Chow!"

"Bitch fuck you!" Peaches said, nudging him. "Your Momma looks like Puppy Chow!"

"Your Momma too!"

Joaquin pulled into the parking lot of the warehouse.

"Park around back," Peaches told him.

Joaquin navigated his Jag around the massive steel building to the back. He parked right next to the structure, and he and his sister climbed out. He followed her to the back door, and then through it. Trap and Vendetta where already inside. They were standing next to a large stack of crates sitting in the middle of the warehouse floor.

Joaquin threw his arms up in the air. "What's up, baby girls?"

Trap and Vendetta both stared at him in silence. Trap folded her arms, and Vendetta smacked her lips. Joaquin strolled up to Vendetta and wrapped his arms around her.

"Let me feel on that booty, girl!" he told her.

Vendetta pushed him away. "Get your young ass away from me!"

"Young?" Joaquin asked. "We all the same age when the lights go out!"

"Boy please!" Vendetta said, shoving him to the side. "I can't do nothing with you but give you a bottle and put your ass to sleep."

"You can let me suck on those big old titties and then I'll put this long stroke on you, and put your ass to sleep," Joaquin countered. Again, he tried to feel on Vendetta, but she knocked his arms away.

"Girl, get your little brother," Vendetta told Peaches. "He gone keep on and one day I'mma give him what he asking for, and he ain't gonna know what to do! I'mma put this muthafucking whip on his ass, curl his toes, and he gonna be following me around for the rest of his life."

Trap and Vendetta laughed and hi-fived.

Peaches pulled the lid off of one of the crates that were sitting on top. The lid had already been pried open, so it was easy for her to lift. Inside of the crate sat dozens of kilos of pure cocaine.

"Good Lord!" Joaquin shouted.

Peaches lifted one of the bricks of cocaine from crate and examined it. It was white, wrapped in clear cellophane. She pulled out a small nail file that she kept on her key chain, and cut through the wrapping. The strong smell of pure cocaine whipped through the air.

"Woah!" Vendetta said, waving her hand through the air, trying in vain to clear away the smell.

"That shit is strong!" Trap said.

"Them fiends is gonna love that shit!" Joaquin said, rubbing his hands together. He was already envisioning the profits that he was going to make. This shipment smelled like it was strong enough to step on multiple times. He may even be able to get eighty or ninety ounces out of a single kilo.

Peaches ran her finger over the raised scorpion embedded in the kilo. It was the symbol of the cartel that had sent it to the United States.

"Damn, my fingers started tingling, and now them bitches is numb!" Peaches said with a wide grin. "This shit is fucking strong!"

"Whew!" Joaquin shouted uncontrollably. He wrapped his arms around his sister and kissed her on her cheek.

"Damn, Peach!" Trap said, shaking her head. "We gonna have to step on this shit."

"A lot!" Vendetta added.

"We don't want muthafuckas to start overdosing and dying," Trap told her.

"It's like we *gotta* make money," Joaquin said smiling. "We gotta step on this shit for the good of the public."

Vendetta laughed and shoved Joaquin's shoulder. "Boy!"

"Y'all ready to ball 'til we fall?" Joaquin asked.

"I don't know about you, but I don't plan on falling," Peaches told him.

"I ain't trying to get in ya business, but this is a lot of shit that I'mma have to cook," Trap told her.

"Five thousand keys," Peaches announced, giving Trap the answer that she was looking for.

"Five thousand keys!" Joaquin nearly shouted. "They fronted you *five thousand* chickens!"

"Naw, fool!" Peaches told him. "I paid for this shit!"

"Bullshit!" Joaquin shot back. "You ain't bought no five thousand keys, nigga!"

Peaches smacked her lips. "I know that. I paid for half, and they fronted me the other half, boy. That's what I meant."

"How much?" Joaquin asked.

"Why?"

"Cause you been holding out, nigga!" Joaquin said with a smile. "Stingy muthafucka!"

"Five G's a bird," Peaches said smiling.

Joaquin recoiled. He always said that he wasn't the brightest bulb in the house, nor the sharpest tool in the toolbox, but if it was one thing he could do, it was count money. He ran the figures through his mental calculator.

"That's two point five, nigga!" Joaquin said excitedly. "You ain't paid no two point five!"

"I sure in the hell did!" Peaches told him.

"Sis, are you *serious?*" Joaquin asked. "You sent them two and a half million cash?"

Peaches nodded.

"Five thousand a key is a helluva price!" Trap told Joaquin. "Are you kidding?"

"I'm not saying that," Joaquin said, slicing his hand through the air. "Five G's is a helluva price. What I'm saying, is that I didn't know this stingy muthafucka was holding like *that!*"

"What?" Peaches asked, shifting her weight to one side. "You thought I was in this shit for free? This ain't no fucking charity work, nigga."

"I know, but *damn!*" Joaquin said, shaking his head. "I didn't know you was balling like that."

"I'm not," Peaches said, sitting the kilo of cocaine back into the crate with the others. "I sent that muthafucka every penny that I had."

Vendetta, Trap, and Joaquin all quickly shifted their gazes toward her.

"What?" Vendetta asked.

"I'm broke," Peaches told them. "I cleared out everything. Every penny that I had. Girl, I could pay a light bill right now if it came in."

"Are you *serious?*" Trap asked.

"Sis, you for real?" Joaquin asked.

Again, Peaches nodded.

"Why did you do that?" Vendetta asked.

"For one, I wanted to jump on this shit," Peaches explained. "We've been running short on dope since the drought begin. Two, ain't nobody got no dope but us, so I knew that I could move this shit. And three, I wanted to get as much dope in hand as possible. Ain't no telling when shit is gonna fall short, or when we'll be able to get more. I wanted to make sure that I scored as much as possible."

"I understand that," Joaquin told her. "But damn!"

Trap shook her head. "Peach, I understand what you're saying, but you took a big ass risk. What if this shipment would have gotten busted? What if it still gets busted? What if we get busted stepping on this shit? Anything could happen. Hell, if a police dog is sitting in an SUV just riding down the street, he's gonna be able to smell this shit from a mile away."

"Girl, you be taking some crazy ass chances!" Vendetta told her.

"Look, you take big chances, you win big!" Peaches told them. "We gonna go for it all, or we ain't gonna go for none of it. Right?"

Trap nodded. Her nod, was followed by one from Vendetta.

"No nuts, no glory," Joaquin added. "That's my sis. But look here, let me get my shit and get on, before y'all asses get busted."

"You sorry as a muthafucka!" Peaches said, laughing.

Joaquin started grabbing some kilos.

"Boy stop!" Peaches said, grabbing him.

"You gotta move this shit and get some money, right?" Joaquin asked, lifting an eyebrow.

"Yeah," Peaches said, nodding. "I gotta meet Jermarcus and Kiantae, in a minute. I'mma get some money back then."

"Man, I ain't gonna drive your ass around all day," Joaquin said.

"I ain't ask you to," Peaches told him. She waved her hand through

146

the air. "You're dismissed."

"How you getting home?" Joaquin asked.

"Oh, so *now* you worried about how I'm getting home?" Peaches asked, lifting any eyebrow.

"I ain't gonna leave your ass stranded," Joaquin said, exhaling. "I can at least take your ass to a bus stop."

Trap and Vendetta laughed.

Peaches pointed toward the exit. "Get the fuck outta here!"

Joaquin laughed. He held up five kilos. Peaches nodded. Joaquin raced for the exit.

"You want me to drive you?" Vendetta asked.

Peaches nodded. "Yeah. Trap, you got this?"

Trap peered at all of the crates and exhaled. "Yeah. I'll get it to a couple of safe spots, and start stepping on it."

"We gonna stop by the east side, step on ten of 'em, and then hook up with Jermarcus and Kiantae," Peaches told her. "I got my phone if you need me."

"Alright, girl," Trap told her. "I'll see you later."

"Later, momma!" Vendetta said, chunking up the deuces.

"Later," Peaches said winking at her.

Chapter Seventeen

Vendetta turned off of South Hamilton onto Eastland Drive, and then navigated her Porsche Cayenne into the Crossroads East Shopping Center. She made her way around the massive Sears store, to the parking lot of the Macy's.

"There they go," Peaches said pointing.

Jermarcus and Kiantae were sitting inside of Jermarcus' white Escalade. Vendetta parked as close as she could, which was about three parking spaces away. She pulled out her Glock, pulled back the slide, and made sure that she had a round in the chamber, and that she was ready to let loose. Peaches climbed out of the Porsche, opened the rear hatch, and pulled out several Payless Shoe Store bags.

Jermarcus and Kiante climbed out of the Escalade, and Jermarcus walked to the back of his SUV, opened the hatch, and pulled out a large Bath and Body Works shopping bag. He started to walk toward the Porsche, but Peaches held up her hand stopping them.

"I'mma come over there!" Peaches shouted.

Jermarcus nodded, and he and Kiantae climbed back inside of the Cadillac SUV. Peaches walked to the driver's side of the Porsche.

"You ready?"

"Yeah," Vendetta said, opening the driver's side door. She grabbed one of the bags from Peaches and the two of them headed over to the Escalade.

"Pop the lock, nigga!" Peaches told Jermarcus.

"Oh, shit, my bad!" Jermarcus said, smiling sheepishly. He hit the power locks on his window sill, unlocking the doors on his vehicle. Peaches and Vendetta climbed into the back seats.

"What's up, Baby Girl?" Jermarcus said.

"Nothing," Peaches said, smiling. "What's up, nigga?"

"It's all you," Jermarcus said smiling. His gold teeth glimmered in the sunlight. Jermarcus' top and bottom teeth were grilled out. He had *'J Daddy'* spelled out in his top grill, and *'killa'* spelled out in his bottom. His gold teeth provided a striking contrast to his rich chocolate, but heavily tattooed skin. He wore his hair in a bald fade, with small waves, and always kept a fresh cut with a design in it. Jermarcus was slim, but muscular, with a nice physique that he wore well over his six foot three frame.

"Naw, nigga, it's all you," Peaches countered. "If I had your hand I would throw mine in."

"Shit!" Jermarcus smiled. "Who you fooling?"

"What's up, Kiantae?" Peaches said nodding. "Long time."

"What up, sis?" Kiantae said greeting her.

Kiantae resembled his old brother. He had is mother's Pacific Islander eyes, high cheekbones, and swarthy complexion, mixed with his father's full lips. He had almost as many tattoos as his older brother. However, whereas Chesarae had the most beautiful teeth she had ever laid eyes on, Kiantae had chosen to cover his perfect teeth with gold. He too was grilled out, top and bottom. He had the word *'Young'* spelled out in crushed diamonds on his top grill, and the word *'Holdin'* spelled out in crushed diamonds on his bottom grill. Had it not been for his gold grill and tatted up skin, Kiantae could have been a male model. Young women swooned over him, with his hazel eyes and prominent cheekbones.

"So, is what this nigga saying true?" Jermarcus asked.

"What?" Peaches asked, shifting her gaze between the two of them.

"This nigga lying like Ches is out of the feds!" Jermarcus asked, pursing his lips.

Peaches shrugged. "What would make you think that I would know?"

"Nigga please!" Jermarcus told her. "If that nigga was out, you would be the *first* to know. He gonna go holla at you before anybody else!"

"Tell the truth," Kiantae told her.

A smiled slowly spread across Peaches' face. "Yeah, he out."

"*Are you fucking serious?*" Jermarcus shouted. "How the fuck that nigga get out?"

Peaches shrugged. "They changed the crack law. His paperwork finally made it through the court, and they cut him loose."

"Where that nigga at?" Jermarcus asked.

"Detroit," Peaches told him.

"That nigga at the crib," Kiantae said. "He up there with the folks."

"For real?" Jermarcus asked, lifting an eyebrow.

"Yeah, that nigga called me," Kiantae told them. "We rapped for a minute."

"How that nigga doing?" Jermarcus asked. "He straight?"

Kiantae shrugged. "Yeah, that nigga straight."

"Well, I know Peach got him," Jermarcus said with a smile. "I know you done looked out for that nigga."

"He's straight," Peaches told them.

"In more ways that one," Jermarcus told her. He peered down at her stomach. "I'll bet your ass already pregnant. You pregnant, Peach?"

"Hell muthafuckin naw!" Peaches told him. "And ain't gone get pregnant."

"Aw, nigga!" Jermarcus said, waving his hand and dismissing her statement. "Your ass know you about to get pregnant. You niggaz about to start a family and shit."

"Don't get this shit twisted," Peaches told him. "I ain't that bitch. I ain't Louise Jefferson, I ain't Claire Huxtable, I ain't that white bitch from Leave It To Beaver or The Brady Bunch. I ain't laying it down, I ain't

151

staying in no muthafucking kitchen, and I ain't the happy housewife. Them days is gone. As a matter of fact, where is my issue, nigga. You about to piss me off."

Jermarcus laughed, and handed Peaches the Bath And Body Works bag. Peaches handed Kiantae the Payless Shoe Store bags. She opened the bag that Jermarcus gave her, and found stacks of bills banded together. She began going through the bills and counting.

In the front seat, Kiantae opened the Payless bags and pulled out two shoe boxes. He pulled the lid off of one of the shoe boxes, and spied its contents. The shoes box was filled with bricks of cocaine.

"Hot damn!" Kiante said excitedly. "We back in power, baby!"

Jermarcus held out his hand and Kiante slapped it.

"It's six and six?" Kiante turned and asked Peaches.

Peaches nodded. "Six in each shoe box, nigga. Don't mess up my count."

"It's all there, baby girl." Jermarcus told her.

"Yeah baby I trust you," Peaches said with a smile. "I just love to count. Like that muthafuckin vampire on Sesame Street. One one thousand, Two one thousand. Three, three one thousand."

Jermarcus and Vendetta broke into laughter.

"Bitch you crazy!" Vendetta told her.

"So, what's been happening, V?" Jermarcus asked.

"Chilling, baby."

"What my nigga Tavion up to?" Jermarcus asked.

"The same shit all you muthafuckas is always up to!" Vendetta told him. "Being a lying ass hoe, and letting these tricks get you for your score fair!"

Jermarcus and Kiantae burst into laughter.

"That's fucked up!" Kiantae told her.

"That's the truth!" Vendetta shot back. "You muthafuckas ain't no earthly good."

"So, my nigga must be in the dog house then?" Jermarcus asked.

"That bitch stay in the dog house!" Vendetta told them. "He keep a bitch aggravated."

"It's all here," Peaches declared, placing the bundles of money back inside of the shopping bag.

"You really think I would cheat your tight wad ass?" Jermarcus asked.

"Yeah, nigga!" Peaches said nodding. "You're known to go shopping first, and pay your connect later."

Jermarcus laughed. "It ain't even like that. Say, tell that nigga Ches I said to holler at me."

"You'll see his ass before I see him again," Peaches told him. "Hell, Kiantae will probably see him before both of us!"

"Me and that nigga already rapped," Kiantae told her. "Which brings me to something else. That nigga was tripping. He was talking about why I didn't check up on you and make sure you was straight. Hell, you was doing better than everybody else!"

"He was talking about that shit before he left," Peaches told him. "He was talking about you coming by and calling me and shit."

Kiantae shook his head and looked down. "I mean, damn. It wasn't like I *wasn't* checking up on you. I kept my ear to the street, and kept up with how you was doing through the grapevine. Trust and believe, if word would have gotten back to me that you needed me, I would've been there for you. I ain't have to be all up in your face to watch over you and have your back."

Peaches shrugged. "I didn't ask you to have my back. I didn't tell Chesarae nothing like that. He asked me if I heard from you, and I told him that I hadn't seen you in years. I guess he took it upon himself to holler at you about that. Maybe that was something that bothered him, because I wasn't tripping. Hell, everybody was doing they own thing, you know?"

Kiantae and Jermarcus both nodded. Both had been guilty. Jermarcus less so. He saw Peaches at least twice a month to score from her. Kiantae hadn't seen her in years.

"So big brother made you feel like shit, huh?" Vendetta asked with a smile. "You wasn't handling ya business and checking up on his woman, so he let you know that was some bogus shit, huh?"

153

"Fuck you, V!" Kiantae told her.

Peaches nudged Vendetta.

"A whole lotta muthafuckas trying to get some get right in they life, now that Chesarae is back," Vendetta continued. "A whole lot of muthafuckas violated the code, and didn't look out. Didn't check up on his Moms, his Pops, his girl, or shoot him no bread for commissary. Time to look a muthafucka in the face and tell him why."

Peaches nudged Vendetta again.

"Girl, stop elbowing me!" Vendetta said loudly. "Hell, it's the truth. Speak that shit! Let it be known. Muthafuckas know when they did some foul shit!"

"Bitch, ain't nobody even talking to you!" Kiantae shouted. "You always in somebody else muthafucking business!"

Vendetta laughed loudly. "*Guilty, guilty, guilty!* A muthafucking hit dog will holler!"

"Bitch get out the car!" Peaches said laughing. She opened her door and climbed out. "I'll holler at y'all later. Let me know what you think when you break that bitch and cook it."

Jermarcus nodded.

Peaches patted Kiantae on his shoulder. "Man, don't sweat that shit. Ain't no hard feelings. We all started doing our own thing. Chesarae thinks that everything was supposed to stay the same, and that time was supposed to stop. He came at me with some crazy ass shit too. He'll understand after he's been out a while."

Vendetta climbed out and chunked up the dueces. "Just fucking with you, dude. No hard feelings, youngster."

Peaches and Vendetta turned and headed for Vendetta's SUV.

"Why you do that boy like that?" Peaches asked.

"Fuck him!" Vendetta told her. "His ass *should* feel bad. He didn't do shit for you while his brother was gone. I'm glad Chesarae checked his ass. He should check all of them niggaz!"

Peaches shook her head, and the two of them climbed inside of Vendetta's ride. "Girl, you too much."

"Where to now?" Vendetta asked.

A smile spread across Peaches' face. "Drop me off at the car dealership."

"What dealership?"

Peaches pursed her lips. "I think I want to check out that new convertible Jag."

Vendetta shrugged. "Suit yourself. I can wait on you if you want me to."

"Naw, girl," Peaches said, shaking her head. "You don't have to do that. You can just drop me off. I'mma drive home in that bitch. Besides, Trap probably needs some help."

Vendetta nodded. "Gotcha. Her ass is probably cursing our asses out as we speak."

Peaches and Vendetta broke into laughter.

Chapter Eighteen

Peaches walked around her brand new salsa red, two seat, F-Type Jaguar convertible. She ran her index finger down the side of the front fender, taking in the sensuous curves and luscious paint job. The car was a rolling piece of art.

"Your keys are in the ignition, ma'am," the kid from the make-ready department told her.

"Thank you," Peaches said without taking her eyes off of the car.

The car's finely stitched black leather interior reminding her of an expensive glove. It was supple, and soft to the touch. Even on the dash and the console. The soft rumble of the 495 horsepower supercharged V-8 engine hinted at the power lying in wait. Even at idle, the gurgling sound pouring melodically out of the dual exhaust pipes seemed to foretell of the car's awesome power and potential dynamics. Her brother had been right; this was the car to get. The smile that spread across her face was now cemented in place. She was going to have fun with the top down, racing around Loop 270, while the wind whipped through her hair.

"So, it's yours, Ms. Espinoza!" the salesman, said, walking up behind her. "Your insurance company faxed over the papers, and we faxed them over to the bank, so you're good to go."

157

Peaches turned and extended her hand, and the salesman shook it.

"Make sure you come back and see me if you need anything," he told her. "How's Joaquin?"

"He's good," Peaches said, making her way to the driver's door. She opened it, and climbed inside. "I'll tell him that you said what's up."

Inside, Peaches synched her iPhone to the car's stereo system, and scrolled through her play list. She wanted something gangster, yet old school. Something banging, yet something to represent who she was. She was on top of the world right now. She was strong, female, and in-charge. She found the perfect song to roll out of the lot. She chose The Conscious Daughters song, *Somethin' To Ride To*.

Peaches cranked up the stereo system, backed out of her parking space, and headed for the street. She pulled out onto the road, picked up speed, and let the sun and breeze do their thing. She reached down and pulled her sunglasses off of her shirt and placed them over her eyes. The only thing she was missing, was a nice fat spliff. And a trip to the hood in her brand new Jag to get one, would be just the thing to really lift her spirits. Peaches turned and headed for East Columbus.

Her music was interrupted by a phone call.

"Hello?"

"What's up, stranger?"

"Darius?"

"The one and only!"

"Humph," Peaches huffed. "What made you call me today? Was your hoe busy today?"

Darius laughed. "Man, don't be fucking tripping with me. Last I checked, AT&T sent calls in both directions. Are your fingers broke, nigga?"

Peaches had to laugh. "All right, you got me."

"So what's up?" Darius asked.

"Shit, nothing. Handling business."

"Too busy to call your man, huh?"

"Oh, so you my man, now?"

"I thought I was," Darius told her.

She could hear his smile over the phone. Peaches wanted to be in Texas. She wanted to be in his arms. She wanted a safe place to just chill and collect her thoughts. Away from Ohio, away from Chesarae, away from Kharee, away from Detective Ward, away from The Get Money Boys, and all of the bullshit that had been stressing her. She had so much bullshit on her shoulders, that she had started getting migraines almost daily.

"You ain't applied for that position yet," Peaches told him.

"I thought I put my application in while you was in Texas," Darius said laughing.

Peaches laughed as well. "Your application hasn't been accepted yet then."

"Oh really? Well, what does it take? If blowing your back out ain't good enough..."

"Okay hold up. Who said that you blew my back out?"

"The way you was hollering and holding on and scratching the shit outta my back..."

"Okay, so you want to go there?" Peaches said laughing.

"I miss the fuck outta you," Darius told her.

"I miss you too," Peaches said softly.

"Come to Texas," Darius told her.

"You know I can't do that."

"Then I'm coming up there."

"Don't do that," Peaches told him.

"Why not?"

"Because you know what I'm doing, and you know what I got to do," Peaches told him.

"And you can't do that with me up there?"

"No!" Peaches said forcefully. "Darius, having you here will just distract me. I'll just chill with you all day, and be bullshitting around, and not handling my business. My attention will be focused on being with you, or getting back home to you, or some other shit. And I can't be distracted like that. I have to focus, and if I don't, then I'll get caught slipping. And if I get caught slipping, I'm dead. You understand?"

159

"I got you," Darius told her. He was crestfallen.

Peaches could hear the disappointment in his voice. "We're going to be together soon, Boo. I promise you that."

"You promise?"

"I do."

"How are we going to pull that off?"

"I don't know," Peaches told him. "But trust me, we will. Believe it, and we're going to make it happen. We just have to do it right. Neither one of us can get caught slipping."

"I'll talk to you later," Darius told her.

The awkward silence over the telephone told each of them enough. The three little words that were not spoken, spoke volumes. Neither wanted to say *I love you*. Both knew that the words would be devastating. Their relationship was too complicated for love to come into the picture. Those words would force them to take chances that they both knew they couldn't afford to take. They would force her to run to Texas, or make him sneak to Ohio. Peaches knew that the last thing she needed with Chesarae running around, was for Darius to be in Ohio. Chesarae would kill Darius, or Darius would kill Chesarae. And if Ches killed Darius, once the Reigns family found out that it was her ex-boyfriend that did it, they would come after her in full force. And if Ohio found out that Ches got killed by Darius, her supposed to be new man, then Ohio would revolt against her. She would be dead in a week. The best thing she could do for her survival would be to keep both men apart. If anyone was going to put a bullet in Chesarae's head, it would have to be her. She owed him that much. It would have to be a clean kill, a kill about the business, and it would have to be about her remaining in control of the organization that she built up. Ohio could take that. They would accept a power play, but not a cross action bitch who resulted in her nigga getting killed.

"I'll holler at you later, stranger," Peaches said, swallowing hard. "And don't take so damn long to call me again."

"I won't," Darius told her. "It's just that when I do call you, I'm depressed as a muthafucka when I get off the phone, because I want you here with me."

Peaches momentarily closed her eyes. No man made her feel like that. Not even Chesarae.

"I feel the same way," she said softly. "I'mma hit you up soon."

"All right. Peace."

"Peace."

Peaches hung up the telephone, and for the first time, actually paid attention to her surroundings. When she first left the dealership, she was so enamored with her new whip that she had paid little attention to anything but the car. She had fiddled with the gauges and switches, and watched as the passengers in the cars surrounding her pointed toward her car. And then the phone call from Darius had thrown her for a loop. And now, for the first time, she realized that she had the same car in her rear view since she left the dealership. It was an old Lincoln Town Car. A white one, filled with black faces. And they were following her, without trying to *look* like they were following her. She decided to hit a couple of corners to see if they would follow.

Peaches made a right on Fairwood, and then another right on Whittier. The Lincoln followed. She made a left onto Lockbourne and picked up the pace. The Lincoln did the same. She knew for sure now that she was being followed.

Peaches hit the telephone button on her steering wheel. Her smart phone was still linked to the car's system by Bluetooth. "Call V."

"*Calling V,*" the system repeated.

Peaches could hear her phone dialing Vendetta's number.

"Hello?"

"V, girl, I gotta tail."

"Are you sure?" Vendetta asked nervously.

"No doubt."

"Where you at?"

"Eastside. Rolling down Lockbourne"

"Damn!" Vendetta shouted. "I'm all the way across town! What the fuck you doing over there?"

"I was rolling to the hood to score some weed."

161

"Girl, head back this direction, I'm on my way," Vendetta told her. "I can meet you in the middle. Probably around Victorian Village."

"Girl, I don't think they gonna follow me that much longer," Peaches told her. "They gonna make a move soon. They been following me since I left the dealership."

"Damn! I knew I should have stayed with you!"

"Once I got the whip, we still would have gone our separate ways."

"Who is it? Can you see them."

"Just some niggas in a beat up ass white Lincoln."

"Girl, I'm on my way! Just try to get to Victorian Village."

"All right. I'mma hit you back in a minute."

"All right."

Peaches disconnected the call. She needed to think about her next couple of moves. She was close to one of her old stomping grounds. Perhaps she could roll through, and see if that would spook them. Whoever they were, if they wanted to harm her, they wouldn't be members of Young and Holding. If she could get to one of Young and Holding's hoods, them maybe they wouldn't trip. Maybe that would buy her some time.

"Think!" she told herself.

She was in Young and Holding territory, but it would be even better, if she could turn around, and head north. She needed to get north of Livingston, and then she would be safe. They wouldn't dare come at her once she was north of Livingston. That was her home turf for sure. Peaches busted a right onto Deshler, and then another right onto Linwood Ave. The Lincoln did the same.

"Fuck!" Peaches shouted. She banged her fist on her steering wheel.

Peaches picked up her speed once again. She raced down the streets of Columbus, until she was able to make it to East Columbus Street, where she made a right. This took her back to Lockbourne, where she made a left. The Lincoln was right on her tail. But now, they were no longer being subtle. They realized that she was now on to them, and all subtlety went out of the window. The windows on the Lincoln came down, and a gunman leaned out of the window. Peaches floored her Jag.

The convertible Jag flew to Lockbourne and over E. Livingston. To her surprise, they pursued her.

"Are you fucking crazy?" she shouted. Her answer came in the sound of gunfire. The gunman leaning out of the rear passenger side window opened fire.

"Fuck!" Peaches shouted. She ducked slightly, as the bullets whizzed over her head.

The gunmen opened fire continuously, sending multiple rounds towards Peaches' brand new Jag. She prayed that none of them strike her car, because getting it painted the day after driving it off of the show room floor would really suck. She hit the accelerator, banking on being able to outrun and out maneuver the old Town Car.

"Oh shit!" Peaches cried out, banging on her steering wheel. She remembered that Lockbourne came to and end on Kent Street, and in order to get to the East Freeway, she would need to turn on Kent and take Miller Ave in order to get on the I-70 access road. The thought of having to slow down and turn onto Kent, and then slow down and turn onto Miller, was not something she relished. The Town Car was too close and coming at her at top speed. The last thing she wanted to do was to slow down. She was going to have to take a chance, and make the turn as fast as she could, without flipping the small, lightweight Jag over. Dying in a roll over in a convertible was no better than dying from a bullet to the back of the head. Dead was dead.

"Here we go!" Peaches said to herself. She came to the corner of Kent Street, and yanked her steering wheel to the right. The tires on the Jag squealed and squelched ferociously. And being that they were brand new tires and not properly broken in, they were still slick. The Jag slid across the intersection and hit a curb hard. The side of her rim crashed against the curb so hard, that she popped both of her tires on the left side of her vehicle. She had no choice. A Jag with two flat tires wouldn't be able to move fifty feet. The dudes in the Lincoln would simply rolled up behind her, pop her in her skull and keep on rolling. She had to abandon her car and get away on foot.

Peaches threw open her car door and leaped out of her vehicle. The

Lincoln screeched to a halt at the corner of the intersecting roads, and four men poured out of the vehicle. She was trapped. She couldn't run, at least not at that moment. She dropped down onto her knees and using her disabled Jag as cover, took aim and the first assailant and fired. Her bullet ran true, and a nine millimeter round swept him off of his feet. It was a clear shot through his heart.

The three remaining assailants hesitated. Two began to back up and find shelter behind the Lincoln, while the third raced across the intersection in an effort to find cover, and then outflank her. Getting caught in a crossfire wasn't on her agenda today. Peaches quickly shifted her aim and let loose on the charging gunman. Her bullets riddled his legs, causing him to fall in the middle of the street. Cars had to hit their breaks and swerve to avoid hitting him. The other two gunman opened fire in an effort to give their wounded comrade some cover. Peaches ducked down behind her Jag, as the bullets whizzed overhead.

Peaches opened the driver's side door on her vehicle, reached beneath the seat and found her purse. Inside, was a second clip. She pulled the clip out of her bag, dropped the one that was inside of her gun, and slid in the new one. She was ready. As long as they didn't press on the attack, she was fine. She just hoped that the Lincoln didn't try to race forward and ram the car that she was hiding behind. She paused for a few seconds, before peering over the crippled Jag. To her relief, the two remaining gunman had climbed back inside of the Lincoln.

The Town Car pulled forward stopping near the wounded gunman. The rear door flew open, and one of the men hopped out and helped his wounded comrade up. He was hurriedly trying to get him inside of the Lincoln so that they could make their escape.

"Fuck this!" Peaches said, shaking her head. She rose up, chambered another round, and then opened fire. Her bullets struck the back of the man helping his buddy. The driver of the Lincoln stuck his gun out of the window and returned fire, while the last assailant, pulled both of his buddies into the back of the Lincoln. Crouched behind her vehicle, she could hear the screeching tires of the Lincoln as it peeled off. Peaches rose, and watched as the Town Car sped down the street. She had survived another one.

She turned to her Jag. The bullets had flown over the low slung sports car, but the wheels on the driver's side where done. Peaches shook her head and exhaled. She was planning on ditching the factory rims anyway, and throwing some chrome Lexani's, Asanti's, or Giovanna's on it. She would have to do just that tomorrow she thought. She just hoped that the impact hadn't damaged the axles on her car.

Peaches' pulled out her cell phone and called Vendetta.

"Girl, where you at?" Vendetta shouted.

"Lockbourne and Kent," Peaches told her. "They hit me. I was trying to get to 70 but they got to me before I made it. My car is dead."

"Are you okay?" Vendetta asked frantically.

"I'm fine," Peaches said, exhaling. Her heart was still racing a million miles an hour. Her hands begin to shake. "Girl, I'm sitting dead in the water here. If they come back, I'm in trouble."

"Go somewhere safe!" Vendetta told her. Get the hell off the street!"

"I'm okay," Peaches said peering around. "I can hear the sirens coming. I'mma clean this mess up. I have to get rid of my shell casings, and make it look like they was just shooting at me."

"Don't forget to wash the gunpowder off your hands," Vendetta told her. "I'm on my way. I'm on 70 right now."

"Girl, call Joaquin, and tell him to get his ass over here," Peaches told her.

"Okay. Hell, he might be somewhere in the area," Vendetta answered.

"I'm sure he is," Peaches said. "Probably fucking with one of these chicken head bitches in the hood."

Vendetta laughed. "I'm glad your spirits are up. If you can laugh about it, then I know you're okay. Any idea who it was?"

"Not the slightest. And that's the problem. I need to take some of these muthafuckas out of the equation."

"What do you mean?"

"I mean, I need to call a meeting," Peaches explained. "I need to meet with Sweet Pea's people, I need to meet with Bug's people, and I need to meet with Poocus' people. I need to squash this shit with them, and get them to join me. Instead of me trying to kill off all of these niggas' peeps, maybe I can get them to see the writing on the wall and hook up with me."

"And what's going to make them want to do that?" Vendetta asked. "Home girl didn't just kill they bosses, she killed people who they considered friends, people who they were loyal to, people they came up with. I can't see them rolling like that. And if they did, then why would we want some disloyal muthafuckas rolling with our click anyway?"

"I can get them to do it, if I let them keep their territories," Peaches explained. "The only difference, is that they work for me now. Hell, at the end of the day, money is money, and war is expensive. And at the end of the day, neither Bug, nor Sweet Pea, nor Poocus is coming back. So they have a choice to make. Maintain they status and come up with me, or fight a war, lose money, and eventually go down in the process. Muthafucka's got mouths to feed, you know what I'm saying?"

Vendetta exhaled. "I'll set it up."

"Not with all their under bosses," Peaches told her. "Just the main three. One from each. The ones with the power and juice to influence the others in they organizations."

"All right," Vendetta said exhaling. "I'm exiting 70 right now."

"The cops are here," Peaches told her. "I heard gunfire, and then I crashed. That's the story. When you pull up, you saw the whole thing. They was shooting at some niggaz standing on the corner behind where I crashed. They started shooting at them behind me, and that's why I panicked and crashed. That's the story."

"Got it," Vendetta told her. "I'm pulling up in a second."

"See ya, Boo."

"Bye, girl."

Chapter Nineteen

The meeting was held in one of the back rooms at Chi-Chi's, Peaches' famous strip club. The club was growing in reputation and revenue, and it was now the hottest strip club in all of Columbus. Chi-Chi's was known as having the finest Black girls in the city. Girls with giant, firm, round booties, and tiny waist. It had even began to develop quite a significant White clientele, many from professional backgrounds. Chi-Chi's had done two office parties this year, and had another one scheduled in the near future. Peaches had quickly learned one of the best kept secrets in the country. Professional White men, loved ebony booty. And she was capitalizing off of this discovery, and growing extremely rich in the process.

The backroom at Chi'Chi's had been converted to a meeting room. A large conference table had been brought in to accommodate her guest. She also had large, plush, swivel chairs arrayed around the table, so as to make her guest as comfortable as possible. A bar had been set up in the corner, and it was staffed by a bartender from the club, as well as two assistants, whose job it was to make sure that everyone's glass stayed full. She wanted to show off. She wanted them to see what rolling with her would be like. And so, she made sure that everything had been done first class.

Her guest were seated around the table. They were all enemies themselves, and had little to say to one another. They were here to see what Peaches had to say, and what offer she wanted to make to them. Each knew that business had been down of late, and each of them knew that without their old benefactors, finding a new source of supply was going to be difficult, especially during the drought that was gripping the country. So each one decided to attend the meeting and see where it would get them. A reliable supply of cocaine was a lot better than war on the streets of Columbus.

Fat Cat leaned back in her seat. She had been Poocus' main mover, and his most loyal and powerful underling. She was six foot two, and weighed close to four hundred pounds. She had fat hanging from her neck, and her jowls always appeared as though they were full of food. She spoke with a heavy nasal tone, as if her breathing was labored. And yet, she was always dressed immaculately. She had her clothes tailored with the finest materials, by the finest tailors in Columbus. She wore numerous rings on her sausage like fingers, as well as several bracelets, and chains around her neck. Despite her enormous weight, and the ridicule she incurred behind her back, she was feared to no end because of her ruthlessness. Fat Cat was a woman to be reckoned with.

"Would you like a drink, sir?" the waitress asked.

Zeus nodded. He, like his counterpart, was enormous in stature. He was six foot four, and weighed over three hundred pounds. His however, was a combination of muscle and fat. He was big, with huge arms, a thick neck, and solid frame. His enormous muscles were present, they just lacked definition. He was a big dude, and had knocked out many an opponent with one punch. An ability that he honed in the ring from his days as a semi-pro boxer. It was in this capacity that Sweet Pea found him, and took him in. Sweet Pea became his sponsor, and eventually he made his way from being outside of Sweet Pea's organization to being his bodyguard, and then his principal under boss. Big Zeus was another to be feared. While he was less treacherous than the others around the table, he did have a lot less tolerance for bullshit. He was straight forward and direct, and not for playing games. He was a punch/counter punch type of guy, a trait that he brought with him from his boxing days.

The third member of the group that Peaches had invited today was an old school gentleman named Catfish. Catfish worked for Bug. He was a old school pimp, just like Bug, and had moved over to the dope game along with Bug. The two men had grown up together in the same hood together back in the day, and both came up running numbers, gambling shacks, and hoes. They were both old school through and through, and Bug wasn't just Catfish's boss, he had been his best friend. They were kindred spirits, like twins separated at birth. He was loyal to Bug, and missed his friend dearly. The only reason he showed up today, was at the behest of Bug's other under bosses who wanted to stop the war. He considered them to be disloyal low lifes, boot lickers, opportunist, and sycophants who jumped ship as soon as the wind changed. He wanted to fight Peaches until the last man died, but he was outnumbered by his brethren. They wanted peace, and he couldn't continue the fight against her alone. Reality brought him to the table, but loyalty would never allow him to cut a deal. He would rather strangle the bitch than sit across the table from her.

The first one to enter into the room was Vendetta, followed by Trap, and finally Peaches. All three of them were rocking white business suits. Trap had on a white, thigh-length skirt and a short, fitted jacket by Escada. Vendetta was wearing a white, fitted jacket with matching pants from Chanel, while Peaches was rocking a white pants suit from Yves St. Lauren. Their outfits had been chosen for impact. It was common knowledge that Young and Holding wore white. And Peaches wanted to remind her guest that although she was a business woman with her own organization, she was also the first lady of Young and Holding. Which meant that she had a massive army of young, ruthless killers behind her. She planned to use every single thing she could think of, to her advantage.

Trap took her seat, followed by Vendetta. Peaches seated herself at the head of the conference table.

"First off, I want to thank everyone for coming," Peaches said, getting right down to business. "The reason that I asked you all here is obvious. There is remaining hostility between us because of some things that happened in the recent past. I want to end that hostility."

"Really?" Bug asked. "You want us to just roll over and lay down? We just supposed to accept what you done?"

"What I'm saying is, I know that shit is fucked up between us, and I ain't asking you to forgive me," Peaches told him. "If I wanted forgiveness, I would go see a priest. What I'm talking about is business. In war, everybody's pockets suffer, and can't nobody do no business."

"Put it on the table," Fat Cat told her.

"I'm saying this, I got supply," Peaches told them. "Let me just put that out there right now. I got plenty of it, and I can get more of it, and I'll always be in power. My shit is reliable. I can supply all of you. I can supply the whole fucking city."

"So you saying, that you want us to buy from you?" Zeus asked, leaning in, placing his hands on the table and interlacing his thick fingers.

Peaches nodded. "I want you to buy from me, I want to stop the war, and even more importantly, I want you to join my family."

"You done bumped your muthafucking head!" Catfish shouted.

"Family?" Fat Cat said leaning back and laughing. "What family? What are you talking about?"

"I'm saying, that it's time for us to stop thinking small, and start thinking big," Peaches told them. "It's time for us to organize, and to get money like they getting money in major cities all across the country. It's time for Columbus to unite. I've started my own family, and I want you to join it."

"You mean like the mob?" Zeus asked.

"That's exactly what I mean," Peaches answered.

"That Short North type of shit a get a nigga life in the feds, baby girl," Catfish told her. "I'm too old for that shit. You know what a conspiracy is? You know what a continuing criminal enterprise charge is? You know they ain't handing out nothing but elbows for one of those."

"They handing out elbows for the amount of shit we moving anyway," Peaches countered. "Whether we doing it together, or separately, the amount will still get us a life sentence."

"You want to start a family, and you want us to be up under you?" Fat Cat asked with a smile. The thought of answering to a young whipper snapper made her want to laugh. Peaches was nothing but Chesarae's girlfriend, and that's it. She was just carrying on for her man. She didn't have what it took to pull off what she was proposing, and she was going to get them all fucked off, Fat Cat thought.

"I want you to be my under bosses," Peaches told her.

"Be up under you?" Fat Cat repeated.

"I have the dope, the organization, the connection, and the vision," Peaches told her. "I'm already putting this thing together."

"What's in it for us?" Zeus asked.

"You keep your territories," Peaches told him. "You lose nothing. Also, you get an even bigger slice, because you get to divide up what your old bosses had. Also, you get a reliable supply, and if we are all together, that means no more war. Everybody makes more money, everybody has a reliable supply, and we pool our power to keep everyone else out of the game. This is *our* city, and we will own this muthafucka."

Zeus nodded, and peered over at Fat Cat.

"I can't believe y'all gonna ride with this shit!" Catfish shouted. "She killed Bug, she killed Sweet Pea, and she killed Poocus! And now, she wants everybody to let their guard down, so she can kill us too. I ain't buying what you selling, sweetheart. I'm too old of a cat, to be fooled by a kitten!"

Peaches laughed. She expected Catfish to be a hard sell. He and Bug were close.

"Okay, so, what's in it for you?" Zeus asked suspiciously. "My momma always told me that you can tell what a person's motivation is, by finding out what they getting out of the deal."

"And I'm sure she told you that everythang that sound good, ain't good!" Catfish told him. "And if it looks like a duck, walks like a duck, and quacks like a duck, it's a goddamn duck! This is an underhanded snake who done bit us all once, and now you want to pick it up and trust it? Y'all some damn fools!"

Peaches exhaled. "What's in it for me, is that I get to supply all of

171

you, and we all get peace out of the deal."

"And what are you going to do with that peace?" Fat Cat asked.

"What do you mean?" Peaches asked.

"What are you going to do with it?" Fat Cat repeated. "Why do you want it so bad. Peace for what? To consolidate? To recruit more soldiers? What?"

"Yeah, why should we trust you?" Zeus asked.

Peaches leaned back in her seat and turned her palms up toward the ceiling. "I got dope."

Zeus and Fat Cat exchanged glances once again. No one could dispute the fact that dope was hard to find.

"You might not want to hear this, but Sweet Pea, he ain't coming back," Peaches told them. "And neither is Poocus. And I know that Bug was your friend, but he's gone. And so now, you have to look to yourselves. You have to do what you have to do to get money. And even though you don't want to hear it, Bug was a fuckin child molester. He was fucking young ass girls, and everybody knew it."

"Who made you judge and jury?" Catfish asked. "How you just gonna pull the trigger on that man because some young bitches wanted to give him some pussy!"

"He took advantage of those girls!" Vendetta shouted.

Peaches placed her hand on Vendetta's arm, calming her down.

"Thirteen year old children, don't have the mental capacity to make those kinds of decisions," Peaches told him. "They see his money, his shiny new Cadillacs, all of his power, and they are blinded by it. He's buying them clothes and jewelry, and talking sweet in their ears. They mommas ain't around to tell them no better. They either gone, or strung out, or dead, or working trying to put food on the table. And then this slick ass predator catches them, and throws them more money than they done ever seen in they life. And you think they can turn that down?"

All eyes turned to Catfish.

"You can't disrespect that man's memory!" Catfish shouted. "You accusing him of shit, and he ain't here to defend himself! And why you think you so high and mighty, like your shit don't stink? Like you can give out justice to all the muthafuckas in the hood doing wrong? You do wrong too!"

"I ain't fuck with no kids," Peaches said calmly.

"You selling that shit!" Catfish countered. "You the reason half they mommas is strung out. They see you rolling through the hood in your shiny new cars, and they wanna be just like you. So yeah, they gonna take the money, cause they wanna be like you. You talking about him, but what you done showed them?"

"This conversation ain't about save the muthafuckin children!" Fat Cat chimed in. "That nigga is dead, and the shit he did was disgusting and way outta line."

"Ain't nobody talking to your ass!" Catfish told her. "They see your fat ass rolling through the hood in fancy cars too. And you stopping in the hood picking up every piece of pussy you can eat. And now, y'all wanna pass judgment like y'all all high and mighty!"

"The question remains, what's in it for you?" Zeus asked loudly, focusing the discussion.

"I answered," Peaches told him.

Zeus shook his head. "That answer wasn't good enough. You can gone on with that world peace bullshit. What do you get out of it? What are you really after?"

"I see the potential," Peaches said, swallowing hard. "We can be so much more, if we put our shit together. We need to form a real family. A real organization. And I want you to be my under bosses. As a matter of fact, not only do you get a reliable supply, but you can also get a slice of my shit."

"What?" Zeus asked, leaning in.

Trap and Vendetta both did a head snap toward Peaches.

"You are going to be my *real* under bosses," Peaches told them. "And you are going to run the other bosses that worked for Sweet Pea, Bug, and Poocus. And you're going to get some of my territory as well. Plus, you get your old bosses territories. This is real money we talking."

"You goddamn right this is real money!" Zeus said, cracking a smile for the first time. He began to nod. "You can count me in. If what I'm hearing is true."

"You get to keep all of your soldiers," Peaches told them. "In fact, get more soldiers. Have as many as you like. They more, the merrier. I want us to be an enormous organization, capable of taking on anyone who tries to set foot in Columbus. I want us to rule this city for real."

"Ahhhh," Zeus said nodding and leaning back. "And there it is. We join forces, and you get help with your battle against Kharee. I see now."

"Make no mistake, Kharee ain't controlling shit in Columbus," Peaches told them. "It ain't happening. I'm here, and he's way the fuck over in Cleveland. And you are going to have to chose. You can roll with a nigga hundreds of miles away, of deal with your peeps in Columbus. And make no mistake about this, if you join me, *we are family*. And we are going to act like family. We need to organize. Them niggaz in Detroit are organized, you can bet your ass on that."

Nods went around the table. Playing the Detroit card was one surefire way to unite Ohio.

Zeus nodded again. He was no punk. If Kharee want to beef with him for joining with Peaches, so be it. She had dope, and Sweet Pea wasn't coming back. He had to look out for number one. Besides, he was going to keep all of his loyal soldiers around him just in case she tried something. It was a no lose situation as far as he was concerned.

"I'm in," Zeus said again.

All eyes turned toward Fat Cat, who quickly began to feel the pressure.

"It sounds good," Fat Cat declared. "But what exactly does being a family mean?"

"It means that we are one," Peaches told her. "No bullshit. You run my shit for me. I supply, you buy. Somebody needs soldiers, we all send soldiers. No beefing between us."

"So, does that mean you can take territories away from somebody if you feel like they ain't doing right?" Fat Cat asked.

Peaches shook her head. "You run all the people who worked for Poocus, it's just that simple. If they ain't doing right, you let me know, and we'll come up with a solution."

"I'm talking about one of us, here in this room." Fat Cat told her.

"I don't see that happening," Peaches told her. "For one, you keeping your soldiers, and two, we are all in this together. We are all on the same page. This shit is going to be about money. And as long as we focus on getting money, and protecting our shit from outsiders, then we all cool."

Fat Cat nodded. She still wasn't convinced. She couldn't see herself answering to Peaches' young ass. But still, she saw no harm in going along for right now.

"Okay, I'll do it," Fat Cat announced.

"I need you to convince the rest of Poocus' people, and the rest of Sweet Pea's people to come along," Peaches told them. "I don't want no bullshit. I don't want my people thinking it's all cool, and then one of your peeps guns them down in the street."

Zeus nodded. "They gone roll with me."

"Fat Cat nodded too. "I can get them to come along."

All eyes turned toward Catfish, who sat in his seat pouting.

"I can't make no decisions," Catfish said sharply. "All I can do is take it back to the rest of them and see what they say."

"And when can I expect an answer?" Peaches asked.

Catfish shrugged. "I'll see when everybody can get together. I'll put it to everybody and see what they say."

Peaches nodded. "That's all I can ask."

Peaches, Vendetta and Trap exchanged glances. Zeus caught them staring at one another and smiled.

"Whoah is he who swims with the fishes," Zeus said laughing.

The four of them burst into laughter.

175

Chapter Twenty

Vendetta fixed her a drink at the bar, and turned toward Peaches. "Okay, so, you wanna tell me what that shit was about yesterday?"

Peaches strolled across her living room, and seated herself on her creme colored leather sectional. "What?"

"That shit about giving up territory to Fat Cat, Catfish, and Zeus," Vendetta told her, lifting an eyebrow and taking a sip from her glass.

Peaches waved her hand dismissively. "Oh, that. Girl, that ain't nothing. I'm giving them what I took from Sweet Pea initially. They vultures, and they needed something to sweeten the deal. If it brings them in, then cool."

"Yeah, but Catfish ain't having it," Trap chimed in. "That nigga would just as soon strangle us, than join us."

"As long as he puts my proposal to Bug's people, I don't give a shit," Peaches told her. "Hey, fix me one of those."

"I got it," Vendetta told her. She began to fix Peaches a drink from the bar.

"Yeah, but he ain't gonna put it to them in no way that sounds good," Trap told her.

Peaches nodded. "That's why I asked, Zeus to put it out there to them as well. He knows that Catfish wasn't feeling it, and that he was liable to sabotage shit. Zeus ain't feeling no war. He ready to do business."

"And Fat Cat?" Vendetta asked from the bar. "She didn't seem like she was feeling it too much either. And the way she kept repeating herself about *being up under you*?"

"Ego," Peaches said dismissively. "Her fat ass just mad cause she look bad. And she been trying to eat this pussy for years. It's just her ego. She'll come around."

"Fat Cat about money," Trap said nodding. "And she can't stand Kharee. So, she gone play ball."

"So you organizing this shit into three sections?" Vendetta asked. "North Side, West Side, and East Side?"

Peaches shook her head. "Six under bosses."

"Six?" Vendetta recoiled. "Where the other three come from?"

"I wanted to ask y'all about that," Peaches told them.

Vendetta handed Peaches her drink and then peered over at Trap. "I sense some bullshit coming on."

The three of them shared a laugh.

"I want to bring in Chi Chi," Peaches told them.

Trap and Vendetta exchanged glances, and slowly both of them began to nod.

"Chi Chi," Vendetta said. "That would be a bad move. You think she'd be willing to come in and get down and follow orders?"

Peaches nodded. "No doubt. You know, Chi Chi my girl. She's always been my girl. She'll listen."

Chi Chi and Peaches had grown up together. Chi Chi had been her ace back in middle school, before the two of them started seeing less and less of each other. It wasn't that they had fallen out, it's just that both had discovered boys, and the hustle game, and were too busy up under some dope boy to find time to kick it like they used to. While Peaches had went from dope boy to dope boy, until finally rising in the game, Chi Chi jumped in the game on her own, and made a name for herself early on. She was no nonsense, and had a fantastic business mind. She had her hand in beauty shops, a couple of car stereo shops, a small telemarketing business, and was even pushing Mary Kay Cosmetics and Tupperware to White woman all across the city. She was a hustler, and always had something going on. Most of it illegal. If there was a scam to make money, Chi Chi had a hand in it. And she still pushed weight on the streets.

"Okay, so who else?" Trap asked. "Chi Chi makes four."

"Katt," Peaches said with a smile.

"Katt?" Trap shouted. "Oh hell no! I'll have to kill that bitch!"

Katt was known for fucking everything that moved. She was fine as hell, and she was considered the biggest ho in Columbus at one time. Trap hated her ever since they were in junior high, and she caught her giving head to her boyfriend beneath the bleachers next to the football field. Katt had since used her talents to recruit others, and form her own agency. Officially it was a dating service, unofficially, it was a prostitution and cocaine ring, with a phone sex operation on the side. She had her hand in internet video porn service, a sex toy shop, and even an extortion ring for ex clients who tried to stray from her service. She was ruthless, shady, underhanded, and didn't let anyone or anything get in the way of her getting her money.

""Girl, Katt don't want your man," Peaches told her. "Let that shit go. That was in middle school."

"If I see that bitch go anywhere near Ashaad I'mma kill her!" Trap declared.

Peaches tilted her head to the side and pursed her lips. "Girl, this is business. We are putting together a real family. People who are going to come to the table with different talents, fresh ideas, and new ways to get money."

"Yeah, Peach, but don't none of these bitches know nothing about the dope game," Vendetta told her. "At least not at this level."

"They baller bitches," Peaches told her. "But more importantly, they *business* women. I don't need them to know nothing about the dope game at this level, because *I* know about the dope game. I just need them to manage my shit. I need them to run territories with a ruthless hand. Keep muthafuckas in line. And to bring in fresh hustles to invest my dope money in. It's time to think bigger, remember? And that means bringing in bitches that know how to get legitimate money as well. I can't walk into JP Morgan and throw piles of crack laced twenties on the table and tell them to invest that shit. But if I got a plenty of legit shit that I'm running money through, and putting that shit in the bank, *then* I'm coming up."

Vendetta and Trap nodded.

"So this is the shit they taught you in Texas?" Vendetta asked.

"They told us about getting legit money, to cover up the dope money," Peaches told them. "They want us to get organized, and get our families together, and get right. They gonna take us to the next level, if we follow they examples and instructions."

Trap nodded. "I can feel that."

"Okay, and who's the third?" Vendetta asked.

A smile slowly spread across Peaches' face. "Spooky."

"Spooky!" Trap shouted.

"Spooky?" Vendetta threw her hands up. "*What*, are you smoking? Did you inhale a little too much of that shit the other day?"

"C'mon, now, Peach," Trap said, lifting an eyebrow. "Spooky?"

"Have you forgotten that she's a dope fiend?" Vendetta asked.

"Ex drug addict," Peaches said correcting her.

"Yeah, and you put her around a bunch of dope, what do you think she's gonna do?" Vendetta asked.

"Nothing," Peaches said, shaking her head. "Spooky's been through the ringer. She knows what's up. She knows how bad shit can get. And she's been clean now for two years."

"That doesn't mean that she's gonna stay clean!" Trap told her. "You never know when she's going to fall off the wagon again. And she could do that shit at the wrong fucking time! We could all get caught up behind some dumb shit!"

"And she used to be a booster!" Vendetta chimed in. "Don't forget that shit! She's a thief by trade. She's liable to run off with our shit as soon as she gets it."

Peaches shook her head. "The old Spooky, yeah. Not this one.

She's been on her grind for the last two years, and she's been scoring bigger and bigger amounts from me since she's been clean. That bitch is a *hustler*! Have y'all forgot. Who knows all the dope fiends, and all of the ballers, and all of the niggaz in the hood coping zones and quarter keys and shit? *A damn dope fiend*! How do you think she was able to come up like that? Nobody knows how to get over on a fiend like another fiend. Nobody knows all the dope boys like a dope fiend. She used to score from them niggaz on the Eastside, and now she's supplying a lot of them!"

Vendetta shook her head. "Bad move, Peach."

"Yeah," Trap concurred. "Why you trying to get all of these hood bitches?"

"Because they loyal!" Peaches shouted. "And that's what matters more than anything in this game! They are all bitches who been on the bottom, who knows what it's like to be hungry and to not have shit. And they've all worked they way up. And with us supplying them, organizing them, and uniting them, there ain't nothing they can't do. With them on the team, there ain't nothing *we* can't do! We grew up with them! All of them! These are our girls from the hood. Remember hop scotch, jump rope, hide and go seek? These are the bitches we shared our dreams with, who used to spend the night and play dolls with. They will go to prison for life, rather than betray us. Think about that shit!"

"You used to play hide-and-go-get-it, cause you was a fast little trick back in the day," Vendetta said smiling.

"I wasn't alone!" Peaches said laughing.

"You bringing Spooky ass in on this, please have that bitch fix her hair!" Trap said. "And put some lotion on her ashy ass legs and feet."

The three of them burst into laughter.

"I'll pay for it," Vendetta told them. "She definitely needs to hit the salon, and the nail shop. That bitch needs a manny, a pedi, and some cosmetic surgery on them rough ass feet."

"And that hoarse ass voice of hers!" Trap said laughing. "Oh my god! And them big ass eyes!"

"Y'all gone get off my girl!" Peaches told them. "She ain't the cutest thing in the hood, but that bitch is down."

Trap nodded. "Yeah, she's a hustler. And she ain't scared of a muthafucking thang. She'll walk right into Neiman's and run out with a hand full of purses."

"She ain't scared to go to jail, or to prison," Peaches added.

Trap shrugged. "Your call."

Peaches nodded. "Y'all a see. At the end of the day, we may not be as big as Kharee, but our people are loyal. We trying to build a family. A lot of organizations are based on money, and self interest. Our shit is going to be super tight, because it's based on loyalty. Chicks who grew up together. We called each others mommas, momma. I'll take five loyal sisters, over twenty outside bitches any day of the week."

Vendetta nodded in agreement.

"Well, that brings us to the next order of business," Trap told them. "What are we going to do about Big Meech?"

Peaches turned and stared out of her rear windows into her backyard. "I've been thinking about that."

"I have a crazy idea," Vendetta announced. "How about we send overtures to that fool. See if we can get him on board."

"Big Meech?" Trap asked, pursing her lips. "Yeah, right!"

"No, wait a minute," Peaches said, lifting her hand. "I was thinking along the same lines."

"What if we met with that fool, and laid everything out on the table," Vendetta proposed. "He can't match our strength. Especially once we get organized, and roll the other three organizations into ours. We'll outnumber that fool something like seven to one. If not more. We'll control about eighty eight percent of the city. He can't win."

"Yeah, but this is Big Meech we're talking about," Trap said. "We could outnumber that nigga a hundred to one, and he still wouldn't see the writing on the wall. And even if he did, he would rather go out fighting."

"That's his ego," Peaches told her. "But what if we did it in a way that didn't fuck with his ego?"

Trap shook her head. "Them niggas around him wouldn't go for it. Him, joining us? An organization run by women? *Him*, answering to *you*? It ain't happening."

"We would need to get rid of his chief big mouth, that nigga D.P."
Vendetta told them. "He's the chief caveman over there. And he's also
Big Meech's main adviser."

"And if we clip him, them Big Meech would really be pissed,"
Peaches told them.

"We're at war!" Vendetta said forcefully. "How much more pissed
can you get, than someone trying to kill you!"

Peaches stared off into space, and began to nod. "You're right."

"And you think clipping D.P. would bring him on board?" Trap
asked, lifting an eyebrow. "Are you serious, V?"

"No," Vendetta said, shaking her head. "Clipping D.P. would take
away a major asset of Big Meech. His chief under boss, and closest
adviser. Also, it would help push forward our point, that this war is
fruitless, and that he can't win. It'll get his ass to thinking."

Peaches nodded. "I agree. Trap, V..."

"What's up?" Trap asked.

"Yeah?" Vendetta asked.

"Put D.P.'s ass to sleep."

Chapter Twenty One

A Green Thumb Commercial and Residential Landscaping Company was one of the biggest in Columbus. It was D.P.'s pride and joy. D.P. had poured all of his initial drug profits into the company, insuring its continued existence, and eventual growth. At first it was partly to wash his drug profits, and then the company became a profit machine on its own. It was now turning out more money than his drug dealing enterprise.

A Green Thumb had been D.P.'s baby for years. Ever since working for his uncle's lawn cutting service back in his teenage years, D.P. had dreamed of owning his own lawn service. His opportunity came when one of his partners landed a gig as a maintenance man at a Columbus apartment complex, and learned that they needed someone to handle the complex's landscaping. He slid the job to D.P., who rounded up some homeboys from the hood, some lawn equipment, an old truck, and jumped into the gig with both feet. He got a chic from the hood who was talented with tattoos to draw him up a logo, and eventually coped a riding lawn mower. From there he eventually bought a trailer, some blowers and weed eaters, an old U Haul truck, and a couple more workers. His second apartment complex contract came shortly afterward. The rest was history.

D.P. had always been an outdoors, get his hands dirty type of nigga. He was at home mowing lawns, tinkering with engines, rebuilding transmissions, fixing up houses and repairing shit. If it was manual labor, he was all in. And so, building up a landscaping business came natural to him. Well, that, and selling dope. Despite his many talents as a handyman, D.P. was a hood nigga at heart, and had his hand in everything that being a hood cat entailed. He also ran a gambling shack in the hood, as wells as a ragged old shack that he had fixed up as a night club, and then there was the dope game. D.P. had came up by moving weight.

Big Meech was rough and rugged. And D.P. was his right hand man. Their entire crew was nothing but rough necks. They were dope boys, but they were the rough and rugged dope boys. There was nothing soft or pretty about their crew. They weren't pretending to be pimps, or players, or ladies men. They were muscle bound ex- jocks, big ass ex-convicts, mechanics, plumbers, pipe fitters, welders, ex soldiers, and out-of-work union tradesmen. They were the cats in the projects who ran around bare footed over broken glass and searing hot streets. These were the niggas with the scars, the gunshot wounds, the stab wounds, and the cigar burns. They were big, rough, field niggas, and D.P. was the high priest of the group. He was Big Meech's chief adviser. He was the *Consiliere*.

The Broadway Condominiums in Dublin were one of D.P.'s most important contracts. The owners of The Broadway condos, also owned several other high end apartment communities within the Columbus area, and because of this, D.P. liked to go and check up on his workers. He was now employing over a thousand workers, and had more than a hundred trucks with trailers, and more than two hundred reconditioned, repainted, U-Haul type trucks in his company. He not only did commercial landscaping, but also residential landscaping within all of the finest communities in the Columbus metro area. He put his best guys on The Broadway.

D.P. walked through the complex, surveying the landscaping. He checked the hedges, the edges on the grass that bordered the pathways throughout the community, and more importantly, he checked the community's elaborate entrance. It was the entrance that landed the contracts, and kept them. If the workers, and the corporate honchos were impressed with the landscaping and maintenance around the community's entrance, then the contract was sure to remain his. It was a trick of the trade that he learned long ago. The entrance was the first thing they saw coming in, and the last thing they saw when they left. So he always made sure that the entrance was hooked up.

D.P. made his way through the complex, pointing things out to the minions that he had following him.

"Don't forget the edging around the pool area," D.P. told them. "And reshape the hedges around the office. And the area around the fitness center needs some color. Plant some annuals perennials with some color in the front at the entrance to the workout room."

"Yes, sir," one of the men said nodding, and jotting down notes.

"Make sure that they sweep up all of the grass clipping from the concrete areas, the pathways, the parking lot, where ever we cut," D.P. continued. "The manager says that corporate is coming over to check out the complex. So make sure that everything on our end is tight."

"Yes, sir."

The golf cart swung around the corner with one of the sales girls driving. She was carrying two passengers, apparently taking them to see one of the condo units. The girl in the front passenger seat looked vaguely familiar to D.P. She was wearing large Versace shades, but still, the rest of her face looked familiar. And then she smiled at him.

The smile that she gave wasn't a flirtatious one. She was cute, and a smile from a cutie pie would have definitely made him smile back. This smile was different. It raised the hair up on the back of his neck. It was an *I got your ass'* smile. She reached into her purse, and pulled out a micro Uzi.

The sales girl screamed and slammed on the brakes to the golf cart. Trap leaped out of the front seat, and began to spray. Vendetta hopped off of the back of the golf cart, pulled out a matching micro Uzi and also began taking out targets. They didn't know which of D.P.'s men were armed bodyguards, armed landscape workers, or just unarmed workers.

187

They weren't taking any chances, so they were going to take them all out.

"Shut up, bitch!" Vendetta shouted to the screaming apartment sales counselor. She pulled her by her hair and yanked her out of the golf cart. The cart was going to be their escape out of the complex, and she didn't need the sales girl driving away in it.

Vendetta and Trap sent rounds at D.P. and his fleeing men, dropping them quickly. They had all been caught completely off guard, trapped on a walkway in between two long apartment buildings. They were ducks in an alley.

With military like precision, Vendetta took out the men on her right, while Trap eliminated the threats to their left. The bodyguards fell like wheat to a sickle. Trap got off the money shot, striking D.P. in the back of his leg, blowing off his knee cap. He fell in the grass next to a row of neatly trimmed hedges.

"Oh! Ahhha, shit!" D.P. rolled around on the ground, clutching his bloody leg, where his knee cap would have been.

Trap walked up on him and kicked him in his side.

"Fuck!" D.P. shouted. The pain was excruciating. "Bitches!"

Trap smiled, and lowered her sunglasses. Vendetta grabbed the still screaming sales girl, and hurried over to where Trap was standing. She spied several men trying to peek around the corner and she squeezed the trigger on her weapon letting loose a barrage of bullets. Her bullets struck the corner of the building next to where their heads were, causing them to duck back around the building.

"What are you doing?" the salesgirl shouted.

"Shut up, bitch!" Vendetta said, dragging her along by her blond ponytail.

"What the fuck do you bitches want?" D.P. shouted.

"We're here for you," Trap told him.

"Then get this shit over with!" D.P. shouted.

Vendetta let loose again on the guys peering around the building.

"I got your back," Vendetta said, walking up behind Trap.

"I have a question for you," Trap told D.P.

"Fuck you!" D.P. shouted. He managed to muster enough moisture in his mouth to spit at her feet.

"Pitiful," Trap said, unimpressed. "We need Big Meech to cut a deal."

"Never!" D.P. shouted. "He'll never cut a deal with you scandalous ass bitches. He's going to fuck you in your stanky ass, bitch! And then nut on Peaches' face!"

Trap smiled and shook her head. "He's outnumbered. We've rolled Bug's family into ours. Same thing with Poocus' family. Same thing with Sweet Pea's. We cut a deal with all of they people. They are all rolling with us now. We control the city, and your big daddy is outnumbered."

"Then you don't need to cut a deal then!" D.P. said, writhing in pain.

"If the writing is on the wall, will he cut a deal?" Trap asked.

"Never!" D.P. shouted. "I won't let him. I'll tell him to go to war until the last man let's out his last breath."

Again, Trap laughed. "The last man who lets out his last breath, just might be you."

D.P. frowned at first, and then realization set in. "He still won't deal with you. You kill me, he'll really fight you to the last man! You've fucked up! You tell that bitch Peaches, that she's just fucked up! Any hope of peace, just went out the window today!"

"Will he deal with us once you're dead, and he sees that he's outnumbered?" Trap asked.

"Find out for yourself," D.P. told her. He laid back on the ground, released his knee, and relaxed himself. "Do it."

"Fuck you," Trap said, aiming her weapon.

"No!" D.P. told her. "Fuck you! Fuck Peaches, fuck your mommas, your grannies, your kids..."

Trap squeezed the trigger on her weapon, sending four bullets across D.P.'s chest. Smoke pouted from the bullet holes in his body. Trap turned back to Vendetta and shrugged. Vendetta peered down at D.P.'s body and shrugged as well. She shifted her weapon, and fired into his body as well. His body jumped.

"Just in case," Vendetta said shrugging again. She clasped the salesgirl's hair, and pulled her to the golf cart. She stuck the sales counselor behind the wheel, while she climbed in the front, and Trap climbed in the rear. Both reloaded their weapons. Go back the way we came, and don't stop at the office. You're taking us out of the complex.

The salesgirl nodded, released the parking brake on the golf cart, and headed off. Trap lifted her cellphone.

"Yeah?" Peaches answered.

"Lullaby baby," Trap told her.

"Sweet dreams," Peaches said laughing. "Any problems."

"Naw," Trap said. She peered over her shoulder at the salesgirl. "Got a little birdie with us. A civy. A young un."

Peaches lowered her phone and stared out the window into her backyard. She closed her eyes, and lifted her drink to her lips and sipped. The Moscato was ice cold and super sweet. It was good.

"Peach?" Trap asked.

"Let her go," Peaches told her. She exhaled. "There's going to be enough killing. There's already been enough killing. Let her go."

"Gotcha," Trap said, disconnecting the call. She turned toward Vendetta. "We gonna let the little birdie fly."

Vendetta turned to the salesgirl and smiled. "Today is your lucky day. I know it might not seem like it, but it is. You better go to church this weekend, and you better say a thank you prayer like you ain't never said before, you got that?"

The salesgirl nodded and burst into tears.

Chapter Twenty Two

Omar climbed out of his Lexus and peered up at the massive black and gold sign on the building. He smiled and shook his head, and then headed inside of the luxurious establishment.

Hassan was standing in front of one of the glass counters giving orders.

"This how we doing it now days, baby?" Omar shouted in his gruff and raspy voice.

Hassan turned and spied Omar. "Old black ass nigga!"

Hassan and Omar embraced tightly.

"What's up, nigga?" Hassan asked.

"Shit, you!" Omar told him. He turned and took in the massive jewelry store. "Hassan 's Fine Jewelry? I see your work, Big Pimpin! Damn, this place is like that!"

Hassan beamed with pride. "Shit, aint' nothing."

"Shit! It is something. You ain't got to be modest, nigga. This is something to be proud of. A few years ago, they wouldn't even let us in a place like this, and now you own one!"

"Shit, just trying to make it do what it do," Hassan told him.

"When it open?" Omar asked.

"Opening in two days," Hassan told him. "Grand Opening two

weeks after that."

"Damn!" Omar said, shaking his head. "Man, I ain't trying to get in ya business, but..."

"Nigga, you don't even want to know," Hassan told him. "It cost a grip. But shit, gotta put it somewhere and make it legit, you know what I'm saying?"

"Shit, I hear ya, baby!" Omar said, taking in the glass counters and display cases, the marble floors, and the chrome chandeliers. Young women where scattered throughout the store cleaning the glass, while others were setting up the displays. Omar walked to a counter and peered inside. It was already stocked with jewelry. "Damn, can I see that?"

The girl behind the counter stared at Hassan, who nodded. She pulled the platinum, diamond filled bracelet from the display and handed it to Omar.

"God damn!" Omar said, placing the thick bracelet around his wrist. He held it to the light. "This shit will blind a muthafucka!"

Hassan laughed.

"You balling so much you got a whole jewelry store, nigga!" Omar told him.

Hassan waved him off. "Most of this shit is on consignment. I got a connect in Israel, a connect in Belgium, and a connect in China."

"This shit real?" Omar asked.

"Hell yeah!" Hassan told him. He turned, grabbed a clip board, and signed some papers. He handed the clip board back to the waiting worker who scurried off.

"Even the Chinese shit?" Hassan asked.

"Yeah, nigga!" Hassan told him.

Omar shook his head. He pulled off the bracelet and handed it back to the girl.

"Let me see that Rolly," Omar told her, pointing at a platinum Rolex, with a diamond studded bezel, and diamond encrusted face. "That muthafucka is clean!"

The girl handed Omar the Rolex.

Omar placed the Rolex on his wrist, and held it up to the light.

"How much is this one?"

"Nigga, we ain't even open yet!" Hassan told him. "I'm just putting this shit out for the photo shoot for our advertisement, and for the T.V. commercial we gonna shoot announcing the grand opening."

"Nigga, this a jewelry store!" Omar told him. Sell some muthafuckin jewelry! How much is this bitch?"

Hassan smiled. "For you? Fifteen grand nigga!"

Omar nodded. "I'm good."

"Give me my money, Omar!" Hassan told him.

"Nigga, I got you!" Omar told him.

"All right!" Hassan told him. "Don't make me come and look for your ass!"

Omar laughed. "I'll give it to you tonight. "I know you gonna be at the club?"

"Club?" Hassan lifted an eyebrow. "I don't do too much clubbing no more."

"Oh, you a business man, now?"

"You damn right!" Hassan told him. He turned, and signed another invoice.

"We hitting the club to celebrate with ya boy," Hassan told him.

"Who is that?"

"Ya boy! Ches!"

"Oh, yeah!" Hassan nodded. "I heard that nigga was out. That shit for real?"

"You damn right that shit for real!" Omar told him. "Come hit the club with us tonight. It'll be like old times! We'll tear up the muthafuckin town!"

Hassan smiled. "I'll try to make it."

"C'mon now, what the fuck is that? Ya nigga outta the joint, and you gone try to make it?"

"Shit, we ain't kids no more, O," Hassan told him. "We got responsibilities, and other shit to do. We can't follow Ches around all our life."

"Follow Ches? Nigga, what the fuck is that? Ain't nobody

following nobody! We celebrating 'cause the fam is out. Shit, a nigga can't celebrate freedom, what the fuck can he celebrate? It's all good, baby!"

"I'mma try to make it," Hassan told him. "So, is this what you wanted to holler at me about?"

"Shit, I just wanted to see you," Omar told him. "I ain't seen you in a minute. I just wanted to put eyes on you, and my arms around you. Make sure everything is everything. We always gone be kinfolk."

Hassan nodded, and held out his hand. "Always."

Omar clasped Hassan's hand, and the two embraced once again.

"Where that nigga Ches at?" Hassan asked.

"He here," Omar told him.

"In D-Town?" Hassan asked. "Already?"

"Already," Omar nodded. "This home, baby."

"He headed back to Ohio?" Hassan asked.

Omar smiled. "I don't know. Shit, he was in a hurry to get back home. He might be trying to camp out here for a minute."

Omar stared at Hassan face, taking in his reaction.

"Word?" Hassan asked.

"Word," Omar said smiling. "I know once he got here, you two niggaz was gonna hit the town, and tear this bitch up. Y'all wasn't gonna have fun without me."

"Yeah, yeah," Hassan said, staring off into space. "I wonder where that nigga is? He been up here, and he ain't even got with me yet. Who he up here with?"

Omar shrugged. "Shit, you know Ches. He got homies everywhere."

Hassan hesitated. "Yeah, yeah. That nigga probably got some bitches up here he laying low with."

"Probably," Omar said smiling. He was enjoying fucking with Hassan's head. "Bitches, and probably a gang of homies."

Silence permeated the room for several moments.

"Tell that nigga I said to get at me," Hassan told him.

"We all gonna see each other tonight, right?" Omar asked, lifting an eyebrow.

"Oh, yeah, yeah. That's right."

"Shit, kinfolk, I'm outta here," Omar told him. "I ain't gonna hold you up any longer. I know you gotta lotta work to do getting shit together. But I'll get 'em up wit you tonight."

"For sho!" Hassan told him. The two of them embraced once again.

Omar headed out of the jewelry store. He lifted his cell phone and dialed a number.

"Yeah?"

"That nigga full of shit," Omar said. He pulled out a pack of cigarettes, and pulled one out. He lit up a square and headed toward his Lexus. "It ain't all love."

Omar took a long drag off his cigarette and blew the smoke into the air.

"You didn' t call him on it, did you?"

"Naw, I ain't gonna tip our hand," Omar said.

"Get wit me."

"I'll be there as soon as I can," Omar said.

"What up, Black?" a voice called out from behind.

Omar turned. It was a face he didn't recognize. But the gun he did recognize. It was a big ass Smith and Wesson semi automatic.

"You know what it is!" the gunman told him.

"No, I don't know what the fuck it is," Omar told him.

"It's a jack, nigga! Break yo self!"

"A jack! Nigga, is you crazy?" Omar peered toward the jewelry store, wondering if anyone was watching.

"Naw, but you are. You should have kept your bitch ass in Ohio!"

"Ohio! Nigga, I'm from Detroit! D Town born and raised, bitch!"

"Not anymore. Where the jewelry at?"

Omar smiled. He was wearing a long sleeve shirt, and the Rolex was hidden. No one knew he had it, except for the people in the store.

"How you know I got some jewelry?"

The gunman turned nervous. He knew that he had fucked up.

"Fuck you, nigga!"

"Fuck you!" Omar told him. "And tell that bitch ass nigga, that I said fuck him too!"

"Naw, fuck you!" The gunman lifted the weapon, and fired.

Omar fell, and blood poured out of the side of his face. The gunman raced off toward a waiting car, hopped inside, and fled.

On the ground, Omar slumped over. The bullet struck him in his skull. And it was lucky for him, that it did. It struck him in the same place where the doctors had to place a metal plate to hold his skull together, after he was tortured with a Skill Saw. The bullet scraped across the metal plate and exited out the back of Omar's head. Blood poured down his face, neck, and shirt. The force of the bullet gave him a concussion and knocked him unconscious. From inside of the jewelry store, it appeared as though he had been shot in the head, and was now dead.

Chapter Twenty Three

Trap's six thousand square foot house was a study in modernity. It was a futuristic glass design, with ledge stone accents, and a gorgeous metal roof. The geometry of the roof was architecturally stunning, and caused many a traveler to stop and take pictures. The fact that it was nestled on a hilltop with a infinity edge pool in the backyard, and a view of the city skyline, only added to the visual drama. It was a house that was designed to grace the pages of magazines.

Trap found herself chilling on her black leather sectional in front of her massive modern fireplace, staring intensely at her flat screen T.V. She and Ashaad were playing Call Of Duty Black Ops II on X Box Live, and she was kicking his ass. She loved evenings like this. Evenings where she could just chill with her man, and throw back on a couple of Budweiser Black Crowns and relax. She had Earth Wind and Fire playing in the background, and the entire house still smelled like the Purple Haze they had just finished blowing.

"Damn, you always kicking my ass in this shit!" Ashaad said, banging his controller. "Is this what you do all day? Play this shit?"

"Aw, nigga, don't be a sore loser!" Trap said with a smile.

"I got your sore loser!" Ashaad said, pulling her close.

Trap screamed. "Ahhh! Boy, quit playing! You gonna make me

lose."

"Good, I hope they shoot your ass!"

"Well, you should have got on the same team!" Trap told him. "You always wanna play on the opposite team. Play with a winner, nigga!"

Ashaad laughed. He rubbed his stomach. "You hungry?"

"Why?" Trap asked, peering over at him. "You hungry?"

"Hell yeah," Ashaad said, continuing to rub his belly. "I could use some Burger King."

"Some *Burger King*?" Trap waved him off. "I'm not in the mood for that flame broiled shit. I gotta have a taste for it, and I don't have a taste for it right now."

"Shit, what you want then?"

Trap paused and thought for a few moments, before shrugging her shoulders. "I don't know."

"I know what I wanna eat," Ashaad told her.

"What?"

"You!" Ashaad grabbed Trap and pulled her onto his lap and started tickling her.

"Boy stop!" Trap said, striking his shoulder and fighting him off.

"Boy, I just gave you some," Trap said, pretending to roll her eyes.

"I can't get enough of you," Ashaad said, rising from the sofa. He turned and pulled Trap up.

"What?" Trap asked, turning up her palms.

"Nothing," Ashaad said, staring into her eyes. He pulled her close and began to slow dance with her.

The two of them held each other close, slow dancing to Earth Wind & Fire. They were in their own world. At least until Trap's Pit Bulls started barking and growling.

"Damn, they be tripping," Ashaad said, shaking his head. "I'll bet you Tank's ass is right by the back door, peering in the window. That fool know we slow dancing, and he probably jealous. He don't want nobody touching his Trap."

Trap laughed.

Ashaad turned toward the back door and shouted. "She mine, nigga!

Get over it!"

Trap slapped Ashaad's arm. "Don't be doing him like that. He love him mommy, that's all. He can be jelly if he want to."

And then, they heard one of the barking dogs let out a yelp.

"What the fuck?" Trap said. Instantly, she turned and raced toward her sofa, lifted the cushion, and pulled out a Glock.

"Hold on!" Ashaad told her.

"What?" Trap asked.

"You can't go out there by yourself." Ashaad told her.

"Didn't you hear that shit?"

"I know," Ashaad told her. "I'll go."

"Well, c'mon!"

"My strap is in the car, nigga," Ashaad told her.

Trap smacked her lips, raced into her kitchen, opened a drawer, and pulled out another handgun. She tossed it to Ashaad.

Ashaad, caught the weapon, pulled back the slide, and made sure that there was a round in the chamber. He took the gun off of safety.

"Stay here," Ashaad told her.

"Bullshit!" Trap told him.

He knew there was no win in arguing with her. The two of them headed for the back door. Ashaad opened it, and stuck his head out. No one was out there. He could hear the Pits barking, but couldn't see them. They were now barking on the side of the house.

Ashaad turned to Trap. "Go out the front. I'mma go out the back, and I'll meet you on the side of the house."

"Shouldn't we go together and cover each other?"

"Girl, it's probably just a stranger walking down the street."

"Tank and Sheba was in this back yard when they started barking," Trap told him. "And Tank was on this porch when he hollered. Don't be stupid."

Ashaad shook his head. "I got this. We need to come from two different directions. If somebody is back here, and they got a chopper, then we'll both go down at the same time. Go out the front and I'll check out the back. Just be careful and keep ya eyes open."

Trap knew better, but she nodded. She would let Ashaad be a man, and call the shots on this one. She turned and headed for the front door.

Ashaad stepped out onto the back porch, and crept into the grass, heading around the side of the house.

Trap peered out of the side window next to her front door, making sure the coast was clear before opening the door. Once she was satisfied that no one was on her porch, she carefully opened her front door and stepped out, surveying her front yard. She lifted her gun and had it ready, as she began to make her way through the yard to the side of the house.

Ashaad got to the corner of the house, and then whipped around the corner. He could see the Pit Bulls near the front of the fence, barking away.

"Tank," Ashaad said in a hushed whisper. "Get your ass over here."

Tank peered back at Ashaad, and then turned back toward the fence and resumed his barking. Something wasn't right. Something had aroused Tank, and had gone over the fence.

Ashaad turned around in time to see someone running on the other side of the swimming pool. He lifted his weapon and fired two, just as the intruder's boot was clearing the fence.

"Ashaad!" Trap shouted.

"I fired the shot!" Ashaad shouted. "Are you okay?"

"Yeah!" Trap shouted. "Are you okay?"

"Get back inside!" Ashaad shouted. "There was a fool back here. He ran and hopped the fence. I think I got him."

Ashaad lifted his weapon, and carefully made his way back across the lawn toward the opposite side of the lawn, where the intruder had hopped the fence. He heard the guy cry out when he fired, so he knew that the intruder was injured. Whether it was from a bullet, or from hopping the fence, he didn't know yet. But he was about to find out. Ashaad carefully surveyed the lawn again. The intruder had been wearing all black, and he had skillfully hidden himself inside of Trap's shrubbery. Apparently there had been more than one, because the dogs had chased off another. Ashaad knew that if there had been two, there could be three, or four, and any number of them still hiding.

Trap appeared at the back door. "Are you okay?"

"Call the police," Ashaad told her.

Trap nodded, and went back inside.

Ashaad continued to make his way across the lawn, while carefully surveying the bushes against the rear fence.

"Tank!" Ashaad shouted.

Tank and Sheila rounded the corner and raced up to Ashaad.

"Sic 'em!" Ashaad told him. "Get him. Attack! Attack!"

Tank peered around the yard. He raced the the bushes where the gunman had been hiding. It was the only fresh scent he found.

Ashaad made his way to the fence. He peered through the slats in the fence. He could tell by the way the grass on the other side of the fence look, that the intruder had fallen, and perhaps even been drug away. And that meant there was at least another one out there. He backed his way into the house."

Trap hung up her cell phone just as Ashaad was stepping inside and locking the back door.

"What's the deal?" Trap asked.

Ashaad shook his head. "At least three, maybe more. I think I hit one, and someone helped him get away. Tank scared one off. Or maybe more of them. Or, Tank could have scared off the same fool that helped the one that I hit. Don't know."

"How's Tank?"

"I couldn't check him," Ashaad told her. "I'll check him when the cops get here."

Trap lifted her hand to her forehead. "I don't need this shit."

"What did you think?" Ashaad told her. "They can get at you, just like you can get at them."

"Okay, look, let's not get ahead of ourselves," Trap said, taking a deep breath. "It could just be some fools trying to break in. Let's not jump to conclusions."

"And let's not be stupid," Ashaad told her. He held up his pistol. "I know you can do better than this."

Trap nodded. She ran into her bedroom, and came back out with a

Bushmaster assault rifle, and an AK-74 assault rifle. She handed Ashaad the AK-74.

Ashaad pulled back the slid on the Russian assault rifle, chambering a round. Trap did the same for her Bushmaster. She followed Ashaad to the front door and outside. This time, Ashaad headed to the opposite side of the house, where the wounded man jumped the fence. It was a heavily wooded area.

"You not going in there," Trap told him.

Ashaad turned on the flashlight that was attached to the bottom of his assault rifle, and shined the light into the woods. He could see the disturbed leaves where the intruder fell over the fence.

"The cops will be here in a minute," Trap told him. "We need to put these away before they arrive."

Ashaad nodded.

Trap walked over to her driveway where her vehicle was parked. She peered into her Infiniti Q 50, and then dropped down to one knee and peered under it. While she was down there, she peered under Ashaad's ride as well. It was all clear. Trap rose, and stared down the street. She turned back to her car, and pulled her door handle so that the interior light would come on. The light was the last thing she remembered.

The explosion ripped the air, sending Trap flying ten feet in the air, and more than fifty feet into the grass. It also knocked Ashaad off of his feet.

"Trap!" Ashaad shouted. He picked himself up off of the ground, and stumbled to where his girlfriend was lying crumpled on the grass. "Trap!"

Ashaad dropped down next to Trap, and scooped her up into his arms. "Trap..."

Chapter Twenty Four

Peaches climbed out of her soaking tub and wrapped a towel around her body. She walked to the counter, where she lifted a second towel, and wrapped it around her head. She loved nothing more than to wind down a busy day with a nice, hot, relaxing bath. The warm water and gentle scent of chamomile help her to relax and clear her mind. It gave her a peace that was much needed of late.

Peaches dried off her body, lifted her chamomile lotion and rubbed it over her arms and legs first, before applying it to the rest of her body. She loved the scent. It reminded her of the scent of a newborn baby. She thought briefly about the day when she would actually be rubbing some on a baby of her own. But that would come later of course. First, she would need a man. Not just any man, but one that she could call her own. A husband. A faithful husband, she thought. Did that just rule Chesarae out, she wondered?

Peaches smiled, lifted her panties from the bathroom counter and slid them on. She then squeezed the towel over her head, drying out her hair, and then tossed it into the clothes hamper. Next, she pulled on an oversized sleeping t-shirt, lifted her brush, and stared at herself in the mirror.

She still looked good, she thought. She was still young. In her early twenties. She had plenty of time for babies, and husbands, and settling down, and soccer games, and all of the suburban shit, she thought. Right now, she was rocking her new Jag, and she wasn't excited about one day having to roll in a mini van, or a damn station wagon. Even if it was a Benz station wagon. She could be a cool mommy. She would just have to roll in a Porsche Cayenne, or a big Range Rover or something. Yeah, that was it. She could roll up to PTA in a Range sitting on some dub sixes.

Peaches laughed at the thought and shook her head. She examined herself in the mirror. She was heavily tatted, and grilled out, but still, she could be a PTA bitch she thought. She could pull her hair up in a bun, and put on some boring ass clothes, and go to meetings with the stick-up-the-ass suburban bitches.

"PTA, y'all ain't ready for this!" Peaches said laughing and getting her eagle on.

The telephone rang, disturbing her thoughts. Peaches walked from her bathroom into her kitchen, and lifted her cordless telephone.

"Hello?"

"Is this that no good, low down, snake ass bitch Peaches?"

"Who the fuck is this?"

"Your worst nightmare, bitch!"

"Fuck you! I ain't got time for this shit!" Peaches disconnected the call.

The phone rang again.

"Hello?"

"Omar's dead, bitch!"

Peaches disconnected the call. The telephone rang again.

"Look, go fuck yourself! Stop calling me!"

"Joaquin's dead, Bitch! And so is that trick ass dike bitch you call Trap!"

Peaches disconnected the call. The caller rang her telephone again, but this time she didn't answer. Instead, she located her cell phone and dialed up her brother's number.

Peaches let the phone ring until Joaquin's voice mail picked up. She disconnected the call, and then quickly called him again. Again, his answering service picked up. She hung up and called Trap's phone. Again, no answer.

"This is bullshit!" Peaches said, growing frustrated. Still, the tiny micro hairs on her neck began to rise. She walked into her bedroom, opened her nightstand drawer, pulled out her pistol and cocked it. She sat on her bed, and re-dialed Trap's number. Trap's voice mail answered.

"Girl call me as soon as you get this message," Peaches said. She hung up, and dialed Joaquin's number. Her brother's voice mail answered again. "J, this is sis. Call me as soon as you get this message. This is serious, J. Don't wait 'til tomorrow, don't wait 'til later, don't wait 'til you finish fucking, call me now!"

Peaches disconnected the call, and then dialed up Omar's number. She got his voice mail as well. Her house phone rang, startling her.

"Damn, bitch!" she said to herself. "Calm the fuck down. You acting like a scary ass bitch, and you letting your nerves get the best of you. It was just a stupid ass muthafucka prank calling ya ass. That's all."

Peaches lifted her cell phone, and called Vendetta. Again, she got a voice mail.

"Damn, where the fuck everybody at?" Peaches rose. She located her remote, and changed the television from cable T.V. to closed circuit video monitor. All of her security cameras came online, and she could survey the entire perimeter of her home. Her men were outside at their post. Seeing them there caused her to relax a little.

And then she spied Vendetta racing up to her door. Peaches rose, and raced for the door, just as Vendetta began to bang on it and ring her doorbell.

"Girl, what's going on?" Peaches asked, throwing open the door.

Vendetta was in tears. "It's Trap!"

"What?"

"She's been hit!" Vendetta shouted.

"Oh my God!" Peaches shouted. "Is she okay? Please say that she's okay!"

Vendetta shook her head. "I talked to Ashaad. He called me from the ambulance. She's unconscious. They don't think she's going to make it!"

Peaches screamed. Vendetta grabbed her.

"Noooooo!" Peaches screamed again. she raced back into her bedroom and grabbed her cell phone. She frantically dialed her brother's number. Again, she got his voice mail.

"Peach, what's the deal?" Vendetta asked.

"I got a phone call!" Peaches screamed. She hung up and called Joaquin's phone again. "He said that Joaquin was dead! Trap was dead, Omar is dead!"

Vendetta pulled out her cell, and called Tavion.

"What's up, girl?" Tavion asked.

"Have you heard from Ches?"

"Naw, I heard that nigga was out," Tavion told her.

"Have you heard from Omar?"

"Naw, what's up?"

"Have you heard anything about Omar being shot or killed?" Vendetta asked panicking.

"Omar? *Hell naw!*"

"I need you to get on the phone!" Vendetta shouted. "I need you to call everybody you know in Detroit, and I need you to find out anything you can about Omar being killed."

"What the fuck..."

"*Just do it!*" Vendetta shouted. "I don't have time for this right now, T! Just do it!"

"Okay, I got you!" Tavion told her. "Give me a minute, and I'll hit you back."

Vendetta disconnected the call and turned back toward Peaches. "Any word?"

"He ain't answering!" Peaches said nervously. She was now shaking like a leaf. "He ain't fucking answering!"

"Do Chesarae have a cell phone?"

Peaches shook her head. "He didn't when he left. Call Ashaad, see what's going on with Trap."

206

Vendetta shook her head. "He ain't gonna answer. He said don't call, he'll call when he gets some news."

"Dammit!" Peaches shouted. She grabbed her lamp and slung it across the room, shattering the bulb. "Fuck!"

"Peach! We gonna get through this. It's gonna be all right!"

"We should have seen this coming! We should have seen this shit coming!"

"Peach, we gonna be all right," Vendetta told her. "She's gonna be all right. Trap is tough. You know that bitch can't die. And she's gonna be mad that somebody fucked up her hair. Muthafucka's gonna pay."

Peaches smiled.

"That's it, baby," Vendetta told her. "Smile. We gotta smile. We gotta laugh so our asses won't be sitting up here crying."

"I can't stay here," Peaches said rising. She walked into her closet and started gathering some clothes. "I gotta go find Joaquin."

"I understand," Vendetta said, following her into the massive walk-in closet. "But listen to me. It's dangerous. We are under attack. Somebody is taking us out. And if you go out there and get yourself killed, or hurt, then it's all over with. They are going to wipe us all off the map. They are going to kill Trap in the hospital, they are going to kill me, they are going to get to Joaquin for sure, they are going to wipe us all off the map. I know he's your brother, you love him, but you can't help him if you're dead."

"I can't just sit here and my baby brother is out there hurt!" Peaches said breaking down. "Girl, what if he's lying in the street somewhere? What if he's calling for me? What if he's waiting on me to come save him, and I'm sitting my ass here! I need to go, V! I need to find him. He's all I got left!"

"We all we got, remember!" Vendetta told her. "He's like my baby brother too! Girl, he needs you to be strong. We *all* need for you to be strong. A lot of people are counting on you! You gotta use your head, Peach. *Use your head!* You wanted to put together a family, now you have to *command* that family. You can't curl up in a fucking ball as soon as the shit hits the fan. You gotta put all of your emotions in a box, and put that shit in the closet for right now. You got soldiers. We gonna put 'em out there on the street."

Peaches dropped her clothes on her closet floor. "Girl, he *needs* me."

"He *needs* you to be strong." Vendetta told her. She clasped Peaches' shoulders, turned her around, and led her out of the closet. She sat Peaches down on her bed, and then lifted her cell phone, and scrolled through Peaches' contacts. She found the one she was looking for and pressed dial.

"Hello?"

"Fat Cat, this Vendetta."

"Hey, what's up?"

"Hey, Peach wanted me to give you a call. She wants you to get all your peeps to put they soldiers on the street. Something is going on, and she needs to find Joaquin. Have everybody get they soldiers up, and hit the streets. I need Joaquin found."

"You want me to call up all the other bosses, and have then put all they people on the streets just to find Peaches brother?" Fat Cat asked.

"This is some real shit!" Vendetta told her. "We getting hit! Get you some soldiers over to your crib for protection as well. But get every one up. Sound the alarm, and this shit ain't no muthafucking drill. But we need to find Joaquin."

"Got it," Fat Cat told her.

Vendetta disconnected the call. She then dialed up Zeus.

"What?"

"Sound the alarm," Vendetta told him. "This is V. We getting hit. Get everyone up. And put some soldier on the street for me. I need to find Peaches' brother. He's either been hit, or don't know we getting hit. I need him found."

"And the rest of my soldiers?" Zeus asked. "Where we getting hit at? I can get 'em where they needed?"

"Put 'em on the streets for right now," Vendetta told him. "Right now, roll and find Joaquin. Once that changes, I let you know where they needed at. But get everybody strapped and rolling."

"Gotcha," Zeus said, disconnecting the call.

A knock came to Peaches' door. Both she and Vendetta stared at the monitor. It was one of Peaches' men. Both of them headed for the front door, and Peaches opened it.

"What's the deal, Rocko?" Peaches asked.

"This came for you," Rocko said, handing Peaches an envelope.

Peaches eyeballed the envelope with apprehension, so Vendetta took the envelope from Rocko's hands. "From who?"

Rocko shrugged. "Some chick rode up and some little kid hopped out the car and delivered it."

Peaches and Vendetta exchanged glances. Peaches snatched the envelope and tore it open. Inside of the envelope was a folded piece of paper. Peaches removed it, and unfolded the letter. The message was very clear. There were three simple words in bold type. It read;
KHAREE IS HERE

Chapter Twenty Five

Joaquin stepped outside of his condo and peered around. The night was quiet, still, heavy even. The clouds had brought with them a humidity that was so thick, he felt as thought he could slice off a piece of air and take it back inside with him. He could see the orange glow and the faint flash of lightening in the distance. A storm was coming.

"What you gonna do, nigga?" LaQuan asked, stepping out of the condo with a bottle of Grey Goose in his hand. "Nigga, I ain't trying to lose to these niggaz no more!"

LaQuan had on a white wife-beater, showcasing his numerous tattoos and chiseled torso. He had a rich chocolate colored complexion, and wore his hair short with waves. He stood six foot two, and like many other members of Young and Holding, had numerous gold teeth in his mouth. His blue jean shorts hung low, showing off his Perry Ellis boxer briefs, while black gangster house shoes covered his feet.

"I'm coming!" Joaquin told him. He lifted the blunt to his lips and took a long pull off of it, and then blew rings of smoke into the air.

"Look, just follow my lead," LaQuan told him. "When I hold my Dominoes like this, then whatever I play, that's what I'm strong in."

"Nigga, we don't gotta cheat to beat them niggaz!" Joaquin told him.

211

"I'm coming. I'mma bring my A game. I just been bullshitting."

"Man, them niggaz can't go back to Dayton talking about how they whipped our ass!" LaQuan told him. "We'll never live that shit down. *I'll* never live that shit down!"

Terrell stepped outside of the condo and stretched. He held in his hands seven dominoes. "What the fuck you niggaz doing?"

Terrell, like LaQuan, stood six foot two. His complexion was high yellow, and he too wore his hair cut in a bald fade with waves at the top. His body was even more heavily tattooed than LaQuan's, and he even went so far as to have four tattooed tear drops making their way down his left cheek. Like LaQuan he also wore his jeans sagging, showing off his boxers. His shirtless body was less bulky than LaQuan's, but no less muscular. He cut a more sinewy figure, with more tone and definition and nearly zero body fat. And like the others, he too was grilled out. Gold teeth with crushed diamonds highlighted his high yellow skin color.

"What the fuck y'all niggaz doing?" Jakeem asked, suddenly appearing at the front door. "Y'all moving the party out here or something?"

Jakeem was the tallest of the bunch. He stood six four, and like Terrell, had a slim but muscular build. He wore his hair cut short with waves like the others, and also had numerous tats all over his body. But unlike the others he kept his pearly whites natural, and preferred to showcase his perfect teeth instead of covering them with gold. His complexion was identical to LaQuan's, which was only natural, since the two of them were cousins.

"I'm just finishing up this muthafuckin spliff and catching some fresh air," Joaquin told him.

"Pass me that muthafuckin blunt, nigga!" LaQuan told Joaquin, while snatching the Black N Mild away from him.

"These niggaz out here cheating and shit," Jakeem said to Terrell. "They getting they muthafuckin signals together and shit."

"Ain't nobody gotta cheat y'all ass!" LaQuan shouted. "We can beat that ass blind folded!"

Terrell snatched the blunt away from LaQuan. "These niggaz out here looking at the stars and moon and shit. In love ass muthafuckas!"

"Nigga, can't you see it's cloudy?" Joaquin told him. "Old dumb ass nigga!"

"Yeah, ain't nobody pussy whipped out here nigga!" LaQuan chimed in. "You the only in-love-ass muthafucka around here."

Terrell tried to hand the blunt back to Joaquin, but Joaquin waved him off.

"I'm already higher than a muthafucka," Joaquin declared.

LaQuan took the blunt, placed it between his lips, and inhaled deeply. He began to cough.

"Old soft ass muthafucka!" Jakeem said, snatching the weed away from LaQuan. He also took a long pull off of the stuffed cigar. He blew smoke rings into the air. "That's how it's done, nigga."

"What y'all trying to do?" Joaquin asked.

"I'm trying to finish whipping y'all ass, nigga!" Terrell told him.

Joaquin peered down at his diamond encrusted Rolex. It was two in the morning. He had some pussy lined up with a chick who worked at a nursing home up near New Albany. She was scheduled to get off at two, and he was supposed to meet up with her at her crib about two-thirty. He pulled out his cell phone to see if she called. His iPhone was dead.

"Damn, fool," he said, turning to LaQuan. "You got your charger?"

LaQuan nodded back toward the inside of his apartment. "It's in the living room."

"I gotta see if this little old freak done called," Joaquin told them. He hurried back into the apartment, and located LaQuan's charger on an end table. He plugged in his iPhone and turned it on. He had over twenty messages.

"Damn!" LaQuan declared, peering over his shoulder.

Terrell and Jakeem took their seats at the kitchen table.

"What y'all fools trying to do?" Terrell asked.

"Don't be running from this ass whipping!" Jakeem added, mixing up the dominoes.

"Damn, Peach been blowing my shit up," Joaquin said. He had calls from Vendetta, Peaches, and several other numbers that he didn't recognize. He hit redial, and tried to call up his sister. Her phone went to voice mail. Joaquin was a little drunk, and very high, but he knew that if Peaches had been blowing up his phone like that, it must be something. And the fact that Vendetta had called him as well, told him that it was serious. He had to clear his head. More importantly, he had to get in touch with his sister to see what was going on.

"What's up?" Terrell asked, holding out his hands.

"Man, Peach been trying to get at me," Joaquin told him.

"Nigga, don't use your sister as an excuse!" Jakeem shouted. "Bring your ass over here and take this whipping like a man!"

"Hold on fool!" LaQuan told him, holding up his hand.

Joaquin tried Peaches again. Again, his call went to voice mail.

"Man, I gotta see what's going on," Joaquin declared. "Shit might be going down."

"What you mean?" Terrell asked.

"We might be getting hit by them Feds," Joaquin told them. "Shit, I might have to bail outta town and hole up for a minute if them fools is raiding us."

"Nigga, you can't drive all fucked up!" LaQuan told him.

"Nigga, I'll take you over there," Jakeem told him. "I wanna see Peaches' fine ass anyway."

"Fuck you!" Joaquin told him.

"Nigga, what you tripping about?" Jakeem asked. "Your sister is fine as a muthafucka!"

"Don't play with me," Joaquin told him.

"Shit, we might as well *all* roll," Terrell said, rising from the table. "Shit, we can stop and get something to eat."

"What make you niggaz think I want y'all rolling with me?" Joaquin asked. "I got bitches to see."

"Nigga, you ain't getting no pussy tonight," Jakeem told him. "You liable to fall asleep in that shit."

"Nigga that's the muthafuckin plan," Joaquin said laughing. "To fall asleep in some pussy."

"C'mon, old soft ass muthafucka!" Terrell told him. Terrell grabbed his gun from off of the kitchen counter, and then handed Jakeem his weapon. Joaquin already had his on him. Terrell then handed LaQuan his weapon from off of the coffee table in the living room. "Y'all ready?"

The four of them filed out of the apartment, down the stairs and into the parking lot. Jakeem hit the remote start button on his Escalade, bringing it to life. And that was when they saw them.

There were five of them; all waiting near Joaquin's Jag. The attackers thought that their five-to-one odds were going to allow them to ambush Joaquin and dispatch him easily. They were shocked to see that he wasn't alone, and that their five-to-one odds, were now five-to-four. They peered at one another in confusion, and that confusion caused their uncertainty, which in turn caused them to hesitate. Hesitation in the world of drugs and violence meant death.

"What the fuck?" Jakeem said, stopping cold. The sight of five heavily armed strangers around Joaquin's Jag startled them. And by the way the men were dressed, they knew that they weren't feds.

Terrell drew first, *and* shot first. He dropped one of the men instantly with a shot to his chest. Guns were drawn and pointed, and an abrupt gun battle quickly ensued. Terrell popped a second, while LaQuan managed to hit another in the thigh. Everyone quickly scrambled for cover.

"What the fuck?" LaQuan shouted, dragging Joaquin down behind a parked car. He peered over at Jakeem, who had taken cover behind an adjacent vehicle. Jakeem shrugged his shoulders. "T!"

"What up?" Terrell shouted.

"You okay?" Jakeem shouted.

"Yeah!" Terrell shouted back.

"Where they at?" LaQuan asked.

Terrell carefully lifted his head and peered through a car window, trying to spy the assailants. He saw them loading their men into a nearby car, and then spied the car peeling off. He rose from behind the vehicle which he was hiding behind.

"They gone," Terrell shouted.

The others stood.

"Who the fuck was they?" Jakeem asked.

The three of them peered at Joaquin, who shrugged.

"Fool, they was after *yo* ass!" Terrell told Joaquin.

"I gotta get in touch with Peach!" Joaquin said frantically. His mind was becoming more lucid, and the impromptu gun battle had brought back much of his consciousness. "She might be in danger."

"Let's go, my nigga!" Jakeem said, racing toward his Escalade. The four of them quickly climbed inside, and Jakeem peeled off, heading toward Dublin. They were determined to get to Peaches immediately. Unaware that Trap had been hit, and so had Omar, none of them knew that they had just participated in the opening battle, of what was about to become an extremely bloody war.

Chapter Twenty Six

Peaches threw her Jag into park and raced inside of the emergency room of the hospital. Vendetta was right behind her.

"Peach, slow down!" Vendetta shouted. "Girl, they gonna tow your car!"

"Fuck it!" Peaches shouted. She raced up to the desk. She started to ask for Trap's room, and then she spied Ashaad at the soda machine. "Ashaad!"

Ashaad turned. Vendetta raced into his arms, and the two of them embraced.

"How is she?" Vendetta asked.

Ashaad shook his head. "She's still in surgery." Ashaad peered over at the nurse behind the emergency room desk. "And I can't get these *bitches* to give me any more information!"

"Calm down," Peaches said, rubbing her hand across the side of his face. "Calm down, baby."

Vendetta began nodding. "She's gone be alright. I know it. I know she's gone be alright. That's my girl. And she's strong. She's gone pull through this bullshit."

"Come sit down," Peaches told him. She led him by the hand to a nearby set of chairs. "What happened?"

Ashaad shook his head and peered at the floor as the night's events re-played inside of his head. "We was just chilling, getting blunted and shit. And then we heard the dogs barking. We went out there and checked on 'em when we heard one of 'em holla. We grabbed some straps and shit, and when we went outside, I saw this one muthafucka come outta the bushes and run for the fence. I shot. I think I hit that fool right when he was going over."

Ashaad leaned back shaking his head.

Vendetta patted his hand. "It's okay, just relax."

"Man, we went out the front and I walked to the side of the house, you know, where it's real woody and shit," Ashaad continued. "I wanted to see if I hit that fool. Man, she was like right there. Right by my side. And then she went to go and check underneath the cars. She pulled the door handle and... She pulled the handle and..." Ashaad broke down into tears.

Peaches rubbed his back. "It's okay."

"Did you get a look at any of them?" Vendetta asked.

Ashaad shook his head. "I should have made her stay in the house."

"Hey, don't start that shit," Peaches told him. "This shit wasn't your fault?"

"Whose fault was it then?" Ashaad said, staring at her. "Yours then? Was it yours for starting a bunch of bullshit?"

"Hey, this is the business we are in!" Peaches shot back. "This is what we do! We get money. And we take chances getting money."

"Getting money is one thing, but being greedy is another!" Ashaad told her. "Man, this shit wouldn't have happened if you wasn't trying to be greedy and take over everything! You happy now?"

"Chill, baby," Vendetta said, rubbing Ashaad's back.

"Naw, man! Fuck this shit!" Ashaad rose. "Man, this shit wouldn't have happened, if everybody would have just stayed in they muthafuckin lane! Why the fuck you gotta be greedy, Peaches? Was it worth it? Was this shit fucking worth it?"

Tavion strolled into the emergency room, followed by his brother Tyshaun. Vendetta rose and rushed to him. The two of them embraced.

218

"Get ya boy," Vendetta told Tavion. "He bugging. He blaming Peach."

Tavion nodded. He walked to Ashaad and wrapped his arms around him. "It's gonna be straight, my nigga. Don't even trip."

Ashaad shook his head. He shot Peaches a venomous look. Tavion pulled him away. "Let's hit the parking lot and walk, my nigga. We can blow if you want to. You wanna blow some kill?"

Tavion led Ashaad out of the hospital.

Vendetta turned toward Peaches. "Yo, he bugging, Peach. Don't even fade that shit."

Peaches shook her head and stared at the floor.

"This shit ain't nobody fault, but the muthafucka who hit us," Vendetta continued.

Peaches broke into tears.

"Man, why you bugging?" Vendetta asked.

"I ain't tripping about that shit," Peaches said, shaking her head. "I want to go and ask if they brought in any John Does tonight."

Vendetta threw her head back and closed her eyes. She had forgotten about Joaquin.

"I can't ask them," Peaches told her. "I can't."

"Girl, don't even bring that negative shit up in here," Vendetta told her. "He ain't here."

"Then where the fuck he at?" Peaches asked loudly. "They said that he's *dead*. They said that Trap is *dead*. Trap is in there laying up on a operating table. Where is Joaquin? Is he laying up on a table in the morgue? Is he laying in an alley somewhere? Or up in somebody's trunk? Did they dump his body in the lake?"

"Peaches, get a hold of yourself!" Vendetta said, clasping Peaches' arms forcefully. "We gonna get through this shit! Do you hear me? We gonna get through this!"

"What happened?" Tyshaun asked.

Tyshaun was tall, with green eyes and bright skin. He had light freckles on his cheek, and wore his hair short in waves. Unlike a lot of members of Young and Holding, he wasn't grilled out or tatted up. And he dressed more like a jock than a thug or a baller. He could pass for being a straight laced college kid.

Vendetta shrugged. "We got hit. They hit Trap. They left a message saying they hit Joaquin and Ches and Omar. We can't get in touch with none of them."

"Damn!" Tyshaun said, peering down at the floor. "You want me to hit the streets and see what I can find out?"

"Please?" Vendetta asked. "I really need you to do that. Please, please, please see what you can find out. And call me as soon as you hear anything."

Vendetta pulled out her phone. It was dead. Tyshaun saw her blank screen.

"I'll hit Tavion up on his phone if I find out anything," Tyshaun told her.

"Thank you, thank you, thank you!" Vendetta wrapped her arms around Tyshaun and hugged him tightly.

"Thank you, Ty," Peaches said. She wrapped her arms around him and embraced him tightly once Vendetta had finished.

"I got you covered," Tyshaun told them. He turned, and walked through the emergency room exit.

"You want some coffee?" Vendetta asked.

Peaches nodded. "I *need* some coffee."

"There's a store across the street," Vendetta told her.

Peaches shook her head. "I don't want to leave until I hear something."

"We coming right back," Vendetta told her. "We just gonna grab a cup and come right back. She's in surgery, there's nothing we can do right now."

Peaches nodded. Finally, she followed Vendetta out of the hospital toward her illegally parked Jag.

*****

Brandon Reigns' massive French Normandy style estate was nestled on the far northern outskirts of Philly. It was a grand, old world type estate, with dramatic roof pitches, gorgeous steeple turrets, and a custom slate roof. The manor was nestled on twenty two gorgeously landscaped acres, and included horse stables, barns, and a riding ring. A manned gatehouse guarded the entrance to the property, and numerous foot soldiers were on constant patrol. A state of the art security center with numerous video monitors kept a close eye on every inch of the property. Inside of this highly secured mega mansion, Brandon found himself being woken up from his sleep.

"What is it?" Brandon huffed.

"It's Nico," the voice at his bedroom door told him.

Brandon rubbed the sleep from his eyes, climbed out of bed, and opened his bedroom door. "What is it?"

"Sorry to wake you," Nico said, deferentially. "But I got something you *need* to hear."

"At this time of the morning?" Brandon asked, continuing to wipe the sleep out of his eyes. "What?"

Nico nodded down the hall. "He's in the living room."

"I'll be there in a minute," Brandon told him, closing his bedroom door.

Brandon walked into his master bathroom, where he took a long hard piss. He had no idea what Nico wanted at this time of the morning, but he trusted Nico completely. Nico was one of his main men, and he had been with him from day one. So if it was something that Nico thought was important enough to wake him up in the middle of the night, then it was something that he needed to listen to. Brandon flushed the toilet, washed his hands, and then splashed some cold water on his face. He grabbed his bathrobe off of a hook in the bathroom, adjusted his pajama bottoms, and then headed for his living room.

Brandon walked into his living room to find Nico and another gentleman standing and talking. Nico turned to him.

"Brandon, this is my man Winston," Nico said, introducing their late night guest. "Win Dog here is from Ohio, Columbus to be exact. He's been my boy since back in the day."

Brandon nodded. "What's up?"

"It's all good," Winston told him.

"I hooked up with Win Dog at the club tonight," Nico continued. "We got to rapping, and he started filling me in on some things going on in Columbus. It's going down over there."

"What do you mean?" Brandon asked, shifting his gaze from Nico to Winston.

"Man, it's like the Wild Wild West," Winston explained. "Everybody blasting everybody. Fools getting shot all over the place, damn near everyday. Big ass drug war. Cops flipping out, 'cause they don't know what to do."

Brandon shifted his gaze back to Nico. He didn't understand what this had to do with him.

"That chick that you was telling me about, the one that Darius is hitting," Nico explained. "Well, it turns out, that she's right in the middle of the shit. Things ain't what they seem in Ohio."

"Shit!" Brandon said, shaking his head. Now he understood. Darius had sworn him to secrecy, and he knew that his cousin had fallen head over heels for this Peaches chick. The last thing he wanted was for his cousin to get caught up behind some bullshit. Furthermore, she was now a member of The Commission, just like he was. She was supposed to be wrapping up Ohio, consolidating her power, not engaged in an all out drug war. The Commission would go ape shit if they found out. Furthermore, it may put her neck on the chopping block, in which case, Darius could do something really stupid.

Brandon rubbed his tired eyes and thought over the situation for a few moments.

"Okay, here's what we're going to do," Brandon told them. "Nico, you are going to keep this quiet. No one outside of this room knows this. Furthermore, I want you to start checking things out in Ohio. But I need it done quietly. I need a full assessment of the situation. Also, Winston, you now work for me. I need to know everything going on in Ohio, especially as it concerns this Peaches chick. But I want it done quietly. Got it?"

Winston nodded.

"Darius?" Nico asked.

"I'll handle that," Brandon told him, shaking his head. "It might be prudent to get some men into Ohio. Especially Columbus. Get me as many assets in place as you can quietly. The key is for no one to know we're there. People find out that we're there, they're gonna want to know why. And the last thing we want to do, is to get people asking questions and snooping around."

"Got it," Nico said nodding. He turned toward Winston. "C'mon, I'll walk you out."

"Nico," Brandon said softly.

"Yeah, boss?"

"Thanks," Brandon told him. "Now, if there's nothing else, I'm going back to bed."

Chapter Twenty Seven

Peaches woke to find herself in an unfamiliar environment. Her surroundings startled her momentarily, before she remembered the previous night's events. She was at the hospital. She had fallen asleep on a worn sofa inside of the hospital's emergency department's waiting room. Her neck was sore, as was her back. She stood, and had to brace herself because her legs were still wobbly, and then managed to yawn and stretch and shake off some of her fatigue.

Vendetta was asleep on the sofa next to her, while Ashaad was no where to be found. A shift change had apparently occurred while she was out of it, as a different nurse was now seated behind the emergency room intake desk. Peaches turned and tapped Vendetta on her leg, waking her.

"What?" Vendetta said, quickly rising. "What?" She peered around, taking in her surroundings. Unconsciously, she had placed her hand on the handle of her pistol. And then she remembered where she was, and processed the fact that Peaches was standing next to her.

"Girl, wake up," Peaches told her.

"What's the matter?" Vendetta asked.

Peaches shook her head. "Nothing." She peered at the nurse behind the desk. "I don't know. Where's Tavion?"

Vendetta rubbed her face, and wiped some sleep out of the corner of her eyes. "He was with Ashaad."

"Okay, so, where's Ashaad?"

Vendetta peered around the waiting room, and then shrugged her shoulders. "Maybe they outside blowing."

Again, Peaches eyed the desk. She wanted to ask about Trap, but was afraid to receive any bad news. She also wanted to ask if anyone else was brought in last night, but was deathly afraid of the answer to that question. She pulled her iPhone out of her pocket and peered at the blank screen. It was dead. It had been dead since last night.

"You want me to ask?" Vendetta asked her, knowing what her friend was thinking.

"I can ask her," Peaches replied.

Peaches began to make her way toward the front desk, which now seemed like it was a million miles away. She felt as if she were walking through a long tunnel, with the fear of not knowing what lay at the end of it. Each of her steps were slow and deliberate, as her feet felt heavy, and needed to consciously be willed into functioning.

The sliding glass door to the emergency room opened, and in walked Jakeem. He was followed inside by Terrell, who was pulling up his sagging shorts. Terrell was followed by LaQuan, and finally, Joaquin. Peaches' eye flew open wide, and she raced into her brother's arms. The two of them embraced as if they hadn't seen one another in twenty years. Peaches kissed her brother all over his face. Her tears flowed heavily, as she continued to kiss and embrace him.

Vendetta gave them a moment, before also stepping in and embracing Joaquin. Her was like her younger brother as well.

"Where have you been?" Peaches asked, sniffling, and wiping away her tears.

"Trying to get with you," Joaquin told her. "I didn't know what happened to you. I went by your crib, and I've been trying to call you for hours."

"Hours? We've been trying to get in touch with you since last night!"

Joaquin nodded, and pulled out his still dead cell phone. "My phone was dead."

"Mine is dead now too," Peaches told him.

"Ditto," Vendetta added.

"Where have you been?" Peaches asked again.

"I was kicking it with T, and Jakeem, and L," Joaquin told her. "And then, when I plugged up my phone, I saw how many times you had called, and I tried to hit you back but couldn't get in touch. I left the crib to catch up with you to see what was going on, and got hit."

"What?" Peaches shouted.

"They hit us coming out of the apartment," LaQuan told her.

"We handled them fools," Terrell said with a smile.

"Are you okay?" Peaches asked. Her eyes raced up and down her brother, searching for traces of blood.

"Yeah, I'm cool," Joaquin said, nodding. But what's up with Trap? Word on the street is that she's dead."

Peaches shook her head. "Don't say that. We don't know yet."

"She got hit," Vendetta told him. "And we got a note saying that you and Ches and Omar were dead too."

"Where's Ches?" Joaquin asked, nervously.

Peaches shook her head.

"Damn!" Joaquin said, slamming his fist into his palm.

"Yo, I'm out!" Terrell said.

"Where you going?" Joaquin asked.

"They say he went to Detroit," Terrell told him. "I'm headed up there to see if I can find that fool."

"I'm rolling too!" Jakeem told him.

"Y'all be careful," Peaches told them. "And call me as soon as you hear something! Anything!"

Terrell kissed Peaches on her cheek, and then Jakeem hugged her. They both turned and raced out of the emergency room.

"What happened?" Joaquin asked.

"They got her with a car bomb," Vendetta explained.

"Damn," Joaquin said, peering down at the floor and shaking his head.

"What happened to you?" Peaches asked. She began checking Joaquin for injuries. "Are you sure you're not hurt? Were you hit?"

Joaquin knocked his sister's hand away. "Naw, girl. I'm good."

"How many of them was it?" Vendetta asked.

"Five."

"Did you get a good look at any of them?" Peaches asked.

Joaquin nodded. "I got a good look at *all* of them. They was posted up on my ride, waiting to ambush me. I guess they wasn't counting on me having the homies with me."

Peaches turned to LaQuan and hugged him.

"You know how we do it," LaQuan told her. "Young and Holding. Young Thuggin, baby!"

The door to the emergency room area opened, and Ashaad came from the back. He approached the others.

"She's out of surgery," Ashaad told them. "She's still in critical condition. They got her on a vent right now, and they moving her up to the intensive care unit as soon as they get a room up there."

Vendetta hugged Ashaad. "She's going to make it."

No one knew whether she was trying to comfort Ashaad, or trying to convince herself.

"I know," Ashaad said nodding. "She's strong."

Ashaad and Peaches stood staring at one another. A lot had been said between them. Peaches knew how much Ashaad loved Trap, and how much Trap loved Ashaad. She knew that he said what he was feeling, and that it was said out of anger and frustration. Any normal person would have said the same. Ashaad made the first move. He stepped toward Peaches and wrapped his arms around her. The two of them embrace tightly.

"She's going to be okay," Ashaad said. He kissed Peaches softly on her forehead.

"How about you?" Peaches asked. "Are you okay?"

Ashaad nodded. "I'll be straight."

"Where's Tavion?" Vendetta asked.

"He went to go and get me something to eat." Ashaad told her. "He'll be back in a minute. He also had to stop and handle some business."

"Yeah?" Vendetta said, pursing her lips. "What's her name?"

Ashaad laughed and shook his head. "Same old V. I needed that laugh. He handling D-boy business, nigga."

Vendetta folded her arms and nodded slowly. "Um-hum."

Ashaad rubbed his tired eyes. "Y'all go and get some sleep. I'm a call y'all if anything changes."

Peaches shook her head.

Ashaad nodded. "You need to get some rest. You need a clear head right now. This shit ain't over. It's just now jumping off. Go somewhere safe, and get some much needed rest. Ain't no telling when it's going to pop off again."

"He's right," Vendetta told her.

"I need to find Ches," Peaches told them.

"No you don't!" Ashaad said forcefully. "Ches can take care of himself. You need to rest. You ain't no good to nobody if you tired and can't think straight. That's when a nigga gets caught slipping."

Peaches nodded.

"Go to my spot on the outskirts," Joaquin told her. "You know that smash spot I set up on the Northeast side of town."

"Yuck!" Vendetta said, placing her arm around Peaches. "I hope you washed the sheets and shit. And aired that muthafucka out. Don't nobody want to smell no funky ass nuts and stank pussy from your nasty ass hoes."

Joaquin laughed. "Just go!"

"You coming too!" Peaches told him.

"I'm a be up there in a minute," Joaquin told her.

"I don't want you running around these streets!" Peaches said, through clenched teeth. "Not right now. It's too dangerous."

"I coming!" Joaquin told her. "I'll be all right. I got LaQuan rolling with me."

"I got him, Peach," LaQuan told her. "I'll make sure his ass gets up there. He needs some sleep too."

Peaches nodded. "Make sure!"

"I will," LaQuan said, placing his arm on Joaquin's shoulder.

"Make sure you call us," Peaches told Ashaad.

"I will," Ashaad told her. "Get out of here."

Peaches and Vendetta made there way out into the parking lot, where they climbed into Peaches' new Jag. Peaches started up the car, backed out, and headed out of the hospital parking lot. She made it only as far as down the street when she saw the flashing lights of an unmarked police car.

"Fuck!" Peaches shouted, slamming her fist on the steering wheel. "I don't need this bullshit right now!"

Detective Sheila Ward stepped out of the black unmarked Chevy Camaro patrol car, holding a large walkie-talkie. She was dressed in a gray pantsuit, and a pair of matching heels. Her hair was fierce as usual. She strutted up to Peaches' convertible Jaguar.

"You trying to hurry up and get on, huh?" Detective Ward asked. "I was just on my way to the hospital when I saw you pull out."

Peaches rested her head on her steering wheel. "Ms. Ward, I'm tired right now."

"I'll bet you are," Detective Ward told her. "Been busy started a damn drug war, huh?"

Peaches shook her head. "Ms. Ward, I don't know what you're talking about."

"Oh, save it!" Detective Ward said, waving her hand and dismissing Peaches' denial. "Let me tell you something, there's a big ass difference between being innocent, and just not getting caught yet. And you are on your way to getting caught! Nobody looks the other way when bodies are involved! Nobody looks the other way when someone's father, or son, or brother ain't coming home. I don't either! So don't think for one minute, that I'm going to look the other way, or ignore any evidence that I find."

"I ain't doing nothing!" Peaches said forcefully.

"You can save that innocent ass shit for the jury, Sweetheart," Detective Ward told her. "A lot of people are in the grave because of your stupid shit! And more are going to die before it's all over with! Are you happy now? Are you happy with yourself? Look at you! Look at both of you! Your friend is laying up in the hospital on a breathing machine because of what you did!"

"Get off my ass!" Peaches shouted. "I ain't did shit! Go and catch the muthafuckas who did it, and leave me the fuck alone!"

"I will catch them eventually!" Detective Ward shot back. "But right now, I'm talking to the person who is *ultimately* responsible!"

"Man, this is some bullshit!" Peaches said shaking her head. "Am I getting a ticket?"

"No, you getting a warning," Detective Ward told her. "And consider it your last. A world of hurt is coming down on you, Baby Girl. Once all of the pieces are in place, you looking at the whole enchilada. State and Fed charges. Everything from murder, to running a continuing criminal enterprise. Throw in some aggravated assaults, some racketeering, all of the drug counts, and you're looking at spending the rest of your life behind bars. No parole, no hope of seeing the free world again. You'll be in a federal super max prison somewhere in Colorado, where you'll shower every other day, and only be allowed out of your cell for an hour a day. It's coming. You can bet your ass on that."

"Are you done?" Peaches asked.

Detective Ward nodded. "How's Trap doing?"

Peaches shrugged. "Like you said, she's on a vent."

"This might not mean nothing to you right now, but The Lord works miracles," Detective Ward told her. "He'll listen. Just put your hands together, get down on your knees and pray. Pray for her, and pray for yourself. Pray that the Lord lifts you and her and Vendetta and Chesarae and all of your other little homeboys and homegirls up outta here. Pray that He forgives you, and gives you a better life. Pray that He brings piece to all of the peoples whose lives have been shattered. He'll listen. I promise you, He'll listen."

Peaches nodded, and rubbed her tired eyes.

"I want you to come down to the station after you get some sleep," Detective Ward told her. "You hear me?"

231

"For what?" Peaches asked.

"Because I need to talk to you," Detective Ward told her. "I need to find out what's going on. I need to find out what happened last night."

"I know less than what you know," Peaches told her.

"Bullshit!" Detective Ward said, staring at her sternly. "Get some sleep, and then call me. Don't make me have to put out a warrant for your ass. I'll do it. You want a bunch of officers running up in your shit. And I'll do it. I'll get a warrant for you being a material witness in an ongoing criminal investigation, and I'll tell the judge that unless I talk to you, another bombing or shooting could happen. He'll sign that warrant in ten seconds. You got that?"

Peaches exhaled and smacked her lips. "Yes, ma'am."

"All right," Detective Ward said, peering down at her watch. "The clock is ticking."

Chapter Twenty Eight

Chesarae walked into the University of Michigan Hospitals and Health Centers' intensive care ward and stared at the electronic chart on the wall. He found the patient he was looking for, and then continued down the hall and into Omar's room. Omar was fully awake and sitting up.

"What's up, my nigga?" Omar said, greeting Chesarae with a wide smile.

Chesarae held out his hand, and Omar clasped it. "How you doing, my nigga?"

"Shit, I got a hole in my head," Omar said laughing. "How the fuck you think I'm doing?"

"You had a hole in that hard ass head of yours before you got shot, muthafucka!" Chesarae told him. He jabbed his finger at Omar's skull. "I always knew that hard ass head would be good for something."

"Yeah, who would have thought getting my skull opened up by a Skill Saw a couple a years ago would've saved me?" Omar said with a smile.

"See, you never know. You should have let me torture your ass a long time ago."

Omar smiled. "You've been torturing me since I met you."

Chesarae and Omar shared a laugh.

"So, where they hit you?" Chesarae asked, examining the bandages wrapped around Omar's head.

"Shit, fool tried to dome me in the temple," Omar said, pointing two fingers toward his skull as if they were the barrel of a handgun. "Bullet penetrated my flesh and then skidded off the metal plate in my skull. Exited out the back."

Chesarae shook his head. He was hardcore, but Omar was even harder. Taking a Skill Saw to the skull, and then taking a bullet in the skull. Not to mention the other times he's been shot. It went without saying that Omar was a bad muthafucka, he thought.

"You got nine live, muthafucka," Chesarae told him.

Omar shook his head. "Not anymore. Not sure how many of them I got left now."

"Dying is for soft ass muthafuckas," Chesarae said with a smile. "That ain't for us. We built to last, baby."

Omar laughed.

"So what's the dealio, yo?" Chesarae continued.

"Shit, it is what it is," Omar said in his gruff, deep, baritone voice. "Everything ain't everything."

Chesarae peered down at the floor and shook his head. He was clearly crestfallen. "Damn."

Omar shrugged. "Shit, it's been a long time coming. Hell, it's been a long time... period. Couldn't expect for it to be like it was, right?"

"Maybe it *is* like it was," Chesarae said softly. "Maybe I was just blind and didn't see it. Maybe Peach was right all along."

"Prison has a way of enlightened us," Omar told him. "If it's one thing it does, it brings clarity. At the end of the day, you'll know who's with you, and who's against ya."

"Yeah, but damn. When it's ya boy..."

"Fuck that! I'm ya boy!" Omar held up his hand, and Chesarae clasped it. "One muthafuckin monkey don't stop no show."

Chesarae nodded. "You right." He turned, spotted a chair, and pulled it up to the bed.

"What the fuck you doing?" Omar asked.

"Sitting down, what the fuck it look like, nigga?"

Omar shook his head and sat up even further in bed. "You act like you staying for a while."

"I was planning on kicking it with you, unsociable ass nigga!"

"You can sit down if you planning on staying up in this muthafucka by yourself!" Omar told him. "Me? I'm getting the fuck up outta here."

"What?"

"Nigga, that nigga knows, that I know!" Omar told him. "He ain't stupid. He knows the rules. Never leave a real muthafucka behind. And he ain't about to leave *me* behind."

"You in intensive care, nigga!" Chesarae told him.

"No shit! And that muthafucka know where I'm at too! The laws is gone. They asked they muthafucking questions and bounced. I'm sitting up here with nothing but my dick in my hand."

"You want a strap?" Chesarae asked.

"Yeah, for starters," Omar said nodding. "Secondly, I want you to help me get this shit off of me. And I need some muthafuckin clothes. My shit was all bloody, so they cut all my shit off of me, and threw that shit away. Either that, or the muthafuckin police took it."

"I ain't got no extra clothes!" Chesarae told him.

"They got a gift shop, nigga!"

"So, you want me to go to the gift shop and buy your ass some clothes, and then help you disconnect all these wires and tubes and shit, and then help you leave the hospital?"

Omar nodded. "That's about right."

"How many charges is that?"

"Oh, you worried about the law now, nigga?" Omar asked with a smile. "You done turned friendly?"

"Fuck you," Chesarae said laughing.

"Let's get the show on the muthafuckin road."

"All right nigga," Chesarae told him. He shook his head. "The shit I do for you niggaz."

235

"Aww, Sweetheart," Omar said in his gruff baritone voice. "You know we love you back.'"

Chesarae lifted his middle finger, and then turned and headed for the door.

"Hold 'em up," Omar said, calling to him. "Leave me a plink plink. I know you got two of them."

Chesarae smiled. He pulled out one of his trademark Glocks, and handed it to Omar. "I'm just going to get some muthafuckin clothes for your naked ass to wear. I should have your ass walked outta here in that muthafuckin hospital gown. That way I can pinch ya booty when the gown flies open in the back."

This time it was Omar who laughed and shot the middle finger. "Go get my shit."

"I'll be back, old black ass nigga," Chesarae said, exiting the hospital room.

Chesarae headed down the hall to the elevators, where he pushed the button summoning one of the cars. He waited patiently for one to arrive. Finally, two showed up at the same time. Chesarae climbed on board the first one that opened its door. He stood waiting patiently for the door to close. Just as the elevator door was finally closing, the second elevator that arrived, was finally opening its door. Four black men poured out of the elevator. They were street niggaz by the look of them, and he could also tell that they were armed.

"Omar!" Chesarae blurted out. He tried to stick his hand into the door to reopen it, but it was too late. The car's door closed tightly. "Fuck, fuck, fuck!"

He bounced around for a few seconds trying to think about what to do. He could hit the stop button and trigger the elevator alarm, but that would just leave him stuck in the elevator, and it would leave Omar a sitting duck. He hit the button for the next floor, hoping the elevator would stop and deposit him the next floor down. Fortunately for him, it did.

Chesarae raced off of the elevator car and quickly pushed a button summoning a car to take him back up to the previous floor. A quick glance at the buttons above the elevator doors told him that none of the cars were close. It would take too long for any of them to get to him. He turned and raced for the stairs.

Chesarae hit the stairwell, and bolted for the next floor. He barely reached the first stair landing when he heard the gunfire.

"Omar!" he cried out.

Chesarae willed his legs to move faster than they had ever moved before. He had to get to his friend. He was *desperate* to get to his friend. He threw open the door to the stairwell, only to bump into one of the assailants. The man had his weapon out. Chesarae punched him in his nose with one hand, and grabbed the man's weapon with his other. Fortunately, his punch was forceful enough to break the assailant's nose and cause him to release his weapon. Chesarae took the gun, and bashed the man on top of his skull with it. He then turned it around and fired a bullet into the top of the man's skull. He could still hear gunfire erupting in the hall.

Chesarae kicked the dead assailant aside, sending his body rolling down the stairs. He then stuck his head into the hallway. He could see one dead man lying on the ground in the hallway, and a second lifting his weapon and pointing into Omar's room. He lifted the pistol that he took from the assailant in the stairwell, and put a bullet in the back on the gunman's head. He then raced for Omar's room.

Omar flipped the last assailant over, and then lifted a gun off of the bed and fired, putting a bullet through the head of the last attacker.

Chesarae was out of breath, but relieved to see his friend alive. "What..."

"What the fuck happened?" Omar asked breathing heavily. "Are you really going to ask me that?"

Chesarae smiled. Slowly, Omar returned his smile. He pulled the shirt, off of the dead man, and pulled it over his head putting it on. He pulled off the dead man's pants, and quickly put them on as well. Next, he pulled off the man's shoes, and then tried them on.

"Big foot, muthafucka!" Omar said, cursing at the dead man. He turned to Chesarae. "C'mon, let's go."

"That muthafucka!" Chesarae said, eying the dead assailants and shaking his head.

"What? I told you he ain't stupid," Omar said. "That muthafucka can't leave me alive. Not knowing what I know. His boy fucked up. He was supposed to make it look like a robbery, but the only problem is, the Rolley that I had just bought, wasn't even showing."

"C'mon, let's take the back staircase," Chesarae said nodding.

The two of them hit the back staircase. They passed the body of the man Chesarae had killed only moments earlier.

"Your work?" Omar asked.

"Yeah. You didn't think I was gonna let you have all the fun?"

Omar laughed. Chesarae was a real nigga, he thought. And he had saved him again.

"So, what are you gonna do about the bodies in the hospital, and your disappearing act?" Chesarae asked.

"Well, anybody who's been on the force for more than a day can tell that they came up to the hospital to kill me," Omar explained. "And second, I was in the hospital under the name Henry O'Malley."

Chesarae burst into laughter. "Are you fucking kidding me?"

"What, I don't look Irish?" Omar asked laughing.

"Like a muthafucking Irish Wolfhound, nigga!" Chesarae said, still laughing. "You need to do a way better job on your fake ass IDs."

"I can be a muthafuckin O'Malley!"

"The closest you'll ever come to being Irish, is eating some muthafucking Lucky Charms, old black ass nigga!"

Chesarae and Omar burst through the hospital doors, and hurried out into the parking lot. Chesarae pointed toward his rental. "I'm in the Dodge Challenger!"

"A bright ass yellow and black Challenger!" Omar said laughing. "You sure know how to pick a damn inconspicuous getaway car!"

"About as well as you know how to pick a fake ass name, nigga!"

The two of them climbed into the car, and Chesarae pulled away. They could see the police cars pulling into the hospital parking lot, just as they were hitting the corner.

Chapter Twenty Nine

Peaches strolled into the conference room that she had set up in the back of her strip club. Waiting for her to arrive were her girls, Spooky and Katt. Vendetta was just a step behind her. Peaches took her seat at the head of the table.

"What's up, P?" Spooky said greeting her.

Vendetta eyed Peaches and smiled. She was trying to keep from laughing. Peaches rolled her eyes at Vendetta admonishing her. She knew what Vendetta was talking about. Spooky's skin was as ashy as ever, and her hair was pulled up into a tiny ponytail. She looked as if she had never heard of the word 'perm'. She was wearing a yellow and white floral print sundress that was a size too large, and she was wearing semi matching flip flops on her ashy feet.

"What's up, home girl?" Katt said, greeting Peaches as well.

Katt's name fit her perfectly. She had feline features, including high cheekbones, and light green eyes with long seductive lashes. Katt wore plenty of make-up, especially on her full lips. She had a reputation in the hood as a ho, and her lips were legendary. The rumor amongst the homeboys was that she could suck a golf ball through garden hose.

"What's up, Spook," Peaches said, greeting her. "What's up, Katt?"

"V," Spooky said, greeting Vendetta.

"Hey, girl," Vendetta told her.

"Hey, V," Katt said, also greeting Vendetta.

"Hey," Vendetta said dryly. She had warned Peaches. If Katt went anywhere near her man, or if she ever found out that the rumors were true, and that Katt had gave Tavion head, she was going to kill them both.

"So, y'all know what's going on in the streets?" Peaches said, starting the meeting.

Katt peered down at the table and nodded.

"I heard about my girl Trap," Spooky said, in her coarse voice. "How she doing?"

"She's hanging in there," Vendetta told her.

"I'm praying for her," Spooky told them.

"She'll be fine," Peaches told them. "She's tough."

"I know she is," Spooky declared. "That's my girl right there."

"Well, the same people that went after her, went after my brother, and after Omar, and Chesarae," Peaches told them.

"Chesarae!" Spooky said dramatically. "How they go after Chesarae? He in prison!"

Vendetta smiled. Spooky was cool, and she was their girl and all, but she was ghetto as hell. And just as dramatic as she could be.

"Ches is out," Peaches explained.

"Out?" Spooky asked. "Praise the Lord, but how the hell did he get out?"

Peaches and Vendetta exchanged a glance, and both of them smiled. She was definitely ghetto.

"He got out cause they changed the crack law," Peaches explained. "His case finally went through, and they let him out."

"Praise be!" Spooky declared. "Girl, I know you happy!" She high-fived Katt. "Got ya man at home again. I know somebody 'bout to get pregnant!"

"Girl, please," Peaches said, waving off Spooky's ridiculous comment. She knew that Spooky hadn't meant anything by it, but it still irked her that everyone thought that she was about to step aside, and run for the kitchen barefoot and pregnant. "Unless you talking 'about somebody else. Cause ain't no baby fixing to come outta this coochie no time soon. If ever!"

The ladies arrayed around the table broke into laughter.

"Anyway, this is what the deal is," Peaches continued. "We been getting hit. And they coming at me hard."

"Well, you know we got ya back," Katt told her.

"I know that," Peaches said nodding. "And that's why I asked y'all to meet me here. Before all of this jumped off, Me and Trap and V was talking, and we came up with this idea about bringing y'all into the mix. We getting organized. And we starting a real legit organization. And we want you to be part of it."

"What kind of organization?" Katt asked.

Peaches tilted her head to one side and pursed her lips.

"C'mon, now, girl," Spooky said, shooting Katt a side glance.

"Oh!" Katt exclaimed, once it hit her. "Like the mob."

"Something like that," Peaches told her.

"And what you want us to do?" Katt asked.

"I want you to take over my territory, and run it for me," Peaches told them. "I'm dividing my territory up between y'all, and I want y'all to run it. You collect, you supply, you manage, you recruit, you maintain soldiers, you run everything in the area that I give you."

Katt and Spooky exchanged glances.

"Also, we are going to buy into your current enterprises, and be full partners with what you already have going on," Vendetta told them. This part of it was more for Katt's consumption than Spooky's. Katt owned business', while Spooky was strictly a street hustler. "This will give you plenty of cash and allow you to expand the stuff you already have. It's about money. You're about to get rich."

"And it's about loyalty," Peaches added. "I wanted to bring y'all on board, 'cause y'all my girls. We been down since day one, and I know that y'all won't burn a bitch when the shit hits the fan."

"Peach, you know I got ya back," Spooky told her. "I always have, and I always will. Y'all my sisters. And I'll do anything for any of y'all."

"But?" Vendetta asked. She knew that there was a second part to Spooky's statement.

Spooky peered down shaking her head. "Doing this, is going to put me in charge of a lot of weight. I'll be moving weight, supplying niggas, and having access to a lot of supply."

Peaches nodded.

Again, Spooky shook her head. "I don't know."

"What?" Vendetta asked. "Speak your mind, girl. We fam, regardless."

Tears fell from Spooky's eyes. "I don't know if I'm strong enough. Girl, you know about my past. And you know how that shit had me. I try to stay away from it as much as possible. And the hustling that brings me into contact with it, you know, I don't do it for long. I get that shit, and get rid of it as soon as I can. And most of the time, I don't even be wanting to see it, or touch it, or be around it."

This time it was Vendetta and Peaches who exchanged knowing glances.

"If I'm in charge of that much, I just don't know," Spooky said, still in tears. "Every day is a struggle. Every day I have to force my self to stay clean."

"And that's a decision that each and every one of us makes everyday," Peaches told her. She rose, walked to where Spooky was sitting, and placed her arm around her. "Staying clean is hard, girl. I can't say that I been through it personally, but I know 'bout that shit. I seen what it did to people in my own family. I seen what it did to my momma. I ain't asking you to do nothing that's going to hurt you, or that you don't feel like you can do. Spook, you can say no, and it won't be no hard feelings."

"Spook, we gonna be here for you," Vendetta told her. "Anytime you feel like smoking, just call one of us. Whether you do this shit or not, you call one of us. We're here for you regardless."

Spooky wiped away her tears and began nodding. "I can do it."

"Are you sure?" Peaches asked. She peered at Vendetta.

Spooky nodded. "I can do it. I ain't gonna let my sisters down. I can do it for me, and I can do it for y'all."

Vendetta glanced at Peaches and nodded.

"Good," Peaches told Spooky. "I wanted you to be a part of this. I need you, girl."

"I'm here for you, Peach," Spooky told her.

"I'm down, too," Katt told them.

"Good," Peaches said, nodding.

"So, what do we need to do?" Spooky asked.

"As for your organizations, you build them," Vendetta told her. "Most of the pieces are in place. We are going to divide the territory up, and we'll give you the soldiers and the people to get started. I'm going to help you get set up."

"Yeah, but first things first," Peaches told them. "Right now, I need you two to do something else. Katt, I need for you to get with your peeps, and get some of my men, and go to Detroit and find out what you can about Chesarae."

"You can't get in touch with him?" Katt asked.

Peaches shook her head. "No."

Katt nodded. "I'll find him."

"If he's alive, get him back here," Peaches told her. "And if he's not, call me. You don't have to wait and give me the news in person, or face to face. I'm a big girl. You call me as soon as you find out something. Okay?"

Katt nodded.

"You want me to go with her?" Spooky asked.

Peaches shook her head. "No, I need you to do something else. I need you to roll with Vendetta to give Big Meech a lesson. I'm not sure if what's happening is coming from Big Meech, Kharee, somebody else, a combination of the three, or all of the above. I need to take some people out of the equation. Or at least give Meech something to think about. Kharee doesn't live here in Columbus, but Meech does. He's siding with the wrong muthafucka, and he needs to feel pain for doing that."

"I got ya," Spooky said, nodding. "I never could stand that fat muthafucka!"

"After this is done, then V is going to help you build up your organizations and get strong," Peaches told them. "I'm counting on you two to be my main counterweights to the others that I'm bringing into this organization. I'm counting on you two to be my muscle, my rock, my ride or die sisters for real."

"We already are, Peach," Spooky told her. "Girl, you know we already are."

Katt lifted a glass of Moscato from the table. "To sisters."

Spooky lifted her glass. "To sisters."

Vendetta waved her hand, and the attendant brought her and Peaches some glasses of Moscato. Peaches lifted her glass, and so did Vendetta.

"To sisters," Vendetta said, joining in the toast.

"To sisters," Peaches told them. "We about to show these niggas, how *real* bitches do it."

Laughter went around the room.

Chapter Thirty

Peaches shifted the gears on her Jag, slowing her convertible, and turning up into Chi Chi's telemarketing business.   She had scheduled this meeting at the telemarketing center because she wanted to check out the place she had just purchased fifty percent ownership in, and because the telemarketing center had a large and comfortable conference room in which to meet.

Today's meeting was going to be totally different from the previous day's meeting with Katt and Spooky. Those were her girls, and she had known them since the sandbox days. She knew that they would be down for whatever, and that they were going to have her back no matter what. The meeting today was going to be with Chi-Chi, Fat Momma, Zeus, and Catfish. These were her other under bosses. Chi-Chi was her girl, and Chi-Chi would be more loyal than the others around the table she suspected, but Chi-Chi still had her own shit going for her. She was a cold blooded money making bitch in her own right. She was an executive bitch, who was used to being the boss. She didn't know how Chi-Chi would feel about having to take orders from her, or how the various personalities around the table were going to mesh. Today's meeting, was going to be a test run, in a sense. And she was sure that it was going to be an adventure.

Peaches was met at the door by Chi-Chi, who hugged her.

"Hey, girl," Chi-Chi said, greeting her. "They are in the conference room."

"Look at you!" Peaches said, walking her eyes up and down Chi-Chi. "You look good, girl!"

Chi-Chi had cut her hair, and was now sporting a short pixie cut. She was wearing a heather gray pantsuit, with matching heels. Of course the heels had red bottoms. Chi-Chi was a fashion maven. She kept her wardrobe tight, her hair done, and her nails manicured. She had also lost some weight, Peaches noticed. She looked fantastic. She was pushing thirty, with a body that was crushing most twenty two year olds.

Chi-Chi led Peaches into the telemarketing center and began pointing things out to her. "This is the main telemarketing floor. Over there are the executive offices and the quality control rooms where we monitor calls and grade our workers. Upstairs we have our training rooms and our human resources department. In the corner we have our main break room, with a kitchen, several microwaves, a refrigerator, a freezer, and several vending machines. We are an ADA compliant workplace. And over here are the conference rooms."

Chi-Chi opened a large glass door, allowing Peaches to enter. A large conference table sat in the center of the room. Zeus, and Fat Momma were seated at the far end of the table drinking coffee.

"Hey, hey," Peaches said, greeting them.

"Hey, Peaches," Fat Momma told her.

"Hey, baby girl," Zeus told her.

"How you doing?" Fat Momma asked, overly dramatic.

"I'm good," Peaches said, taking a seat.

"I was so worried about you when I heard what happened," Fat Momma told her. "How is Trap doing?"

"She's good," Peaches told her.

Chi-Chi sat a cup of Starbucks coffee down in front of Peaches, and then took the seat next to her. "We have a Starbucks station in the break room next door."

"Y'all know Chi-Chi, right?" Peaches asked.

"Yeah," Zeus said, eying her. He bit down on his top lip and winked at her.

"Yeah, we know each other," Fat Momma answered. She too smiled at Chi-Chi. She had been wanting some of Chi-Chi for years.

Fat Momma leaned in over her coffee. "So what happened the other night?"

Peaches leaned back in her chair. Fat Momma was being a nosy bitch, she thought. Still, these were the people she was in bed with. They were now her under bosses, and they needed to know what was going on.

"We got hit," Peaches explained. "I don't know by who. All I know is that we got hit. Trap got hit, and I'm pretty sure V was on the list. They went after Joaquin, maybe even Ches, maybe even Omar. I couldn't get in touch with any of them the night it went down. I still haven't been able to get in touch with Ches."

"I didn't know Ches was out," Chi-Chi told her.

Peaches nodded. She wasn't about to explain for the millionth time how or why, it was a question she was tired of answering.

"So, you think they got him and Omar?" Zeus asked, frowning.

Peaches shrugged. "I don't know. I got people in Detroit looking for them as we speak."

"Damn, that's fucked up," Fat Momma declared.

"So, what do you want us to do?" Zeus asked, always getting straight to the point.

"We're moving forward," Peaches explained. "I'm bringing in Chi-Chi, and two others. I'm bringing in my girls, Katt and Spooky. The six of you will be my under bosses."

And that was when Peaches realized, that someone was missing.

"Where is that fool Catfish at?" Peaches continued.

Fat Momma shrugged. "You know he wasn't feeling this."

"I hollered at Fella, and he's willing to roll with us, and bring the rest of they people along," Zeus told her. "We can by-pass Catfish. He's the only one in they organization that's still up for a fight. Fella said that everybody else wants peace."

247

Peaches nodded. "Good. I need to set up a meeting with Fella, and see where everyone is at. If that's the case, then he can have Catfish's spot."

"And what about V and Trap?" Fat Momma asked. "Where they fit in?"

Peaches smiled. This bitch is *really nosy*, she thought.

"V and Trap are not under bosses," Peaches told her. "They work directly for me. They take care of things, so that everything runs smoothly."

"So, are they up under us, or what?" Fat Momma asked.

The thought of anyone being up under all of Fat Momma's fat rolls made Peaches nauseous.

"No, they aren't up under you, or above you," Peaches explained. "They do what *they* do, so that we can all be free to do what *we* do. I want you to grow your families, and keep doing what you doing. You run your organizations the way you want to run them. I meant that. I ain't gonna be looking over your shoulder. We are a family, plain and simple. No egos, no power plays, no catty ass bullshit, just business. Oh, *and* loyalty."

Zeus smiled and nodded. He was going to like working for Peaches. She was about her business, and her business was to get money. He was definitely down with that.

"So, you want me as an under boss?" Chi-Chi asked. She was intrigued at the thought. Peaches had broken some things down to her when they did the deal, but not everything. The thought of adding cocaine distribution to her repertoire was something that greatly appealed to her. Automatically, her mind shifted from the meeting, to spending big money on shopping sprees at Neiman Marcus. She could do the big time under boss thing for sure.

"Yeah," Peaches said, nodding. "I want you to organize, and run a territory. A *big* territory."

Chi-Chi couldn't help the smile that slowly spread across her face.

"So, what you gonna do about Chesarae?" Fat Momma asked.

"What do you mean?" Peaches asked.

"I mean, if you *can't* find him?" Fat Momma told her. "What if they got to him?"

"I'm gonna keep it moving," Peaches said flatly.

"And you have no idea who did this?" Zeus asked.

"Not yet," Peaches told them. She didn't want to tip her hand. She needed to see where their loyalty lied. If they thought that she was weak, and that Kharee was attacking her, they may want to switch sides.

"I need to know who to look out for?" Zeus told her. "Once word gets out about our little organization, then that makes me and Fat Momma a target as well."

Peaches nodded. He had a point. He had a right to know. "Kharee most likely."

Zeus nodded. It was the obvious answer. They had all suspected who was really behind it. Not many had the muscle and manpower to go after so many people, spread across two different states, all in one night. It had to have been Kharee.

"So, what's the plan?" Zeus asked.

"Get big," Peaches told him. "Recruit. That's the order of the day. Get as many men as possible. This is going to be a big ass war."

"That's expensive," Zeus told her.

"I got ya back," Peaches told him. "That's why we're a family. I will discount the dope so that you can afford to hire, train, and arm as many men as you can."

Zeus smiled. "Shit, you ain't said nothing but the word." The idea of him raising a massive ass army, all at Peaches' expense, was extremely appealing. He could unleash it on anyone, perhaps even her in the future if the situation dictated it.

"You plan on hitting back?" Chi-Chi asked.

"Hell yeah!" Peaches told her. "I plan on sending Big Meech a message, I plan on sending Kharee ass a message, and all the rest of them muthafucka's a message. But first things first, I plan on letting Catfish know, that his services are no longer needed in this world."

Chi-Chi smiled.

"You take care of that for me?" Peaches asked.

Chi-Chi nodded.

Peaches wanted Chi-Chi to get her hands dirty. She needed her to be all in. The best way to keep a muthafucka quiet when the feds come knocking, is to have some dirt on they ass as well. Chi-Chi taking out Catfish would guarantee that she was all in.

"Well, that's about it," Peaches told them. "Zeus, you and Fat Momma get big. Chi-Chi, you send Catfish on to be with Bug, V is handling her business, and Spooky and Katt are handling their business. So, if no one has anything else, this meeting is adjourned."

"Hold on," Fat Momma said, lifting her meaty arm into the air, halting everyone. "I want to get something straight. You bringing in Spooky, the *dope fiend*? I just couldn't let this pass without saying *something*. If you trying to do some serious shit, then how you gonna bring in a hard core dope fiend and try to tell her to run some shit?"

"Spooky is clean," Peaches told her. "She's been clean for a while."

"Yeah?" Fat Momma asked, lifting an eyebrow. "But this shit is also about respect. She done got busy with all these niggaz on the street while she was strung out, and now she's supposed to be running shit? They ain't gonna respect her. And that means, they ain't gonna respect you. And then that means they ain't gonna respect none of us."

Chi-Chi nodded. Fat Momma did have a point.

"They will respect Spooky, once she puts they ass in check," Peaches told her. "A well placed bullet in a nigga's ass, will earn her all the respect she'll need. Don't get shit twisted, Spook will get down for her crime."

"Peaches, I don't know about this," Fat Momma said, shaking her head.

"Trust me, Spook is gonna earn her respect," Peaches told her. "Plus, she's going to earn all of ours. There ain't nobody who's going to be more loyal to this family than she is. You pick a woman up, dust her off, and give her something to live for, then you've just created the most fiercest being on the planet. Don't ever underestimate the power of redemption."

Peaches rose from the table, followed by the others. She made her way through the telemarketing center, and out the front door. The bright sunlight hit her eyes, causing her to lift her arm and shield it. That was when the bullet struck.

The first round burnt a hole straight through her arm. The second round struck Fat Momma in her gigantic belly. The third round hit Zeus in his shoulder. Chi-Chi ducked, pulled her handgun from her purse, and opened fire.

Peaches clasped her wounded and bloody arm, and retreated back inside. She could hear Chi-Chi's gun exploding continuously, and then the sound of screeching tires. Chi-Chi flung the door open and gripped her arm. Peaches screamed in pain.

"It went straight through," Chi-Chi told her. She turned back toward her workers inside. "Call an ambulance!"

Zeus threw open the metal doors and peered inside. He had a handgun in one hand, and his massive musclebound shoulder was bleeding. "Fat Momma needs an ambulance!"

"They calling them!" Chi-Chi said excitedly. She examined Zeus' shoulder. "Looks like it went through you too. Must have been a high powered assault rifle for it to burn straight through like that."

"It was a Bushmaster AR-15," Zeus said in agreement. "I recognized the sound, and saw the fool trying to shoot the damn thing."

Sirens could be heard in the background.

"Don't leave her out there by herself!" Chi-Chi told Zeus.

Zeus nodded, and stepped back outside to watch over Fat Momma.

"You okay?" Chi-Chi asked Peaches.

Peaches nodded, grimacing in pain, while clutching her wounded arm. "I know one thing."

"What?" Chi-Chi asked.

"Only people that knew we were meeting here today, were they people who were invited," Peaches told her. "And that includes Catfish."

Chi-Chi nodded.

"That bitch really just signed his death warrant," Peaches proclaimed. "I don't want his ass to see another Sunday morning. You got that?"

251

Chi-Chi nodded. Catfish was a dead man, living on borrowed time.

Chapter Thirty One

Catfish had been loyal to his friend, and he missed him dearly. He and Bug had been partners their entire lives. They had came up on the streets of East Columbus, learned the pimp game in Detroit together, roomed in Oakland, and then plied their trade together in Chicago, before finally returning home to Columbus to continue their trade. When Bug started moving blow, Catfish tried to discourage it, because it was against their pimp code to get their hands dirty with such a dirty trade. But Bug eventually brought him around to it, by showing him the profits, and by showing him how he could fit cocaine into his expanding repertoire. The rest was history. They built a drug empire in their own little section of Columbus.

Catfish stood over Bug's grave stone, with his hat in hand, staring down at his friend's grave. He wasn't much for prayer, or for words, but what he was for, was revenge. He vowed that that young, childish, immature, underhanded, backstabbing, conniving, low down, dirty ass bitch would pay. He was going to end her life and revenge Bug's death, if it was the last thing on Earth he did. He put that on everything that he was, on everything that he stood for. Peaches was going to pay.

"I carry you with me, Bug," Catfish said softly, touching his heart.

"I carry you with me."

His thoughts turned toward Miami. It was he and Bug's dream to hit the Sunshine State, and semi-retire in South Beach. They knew a couple of old pimp homeboys from Chicago who had done just that. They relocated to Miami, took their bottom bitches, took a couple of their top notch bitches, and started high level escort services. He and Bug had planned on doing the same. They had amassed a small fortune in drug money, as well as proceeds from their other ventures, and they were going to head to Miami and live out the rest of their days fucking hoes, and sipping on Mojitos. Peaches took that dream away from them.

Catfish thought briefly of retirement after Bug's death. He thought about packing up, telling her she could have that shit, telling Columbus good riddance, and heading for Miami himself. It had been a compelling thought, and the idea popped into his head periodically. But something inside of him wouldn't allow him to leave. Something deep inside of his being, his bones, his essence, the very fabric of his soul, wouldn't allow him to hit the road. Not until he had settled the scores that he needed to settle. At least not until he had put Peaches in her grave. Bug would have done no less for him, he thought. He would perhaps head to Miami, but that would only be after he had avenged his friend.

Chi-Chi sat inside of her black Lexus GS 350 staring out the tinted windows at Catfish. She had a couple of her dudes with her, and they were watching Catfish as well. He had brought with him only a couple of bodyguards, and he had made them stay by his Cadillac XTS. He wanted to speak to his friend in private.

Chi-Chi figured that she would be able to catch him slipping here. She knew that Bug's birthday was today, and she knew that Catfish would come and pay tribute to his friend. It was one of the few times anyone would be able to catch him slipping. Nobody thought that they would get hit at a cemetery. As if the dead somehow mysteriously warded off bad shit. Catfish was about to learn different, she thought.

"Let's go," Chi-Chi told her men.

Chi-Chi's men exited their black Lexus, and made their way across the cemetery to where Catfish's men were milling around outside of his black Cadillac XTS. They approached from the other side of the XTS, so that the men's backs were toward them. They completely surprised Catfish's men, and drew down on them in a blink of the eye. Chi-Chi watched it go down from the comfort of her Lexus. Once Catfish's men were out of the picture, she exited her Lexus, and headed over to where they were standing. Catfish was still facing Bug's grave.

"Bad day, fellas," Chi-Chi told the bodyguards. "Or at least, it could be. We'll see."

Catfish's men looked deflated and defeated. All resistance had left their body. They were doomed, and they knew it.

Chi-Chi saw the look on their faces and she knew that she had them. Like Catfish, they were tired. And like most other men in their position, they just wanted to work and support their families. No one wanted war, no one wanted to die.

"You want it to be over, or do you want a job working for me?" Chi-Chi asked.

They stared at one another. The decision was a no brainer. They both agreed to work for her. She had just killed two birds with one stone. She had took out Catfish's men without firing a shot, and she had just gained two more experienced soldiers. Unlike Peaches and Vendetta and Trap, she felt like she didn't need to leave a trail of bodies to get the job done. First and foremost, she was a businesswoman, and she was always willing to do business. And one thing she realized a long time ago, was that most other people were the same way. Everyone was willing to do business. It was just a matter of setting the correct terms.

Chi-Chi turned, crossed the cemetery and headed toward Bug's grave. She walked up behind Catfish.

"Fish Daddy," Chi-Chi said, softly.

The hairs stood up on the back of Catfish's neck. He hadn't been called that in some time. He turned, and a smile spread across his face when he saw Chi-Chi.

"Hey, girl!" Catfish told her. "I hadn't seen you in so long! How you been."

Catfish went to hug Chi-Chi, and she stepped back.

"What are you doing here?" Catfish asked. He peered over her shoulder and behind her, he could see her men standing next to his men. "Oh."

Catfish, began to reach.

"Don't," Chi-Chi told him. She had her hand in her purse, already gripping her silenced weapon. "Don't make this hard."

"What are you doing, Chi-Chi Momma?" Catfish asked.

Chi-Chi shrugged uneasily. "Business."

Catfish rolled his eyes and exhaled. He was genuinely crestfallen. "Damn. Don't tell me that, Baby Gurl. Don't tell me that you done fell in with them snakes."

Again, Chi-Chi shrugged.

Catfish smacked his lips and looked away. He was genuinely disappointed. "Baby Gurl, I know I taught you better than that."

"You taught me how to survive, Fish Daddy," Chi-Chi told him. "That's what you always said it was about, remember? It's about survival. No feelings, no emotions, just using what you got, to get what you want."

"This ain't surviving," Catfish told her. "Jumping onto a sinking ship full of rats ain't what's happening. They going down, Baby Gurl. And don't you be around when it goes down. Get out of here, Chi-Chi Momma. Get out of Columbus. Leave. Take what you have, go to Miami, sit on a beach, and watch the goddamn sun set. You hear me?"

Chi-Chi nodded. "I hear you, Fish Daddy."

Catfish smiled, and started swaying as if her were slow dancing. "You were my best gurl, Cheech. You were my shining star. Ain't none like you. None before, and never none after."

Chi-Chi reached out and caressed Catfish's face. "Why didn't you just take the money and run, Fish Daddy. If you didn't want to join her, why didn't you just take your money, take Bug's money, and run?"

Catfish peered down and shook his head. "Couldn't, Cheech. I couldn't. That gurl is a snake. She's young, and stupid, and inexperienced, and she's gone get a whole lotta folk killed before it's all said and done. Get away from her."

"Why didn't you take the money and run?" Chi-Chi asked again.

"Because I couldn't!" Catfish snapped. "I couldn't. I couldn't let it ride, Ch-Chi Momma."

"And now?" Chi-Chi asked softly. "Could you do it now?"

Catfish's smile answered her question. Slowly, he turned and lowered his head, staring at Bug's headstone once again.

"If there's one thing that I taught you, Cheech," Bug told her. "I hope it was loyalty. Ain't no why in hell I could a left town with that girl still breathing. Ain't no way that I can leave town now, with that gurl still alive."

"She's still breathing now," Chi-Chi told him. "And now, she's bringing in Fella to take your place."

Catfish peered up at her and shook his head. Another smile spread across his face. "Fella? Figured as much. A snake would be quick to jump in bed with another snake." He turned towards her. "But you not like them, Cheech. Don't fool yourself for one minute, and think that you like them. Those are snakes. Low down, dirty ass snake bitches, with no honor."

Tears began to run down Chi-Chi's cheeks. "What makes you think I'm different? What make you think that anything *we* did, was more honorable?"

"We was honorable, Cheech," Catfish told her. "We survived. We came up. We lived."

"We pimped runaways, homeless girls, girls running away from abusive fathers and step-fathers, and their momma's crack head boyfriends," Chi-Chi said, with her tears streaming.

"Get out of Columbus, Cheech," Catfish told her.

Chi-Chi pulled her silenced weapon from her large Hermes' Bag. Catfish peered down at it.

"Survive, Cheech," he told her.

Chi-Chi wiped the tears flowing down her cheeks and nodded.

Catfish turned back toward Bug's grave, knelt down, and held on to the headstone. "I know how I want to die, Chi-Chi Momma. Now it's all on you. Now you gotta decide how you wanna live."

"Good-bye, Daddy," Chi-Chi told him.

"The money is in two Wells Fargo safe deposit boxes," Catfish told her. "Mine, *and* Bug's. The box numbers and keys are in the Caddy. Take care of my hoes. Give them some money, and take care of Misty. She's my bottom, and she knows who you are. She came after you. I used to tell her, there will never be none greater than the legendary Chi-Chi Momma."

Chi-Chi smiled, and sniffled. She lifted her weapon, and put a hushed bullet into the back of Catfish's skull. She watched as his blood and brain fragments splattered over Bug's headstone, and then as his body slumped over it. She burst into tears as she turned, and headed back toward her car.

*****

Big Meech was vain, if nothing else. He was a former pro football player, and he had also grew up in some of the worst projects in the city. Nobody was fucking with him, and nobody was going to fuck with him, he thought. He would rip off their head, and shit down their neck if they tried. He was fucking *Big Meech*, and the whole city was his.

Big Meech's attitude manifested itself in a multitude of ways. One, he wasn't afraid of shit, and he wasn't going to be made to stay indoors and cower behind a bunch of bodyguards. That wasn't for him, that was for pussies. And if that bitch Peaches wanted to try him, then he would be ready for her. He hit the streets, but he hit the streets with an entourage.

Big Meech's reason for hitting the streets today, was to shine up his brand new Bentley. He had just purchased a brand new Bentley Mulsanne, and he was planning on driving it to the club that evening. He had it detailed earlier, but Columbus' fucked up streets had caused him to get the side of it dirty. He hit a small pothole, which did nothing to damage the vehicle, but the puddle of muddy water that was sitting inside of the hole splashed up onto the side of his beautiful, white, four hundred thousand dollar ride. And rolling in a new Mulsanne with a single speck of dirt on it was sacrosanct, let alone rolling in one with dried up mud on the side of it. Nope, he just wouldn't be able to do it.

Big Meech pulled into Buckeye Pride Car Wash and wheeled his big sedan up to the automated wash stall. Normally, he wouldn't dare run one of his vehicles through an automated car wash, but this was supposed to be a new laser based, touch-less car wash system that wouldn't damaged the paint. Besides, he was pressed for time.

Big Meech slid his credit card into the slot to pay for his ten dollar car wash, and waited until the light turned green, telling him that he could enter into the wash. Once he got the green light, he pulled forward slowly, so that the power jets below could work their magic on the undercarriage of his big Bentley. Finally, once he was all the way into the stall, the light changed from green to red, ordering him to stop, which he did, and the car wash came alive.

The robotic wash machine sprayed the big Bentley, washing away the loose dirt and debris with uncanny efficiency and precision. Next, the machine ran back over his vehicle, applying a generous application of lathery soap. And then came the magic. The laser guided rinsing arms sprung into action, using the high pressure circular water jet to clear away any dirt that remained on the vehicle. Inside, Big Meech hit the stereo controls on his steering wheel, turning up the volume on his music. Some old school Keith Sweat was pouring out of the speakers on his satellite radio.

The automated car wash finished the cleaning cycle, and now it was time to apply a thick coat of polish to his vehicle. The machine sprayed a thick envelope of multicolored paint protecting wax over the Bentley, covering it completely. Big Meech was so engulfed in the 2200 watt, 20 speaker Naim sound system, and the cocoon like environment of the Bentley, that he couldn't hear the silenced weapons pouring into his men, nor the sound of the rounds striking their vehicles, nor they yelling and screaming and sheer pandemonium occurring outside of the wash stall. The only thing that he knew, was that the water jets were springing into action again, clearing away the polish that had covered his windows.

Once his windshield became clear, he could see a lone figure standing in front of his vehicle, just outside of the car wash. He recognized her, but it was too late. Vendetta lifted the AR-15 she was holding, and poured fully automatic fired into the brand new Bentley. Instinctively, Big Meech ducked for cover.

Vendetta's rounds raked the vehicle, causing sparks to fly off of the front of it. She aimed toward the windshield, sending rounds into it as well.

"Fuck!" Vendetta shouted, venting her frustration.

Her rounds were striking the windshield and the glass was shattering, but it wasn't breaking. Even with multiple strikes, the windshield was holding. Big Meech was brave, but he wasn't stupid. He had the highest level of ballistic protection one could buy, added to his new Bentley.

Once Big Meech realized that the windshield was holding, he raised up, shifted the Bentley into gear, and mashed the gas. Vendetta leaped out of the way just in time. The massive sedan raced out of the car stall, spun out of control as he turned onto the main street, and then got in the wind. Vendetta stood, dusted herself off and began laughing. Spooky joined her.

"Fucking bullet resistant glass!" Vendetta proclaimed.

"Too bad his boys didn't have any," Spooky told her.

"Damn, this shit could have been over!" Vendetta said, pounding her fist against her assault rifle.

"It's over," Spooky said, peering over at the bodies of Big Meech's entourage. "His main dudes is gone."

Vendetta nodded. "He'll be back. He's got plenty more fools working for him, and there are even more fools that he can recruit to die for him. But our job here is done. He got the message. He had a choice between rolling with the local crew, or rolling with that bastard Kharee, and he chose wrong."

Vendetta handed Spooky her weapon, lifted her arm, and twirled her finger in the air. "Hurry up, let's saddle up and get the hell outta here. And make sure you get the recording from the surveillance camera. And get the disc from the cameras next door and across the street. We are outta here in one minute!"

Vendetta and Spooky headed for their waiting ride and climbed inside. Vendetta patted Spooky on her knee. "You did good today."

Spooky nodded. "I'll do anything to help y'all out. Ya'll my sisters."

Vendetta nodded and peered out of the window. Peaches had been right. Spooky was a down ass bitch, and she would be *extremely* loyal. And loyalty would be more important than anything else during the tough times that they were about to face. One loyal soldier, was worth one hundred shaky muthafuckas, Vendetta thought. Now, if they could just get Spooky to get a perm, and put some damn lotion on!

Chapter Thirty Two

Peaches paced the floor of her home, waiting to hear from Vendetta, Spooky, Chi-Chi, or Ashaad. She had so many things going on at once, and not knowing what was happening, or being able to control events, was extremely nerve racking to her. She was used to being large and in charge. She wasn't used to having to sit around and wait on circumstances or events to take their course. She was proactive by nature. If something needed done, then she got up off her ass and did it. And now, she found herself in unfamiliar territory. She was the boss now, and she couldn't just hit the streets with her girls and wreck shit, like in the old days. No, she had to remain in place, man the communications, coordinate, give orders, plot and strategize. It was driving her crazy.

Peaches strolled into her kitchen and popped open a chilled bottle of Cabernet Sauvignon. She poured herself a stout glass of the spirit, and took a deep, long swig. She needed to relax, she needed to calm down, she needed the type of clarity that came when one imbibed enough of the vine to summon the spirit world's guidance. What to do, she wondered. What to do next, was the even bigger question.

Peaches took another swig from her glass of wine. She had rolled the die. She had gone after Big Meech, and she had gone after Catfish. The play for Big Meech was strategic, she needed him to understand that this was war, and that she wasn't to be taken lightly. He was an old school chauvinistic pig, who thought her weak because she had a cunt between her legs. Well, he needed to be shown. He needed to be made to pause and think. She needed him to realize that at the end of the day, *he* and *she* were in Columbus together, while Kharee lived elsewhere. At the end of the day, it would be *their* men lying in the street dead, while Kharee would be lounging by his swimming pool promising support. At the end of the day, it would come down to him being Kharee's puppet, or her under boss. It didn't get any simpler than that.

As for her hit on Catfish, that was both business *and* personal. It was business, because she needed his ass out of the way, and she needed to make sure that he never threatened her life again. It was personal, because he had tried to kill her, and because Fat Momma was now laying up in a hospital in intensive care. And because of her weight, the chances of Fat Momma leaving the hospital alive, were slim to none. He had really fucked up her plans. She would now need to find someone else to keep Poocus' people in line. And she had no idea who that person would be. Or even who that person *could* be.

The phone rang, and it startled her. She rarely received telephone calls on her house phone. In fact, she didn't know why she still had one. She would have gotten rid of that thing a long time ago, if it hadn't been part of a bundle deal with her cable and internet.

Peaches hurried to her telephone, pressed the answer button, and lifted it to her ear.

"Hello?"

"Peach."

"Chesarae!" she shouted. "Where the fuck are you?"

"I'm still in Ohio," he told her.

"Chesarae, I need you here!" Peaches told him. "I need you to get here right now!"

"I can't," he told her. "I got some things I gotta handle here first."

"Chesarae, we're at war!" Peaches shouted. "I'm getting hit from all directions! I need you."

"Omar got hit," Chesarae told her.

"Oh my God!" Peaches exclaimed. "Don't tell me he's..."

"He's okay," Chesarae told her.   "He made it. And then they tried to hit him again at the hospital."

"Are you serious? Who?"

"Who you think?" Chesarae asked. "We're in Detroit."

"Oh my God, " Peaches exclaimed, resting her hand on her chest. She took another deep swallow of wine. "Are you okay?"

"Yeah," he told her. "They came after me too, but I got away. I went to see Omar in the hospital, and old boy sent a hit squad up to the hospital to finish the job."

"I told you!" Peaches said, shaking her head. "Dammit, Chesarae, I told you! I told you that shit wasn't the same, and I told you to stay the fuck away from up there!"

"You were right," Chesarae said softly.

"Wait, what was that?" Peaches asked. "I can't believe you actually said that. I can't believe that you actually admitted that I was right, and you were wrong."

"I didn't say that I was wrong," Chesarae told her. "I just said that you were right."

"I should have known."

"What's going on down there?"

"We got hit," Peaches told him. "And we got hit hard. Trap's in intensive care."

"What?"

"Car bomb," Peaches explained.

"Where's Ashaad?" Chesarae asked.

"At the hospital with her. "He's okay. But he's staying by her side."

"Dammit!" Chesarae shouted.

"It's been a pretty bad couple of days," Peaches told him. "I need you here."

"I'll be there as soon as I can," he told her. "I need to handle some things up here first."

"Ches, get out of Detroit as fast as you can!" Peaches shouted. "Things aren't the same. Hassan has that town on lock down. That's his town now. They are loyal to him. He's going to kill you if you stay."

"You're underestimating me, and you're overestimating Hassan," Chesarae told her. "Detroit is *my* town, and ain't nobody running me out of it."

"You didn't listen before, will you please just listen to me now?" Peaches pleaded.

"I'll be there, Peach. Right now, I can do both of us a lot of good by being here, and by building up my power base here."

Peaches exhaled. "Ches, I really need you."

"What's going on? Are you okay?"

"I'm okay. Better now that I've heard from your ass." Peaches began to sniffle and tear up. "I thought you were dead. I got a note saying that you were dead."

"Okay, okay, calm down, Baby," Chesarae said softly. "I'm okay. It's going to be okay."

"And they said that Omar was dead," Peaches continued. "And that Joaquin was dead."

"Have you heard from Joaquin?"

"Finally, yes," Peaches said, sniffling, and wiping away her tears.

"I'm sorry, baby," Chesarae said softly. "I had no idea. I didn't know. I just didn't know."

"I don't want to lose you," Peaches told him. "I just got you back, and I can't lose you again, Ches."

"I know," Chesarae said softly. "I can't lose you either, Peach. I don't know what I would do if something happened to you."

"Hurry up and get here, Ches," Peaches told him. "I just need to see you. I just want to hug you. I need to put my arms around you and see that you're okay."

"I understand," Chesarae told her. "I'll be there as soon as I can. Just give me some time."

"Fat Momma is..." Peaches caught herself. Chesarae didn't know that Fat Momma was now working for her. He had no idea that she was trying to build up an organization, or who was a part of it. She would have to break all of that down to him in due time.

"What's up, babe?"

"Nothing," Peaches told him. "Just be careful. Kharee is out there, Hassan is out there, and no telling who else. I've made some enemies Ches. Some powerful ones. And they'll kill you, just to fuck with me. They'll kill you, just to take away some of my strength."

Peach, you just keep your head down," Chesarae told her. "Stay low until I get there. Just stay at the crib. When I get back, we'll start dealing with this shit, and take care of these muthafuckas one by one. You hear me?"

Peaches thought about the direction of the conversation for a few moments. It gave her pause. Yes, she wanted Chesarae back home safely, and yes she would love to have his counsel and comfort. But she didn't want him to think that she was going to move over and become the dutiful wife once he came back into town. That was not what she was asking for. She wanted him to be *safe*, and knowing that he was safe would take one more piece of stress off of her. That was it. She didn't want him to step out of prison and get fucked off by a jealous ass nigga who he thought was his homeboy, nor did she want him to get fucked off because of her shit.

"We'll handle them, Peach," Chesarae repeated.

"Okay," she said softly.

"Be careful," Chesarae said softly. He wanted to say that he loved her. It was the word not said, but implied just as well.

"Be careful, Babe," Peaches told him. She too didn't feel comfortable uttering those three little words. She was uncertain where they stood, and didn't know where she wanted them to stand. She wasn't going back, that was for certain. She was never going to move backwards. She had long ago outgrown her status as the dutiful baller's wifey. She was the boss in her own right, and she was determined to keep it that way.

Peaches disconnected the call, and stared at the phone. Her mind shifted to Darius. She felt a tiny tinge of guilt about the conversation she

267

just had. The words not spoken but implied, made her feel as though she were cheating. She was not that chick to play two guys, or to lead two guys on. One day, after all of this mess was over with, she would have to decide between the two. But that was a long ways away. Right now, she had to focus on today, and the task immediately before her. That task was survival. She had bitten off way more than she could chew, and now she was in a desperate struggle for survival.

*****

Ashaad caressed Traps hand. He was seated by her bedside, and hadn't left it since she arrived at the hospital. He sat quietly caressing her hand and her arm, thinking about the things they done, and the things they had yet to do. He thought about his life, and their life together. Mostly, he thought about the things not said.

Ashaad had told Trap that he loved her. But upon reflection, he felt as though he hadn't said it enough. He should have said it every day, he thought. He should have sung it to her in the morning, and whispered it to her every evening. He grew up hard on the streets, and he was taught to believe that real niggaz didn't show emotions. And so although he loved Trap with all of his heart, he had a hard time saying it. He showed it, but rarely, actually said it. And now, he was having second thoughts about that.

"Trap, you got to come back to me, baby," Ashaad whispered. "I can't do this without you. I can't even think about a life without you. I can't imagine playing X Box, or chilling and smoking a blunt in the hot tub, or muahfuckin gettin on my bike and just hitting the wind. I can't imagine doing any of the shit we do together, you know, doing it without you. I ain't ready for you to go yet, T. I know it sounds like some selfish ass shit, and maybe it is. But I need you. I need you here for me."

Ashaad exhaled. He was trying to find the right words to say, but they came hard for him.

"I don't about tomorrow, baby," Ashaad continued. "I don't know about the next day, or the next day, or the day after that. I can't even think about waking up without you. I need for you to *fight*, Baby. I need for you to fight for us, for me, for tomorrow, for *our* tomorrow. There's so much shit we ain't done yet, and I can't do it without you. I *won't* do it without you. We supposed to hit the road, baby. We supposed to go to Disney World, and to the Grand Canyon, and to Cozumel, and to the Atlantis shit you always talking about. I ain't down for no dolphin trying to hump on ya leg and shit, but I'll still take you there. I just need for you to come back to me, Baby. Come back to me, T."

Trap stirred in her bed. Ashaad's eyes went wide. The nurse said that they had reduced her morphine to nearly nothing, and that her oxygen levels were good. They had reduced the amount of assistance that the machine was providing by a significant margin, and Trap was basically breathing on her own. They just wanted her to take the final steps before pulling her off of the machine completely.

"I love you, T," Ashaad whispered. "I know that I don't say it as much as I should. But that doesn't mean I don't *feel* it, Baby. I love you with all of my soul. Without you, there is no me."

Trap moaned, and she opened her eyes. Her vision was blurred, but she recognized the direction from which Ashaad's voice was coming. She turned in his direction. Ashaad laid his head on her bed and burst into tears.

Trap could feel the tube in her throat, and slowly she began to take in some of her surroundings. Her vision was still blurred, but she recognized enough to realize that she was in a hospital, and she knew that Ashaad was crying next to her bed. She lifted her hand and rested it on top of his head. It only made Ashaad cry even harder. He lifted her hand, and began to kiss it. He kissed each of her fingers, the back of her hand, the palm of her hand, and then interlaced their fingers together. He wasn't a praying man, but he began to thank God for bringing her back into his life, if even for this moment. He thanked God for the opportunity to tell her one more time how he felt about her.

"I love you, Trap," Ashaad said through his tears, after he had finished praying. "I love you so much that it hurts."

A tear rolled out of the corner of her eye, and when Ashaad saw it, he began crying even harder. He knew that she had heard him. And even more importantly, he knew that she loved him with all of her heart as well.

Chapter Thirty Three

Brandon Reigns sat in his office staring at his telephone. He had weighed his options many times since that night his men informed him of what was going on in Ohio. He mulled over calling Dante and filling him in. But doing that would only cause The Commission to doubt Peaches and her ability to control her state. Which would have some on The Commission griping about her, and wanting The Commission to kill her and bring in a replacement. And that would cause a two fold headache. One, because the Reigns family had backed her, supported her selection, and pushed for her admission to The Commission, and two, his little cousin Darius had fallen head over heals for the chick. The second one was perhaps even worse than the first.

Brandon knew that Dante and Damian knew nothing of their brother's fling with Peaches. And the thought of their brother having a relationship with a member of The Commission, especially *that* one, would do nothing but complicate things. What if they need to spank her, or kill her off, what would happen then? What would the other members of The Commission say, if they knew that she was fooling with Damian's younger brother. Every vote she took as part of The Commission would be suspect. On top of that, it was coming at a time when the family was

271

trying to disengage from any and all extemporaneous activities and engagements. They didn't need any more entanglements. Damian was trying to give up territory, and reduce the family's commitments. Taking on another commitment in Ohio, was not something they would be inclined to do. Brandon knew that Princess had warned Darius off, and told him to stay clear of Peaches. But he had went ahead full steam and pursued her anyway.

And *then* there was the matter of Peaches herself. The Commission believed that she was basically in control of the state. If they had known otherwise, she wouldn't have been offered the seat on The Commission for the state. They would have chosen someone more powerful, someone in a better position, and would have simply helped that person bump her off. But since they had backed her, and they had allowed her into the fold, she now knew too much. And the punishment for knowing too much, was death. They couldn't just kick her off of The Commission and replace her. No, they would surely kill her. She saw their faces, she now knew of their existence, she saw how they operated. No, she knew too much to survive now. And that left his young, brash, love struck cousin in a very precarious position.

Darius would certainly do something stupid or rash if he knew that The Commission was going to off his new found love. Perhaps warn her off, perhaps fly to Ohio to be by her side and test his brother's hand, or maybe even try to run away with her. Any of those things would put his life in danger as well, and that was unacceptable. Unacceptable to Damian, unacceptable to Dante, unacceptable to Princess, and unacceptable to him. No, there had to be another way.

Brandon stared at the telephone for what seemed an eternity, before finally deciding on a course of action. If he couldn't kill her off, or risk his cousin's life, then their was really only one other solution. To quietly try to help her. To quietly try to influence events in her favor. But how to do so, was a baffling, if not daunting proposition. His men were *his* men, but many of them were also loyal to Damian, and Dante, and the main branch of the Reigns family. The challenge would be to try to influence her, without anyone finding out, especially his cousins. It was quite the dilemma.

Brandon leaned forward and lifted the phone from his desk. He dialed up one of the numbers that he had on speed dial. It rang in Texas.

"Hello?"

"Darius, what up my dude?"

"Brandon? What's up, kinfolk?"

"Are you alone?" Brandon asked. "Can you talk right now?"

"Yeah, it's all good, what's the deal?"

"You need to get your ass up to Philly," Brandon told him.

"Philly? What's up, B?"

"Listen to me," Brandon told him. "Things in Ohio, ain't what they seem. You know what I'm saying?"

"What are you talking about?" Darius asked, suspiciously.

"I'm talking about old girl, kinfolk. Things in Ohio ain't what they were made out to be. Old girl is in the middle of a big ass war."

"*What?*"

"Calm down," Brandon told him. "Look, you can't get distracted. I need you to clear your head, and listen to me. Listen carefully, kinfolk. Can you do that?"

"Yeah," Darius told him. His mind was still on Peaches. *What the fuck was going on? Was she okay?* Those were just two of the questions that he had.

"I want you to get up here," Brandon told him. "I want you to get up here tonight. But first, I need for you to round up some soldiers. Not just any soldiers, but people you can trust. People who ain't gonna run back and tell what's going on, you got me?"

"I got you, B."

"You get them, and you get up here," Brandon told him. "You get to Philly, and I'm going to have some loyal guys waiting for you. I'm going to put you guys on a plane to Columbus, and you are going to see what the hell is going on. And we are going to quietly tip the scales on this thing, in old girl's favor. It needs to be done quickly, and quietly, before anyone else has a chance to find out. Damian or Dante or Princess find out, the gig is up. Anyone on The Commission finds out, and it's lights out for old girl. You understand that, right?"

Darius closed his eyes and bit down on his lip. He understood it all too well. If The Commission found out that she was engaged in a full blown war, she would be dead within a week. They hated that kind of attention. And they would kill anyone who brought it upon them. "I got you."

"Get some loyal men, and get up here," Brandon told him.

*****

Darius' flight landed at Philadelphia International Airport with thirty men on board. Some were cousins, most were not. All were loyal to him, and all were going to keep quiet. The sight of 30 Black men all dressed in business suits, was a disturbing prospect to many traipsing through the airport. The sight of those 30 well dressed Black men, linking up with another 30 impeccably dressed Black men seemed down right frightening to many of the airport's patrons. Brandon and his thirty soldiers, met up with Darius and his thirty men in the middle of the concourse. It was a surreal scene. Homeland Security was freaking out.

"Lil Cuz!" Brandon said, opening his arms and embracing Darius.

"What's up, B?" Darius said, wrapping his arms around his cousin.

"C'mon, we can talk in the private lounge," Brandon told him. "You're guys can follow my men out onto the tarmac. I've rented a private jet to fly all of you into Columbus. It'll be quieter that way."

Darius turned and nodded toward his men, indicating for them to follow the others. They lifted their bags and followed Brandon's men.

Brandon sequestered Darius into a private corner of the airport's VIP lounge. "You'll arrive this evening. I don't think you should contact her right away. You have reservations at the Hyatt in downtown Columbus. You'll be there under the guise of a 100 Black Men convention. So many Black men congregating in one place is sure to cause attention. So that'll be your cover."

Darius nodded. "Good cover."

"When you get there, find out what's going on, *before* you make contract with her," Brandon continued. "It would be better, if you could do what needs to be done, without her even knowing about it. The less people know, and the quicker it's done, the better it'll be for her. But the key, is to end it quickly. End it, before anyone knows you're there. The longer we're in there, the greater the chance of someone finding out. Your objective is clear and simple, end the war in Columbus, and end it in her favor. And then get the hell outta there. We have a couple of days before Damian starts calling you and asking you where you're at. We have a week at most, before the family starts missing all of these soldiers. Dante is tied up right now in the search for Lucky, but Damian will definitely be aware of your absence, and theirs as well. Got me?"

Darius nodded. Brandon knew his shit, that was for certain.

"If you get into a jam, and need some guidance, I got some good men with you," Brandon told him. "Also, don't hesitate to pick up the phone and call me anytime. *Anytime!* Is that clear?"

Darius nodded.

Brandon nodded toward the waiting charter plane. "Get out of here. Keep your head down. There's no way I could explain it to your brothers if you got killed fucking around in Ohio with a bunch of my soldiers. It'll not only be your ass, but mines and your little girlfriend's as well."

"Thanks, cuz," Darius said, embracing Brandon.

"I hope she's worth it," Brandon told him.

"She is," Darius said nodding. He turned, and hurried off to the waiting jet.

Chapter Thirty Four

The MGM Grand Hotel in Detroit was something to be experienced. It was a massive hotel and casino venture, with numerous luxury retailers, more than six bars and lounges, and six restaurants, including no less than two owned by world renown chef Wolfgang Puck. The hotel's casinos held close to 4000 slot machines, and nearly 100 gaming tables. The hotel itself boasted numerous luxury suites, as well as amenities so numerous as that even the most discerning of clientele was sure to be impress. One such luxury amenity, was the hotel's world renowned spa.

The spa at the MGM Grand Hotel encompassed numerous rooms for personal massages, several hot tubs, and even quite a few private steam rooms. It was in one of these steam rooms where today's meeting was to be held. Kharee wrapped one of the hotel's plush towels around his waist, and proceeded into one of the private rooms. His host was already inside.

"You're late," Malcom 'Baby Doc' Mueller said gruffly.

"My apologies," Kharee told him. "Traffic was terrible."

"Traffic?" Baby Doc huffed. "In this abandoned ass city? Are you fucking kidding me? I can see that we're already starting this meeting off on the wrong foot. Which tells me that pretty much everything else you're going to say is going to be bullshit."

Kharee seated himself on the soft wooden bench across from Baby Doc. They were alone in the sauna, but there was no doubt in his mind that Baby Doc had the entire hotel filled with his men. And at a snap of his fingers, they would be inside of the room with guns drawn in a heartbeat.

"So, what's the deal?" Baby Doc asked. He pulled out a fat Cuban cigar, lit it, and blew rings of smoke into the air.

"The deal with what?" Kharee asked.

"Are you stupid, or just stupid?" Baby Doc asked. "What the fuck do you think we're here to talk about? Columbus, numb nuts! What's the deal with fucking Columbus?"

"I'm working on it," Kharee told him.

"Well, apparently you're not working on it fast enough!" Baby Doc shouted. "What's this I hear about her bumping off Bug, and Sweet Pea, and Poocus? Is this true?"

Kharee wiped beads of sweat from his brow. The steam in the room was already having an effect on him. "Yeah, it's true."

"Are you fucking kidding me?" Baby Doc shouted.

"She did it," Kharee said, shrugging his shoulders nonchalantly. "I don't know how the fuck she pulled it off, but she did it. Look, they were idiots. Stupid ass muthafuckas who couldn't find their asses with a funnel. She took advantage of their stupidity, caught them slipping, and whacked 'em."

Baby Doc leaned back and puffed on his cigar. A deep scowl ran across his brow, as he began to contemplate what he was being told.

"Perhaps, I underestimated this broad," Baby Doc mused. "Perhaps I *overestimated* you."

Kharee leaned back. "What's that supposed to mean?"

"It means, that maybe *I* backed the wrong nigga for a position on The Commission, and maybe *the Reigns family* backed the right one," Baby Doc told him. "I thought that she was a nothing, a nobody, somebody who wouldn't last a day by herself. You said the first sign of trouble, she would wet her pants and go running for the hills."

"Okay, maybe she was a little tougher than I thought," Kharee said.

"But for the most part, she's lasted, because she been going up against the B-Team. She hasn't fully felt what I'm going to bring to her."

"What you're going to bring to her?" Baby Doc asked with a smile. "What the fuck are you waiting on, and invitation? You just told me that this chick has run all of her competition out of town! Maybe you're a little slow and not understanding what that means, so let me break it down to you. The door to Columbus is now open for her. She can consolidate her hold on that shit, and lock it down. If she locks down Columbus, then the game is all over with. She takes Columbus, then that means the entire city becomes her recruiting zone. The entire city buys from her, and *only* her, filling up her war chest. She has Columbus all to herself, Dayton won't be able to stand the pressure. It'll fall. Then Youngstown, then Cleveland, and then Cincinnati, and then the rest of the state, and she'll control all of Ohio. Understand?"

Kharee nodded.

Baby Doc leaned forward, and blew smoke into Kharee's face. "I don't think you do. She controls Ohio, do you know what that means for me? Let me explain. The Reigns family backed her, so that means she *owes them*. Princess will take her under her wing, and that will give those stupid fucks another voice on The Commission who'll vote with them. And I don't want them *gaining* power, I want them *losing* power. Understand, ass wad?"

Kharee frowned. "You're overreacting."

"Quit playing with your dick, Dip Shit!" Baby Doc shouted. "Get this bitch while she's still trying to consolidate. Her people are wounded, she's lost some key people, she's emotional like most broads are, hit her now while she's pissing in her pants!"

"It didn't work," Kharee said under his breath.

"What?" Baby Doc asked, leaning forward.

Kharee shook his head. "I said, it didn't work. I went after her. I took out her people, I manipulated the situation, I followed your advice, and the shit didn't happen. Her dude is still alive. Her ace, Black Ass Omar, is still alive. Her girl, Trap, her entire fucking hit team, they're all still alive."

Baby Doc leaned back. "You gotta be fucking kidding me. What is this? Amateur hour at the Apollo? What? I need to hold your fucking hand in this thing? How hard can it be to kill one bitch? One?"

"Not as easy as you think!" Kharee shot back. "Her people are loyal, I can't get to them. They won't betray her. She's sitting up in a fucking mansion in Dublin, and that place is like a fucking fortress. She has dozens of soldiers guarding her, she has a big ass guard house, dogs patrolling everywhere, fucking cameras all over the place, I can't get to her. Even if that shit would have worked, I still wouldn't be able to get to *her.*"

"If you can't get to her, then you don't deserve the Ohio seat on The Commission," Baby Doc said flatly. "If it's one thing that I've learned in all my years, it's that everyone can be gotten to. *Everyone.* What I also know, is that your window is closing. You want the seat on The Commission, then you gotta take it, and you gotta take it *now.* You hear me? *Now!* No more pussy footing around."

Baby Doc lifted his arm and pointed South. "Right now, the entire fucking Reigns family is busy, looking for Dante's little girl. Every soldier they have, every resource they have, is going toward finding that little girl. This is the opportunity of a lifetime. But once they find that little girl, dead or alive, then the search will be over, and their attention will turn back toward other shit. And what they are going to start wondering, is why this little girl hasn't taken over all of Ohio yet. And if they start digging deep enough, what they are going to find, is *me*. They are going to learn that I've been involved knee deep in keeping this little bitch from consolidating her power. What they are going to find, is my soldiers here in Ohio, supporting your ass, and that sorry ass Big Meech. God only knows where that fuck is now. But what I don't want found out, is that I crossed the decision of The Commission who voted to admit her ass. If they find *that* out, then it'll be my ass hanging out in the wind. And I ain't gonna let that happen. You kill that bitch, and you kill her tonight, or you won't be alive much longer. You got that?"

"What they fuck?" Kharee shouted, rising from his bench. He wasn't one to take threats lightly. He was a man, and he had built up an drug empire with his own spunk. And nobody threatened him. Especially a fat piece of shit whose head he could rip off with his bare hands.

"Sit your five dollar ass down, before I make change!" Baby Doc told him.

Kharee scowled at Baby Doc for a few seconds, before finally re-taking his seat. He would deal with Baby Doc's disrespect in due time. But right now, he needed the fat fuck to help him get a seat on The Commission. But he definitely wouldn't forget today, or all of the other times he had been disrespected.

"I'm not getting into a war with the entire Commission, because I picked the Gang That Couldn't Shoot Straight," Baby Doc told him. "I want this shit over with. It ends... *tonight*."

"I don't have the manpower to end this thing tonight!" Kharee said through clenched teeth. "Ending this would mean taking out her girls, all of her under bosses, all of her key lieutenants, and taking her out as well. And I already told you, she lives in a house that's guarded like Fort Knox!"

"Her under bosses?" Baby Doc asked, lifting an eyebrow.

"Yeah," Kharee said nodding. "She pulled in Bug's people, Poocus' people, and Sweet Pea's people. She folded them all into her organization. You can do the math. Combine all of them with her own people, and she matches me in strength."

"And Big Meech?" Baby Doc asked.

"She hit him yesterday," Kharee said. "Last anyone seen of Big Meech, her was headed to Chicago."

Again, Baby Doc leaned back in frustration and shifted his weight. "You gotta be fucking kidding me."

"I can take her out," Kharee told him. "I can win this war. I *will* win this war! I just need to continue pulling in men and getting bigger."

"It'll be too late!" Baby Doc shouted. "She'll have all of Columbus. I thought I just explained that to you. And with Big Meech out of the picture, she'll really consolidate her hold on that shit. If what you just told me is true, then right now, she basically controls Columbus by default. She is that last man standing. And once she consolidates her hold on that city, you won't be able to match her manpower, or money. She has to be stopped, before that happens. Like I said before, this shit ends tonight!"

"How?" Kharee shouted, turning up his palms. "Do you have a magic fucking lamp somewhere? *I don't have the manpower!*"

"I do," Baby Doc said coldly.

"Gather your men, and hit her lieutenants," Baby Doc said, staring off into space. "Leave this so called fortress to me. You say she has a couple of dozen men? They won't be able to hold off against sixty well armed, well trained men storming that place. I'll take care of Baby Doll, you just get her flunkies."

"I still need time to get my people into place," Kharee told him.

Baby Doc lifted his arm and peered down at his Patek Phillipe watch. "You have five hours to get your men into place."

Kharee leaned back against the wooden walls of the sauna and closed his eyes. He thought about what was about to take place. Baby Doc had backed him. Baby Doc had supplied him with men, money, know how, political protection, and so much more. He had his own army, but he had fucked up, and allowed Baby Doc to bring in just as many men as he had, into his territory. And so now he found himself at Baby Doc's mercy. All in the name of weakening this fucking Reigns family, and getting back at them for killing his boy out in California.

Kharee rubbed his eyes. He was feeling energetic when he walked into the sauna, but now he felt tired. It was as if he had aged ten years while inside. Baby Doc wanted him to pull his entire army from all across the state, and send it into Columbus. It was a giant, bloody, pitched battle that was going to leave bodies piled up four feet high. It was a battle that could make or break him. If he lost, his army would be broken, and he could lose everything that he had worked so hard for. And if he won, then he would have the State of Ohio to himself, and its valuable seat on The Commission. The rewards were great, the risk even greater. But what troubled him greatly at this moment wasn't the risk, but the aftermath. Baby Doc would still have an army in Ohio. And he would owe Baby Doc his loyalty on The Commission. He had made a deal with the devil, and now the devil was ordering him to put up or shut up. It was time to dance.

"Five hours is enough time," Kharee said softly. It was now his turn to stare off into space. He thoughts were on his Grandmother, and her ageless wisdom. She would always tell her grandchildren that if you danced with the devil, you were sure to get burned. The band had struck up the music, and now this fat ass devil sitting in the sauna with him, wanted to waltz.

Chapter Thirty Five

Peaches breezed through her living room wearing her PJs, on her way to the kitchen to fix her a cup of yogurt ice cream. The day had been a busy day, but a good one. It was the best day she had had in the last week or so. Ashaad had called with good news about Trap. She was awake, and the doctors were planning on taking her completely off of the ventilator any time now. Fat Momma was still alive and holding on. It would be a fight, and the doctors had expected her to have passed by now. But miraculously, Fat Momma was still alive.

Peaches was also rejoicing because Joaquin was safe. Having to bury her baby brother would have taken her as well. There was no way she could have survived long after putting him into the ground. Not in any recognizable form. Burying Joaquin would have taken her mind from her. And then there was the fact that Omar and Chesarae were both alive as well. They had tried to get at Omar, but he had survived their attempts. And so had Chesarae. Her people were alive, and her enemies were on the run, and that's what made it a good day. She was free to mop up the small pockets of resistance, and then build her family up. It would not take long before she would be able to take on Kharee.

285

Peaches opened up her freezer, pulled out a bucket of creamy frozen yogurt, and then pulled a bowl from her cabinet. She popped the top off of the frozen treat, pulled a spoon from her dishwasher, and then began to scoop her frozen dessert into her bowl. Once finished, she sealed the top back on it, and then put the yogurt back inside of her freezer. She was just about to indulge when her door bell rang.

Peaches exhaled, and sat the spoon down in her bowl. She walked across her kitchen floor, through her living room, and into her foyer, where she threw open her front door.

"Bitch, you'll fuck up a wet dream," Peaches told her.

Vendetta stepped inside. "You ain't got no dick up in here, so whatever it is, you can stop it and open up the door for ya girl."

Peaches slapped Vendetta on her ass as she walked by.

"Bitch, what are you up too?" Vendetta asked, peering around.

"About to fuck Ben and Jerry," Peaches told her.

Vendetta laughed. "Uh-un. I'mma have to get in on some a that action."

"C'mon, greedy ass," Peaches said, leading Vendetta into the kitchen.

"Uh-un, look at you!" Vendetta said, after spying Peaches' enormous bowl of frozen yogurt. "No you didn't call *me* the greedy bitch."

Peaches lifted her spoon and gobbled some of her frozen cream. "You know where it is."

Vendetta walked around Peaches, opened the freezer, and pulled out the gallon of frozen yogurt ice cream. She pulled open the dishwasher, pulled out a bowl and a spoon, and then began to scoop her some frozen yogurt into the bowl.

"Go easy on my shit," Peaches told her.

"You big baller, you can buy some more," Vendetta told her.

Peaches carried her bowl into her family room, plopped down on the sectional, and then turned on her television. Soon, Vendetta joined her.

"Bitch, what you watching?"

"Love and Hip Hop Atlanta," Peaches told her, pulling up her legs and getting comfortable. "Girl, I got to see what Stevie and Jocelyn asses is up to now!"

"Girl, did you see the Real Housewives last week?" Vendetta asked.

"Naw, I Tivo'd that shit though!" Peaches howled. "Girl, don't you tell me shit about it!"

"I ain't," Vendetta smiled. "Whew, ain't been this happy in days."

Peaches turned to her friend and smiled. "I know, right?"

"That bitch ass Big Meech ran like a little bitch," Vendetta said laughing. "I heard that nigga hit the road and kept going. Didn't stop to change cars, fix a flat, get a change a clothes, nothing!"

Peaches joined in the laughter. She and Vendetta hi-fived one another.

"That muthafucka was ducking down in that seat like a nigga eating pussy!" Vendetta shouted.

"Girl, I wish I could've been there!" Peaches said, howling laughing.

"Chi-Chi handled Catfish, huh?" Vendetta asked.

Peaches nodded. "Quick and clean. Put that bitch to rest right on top of his boyfriend's grave."

"Should have dug a hole, and threw his ass right on top of that nigga," Vendetta said, laughing. "Girl, you know that's where he wanted to be. I swear they acted like they was fucking."

"Hell, they probably was," Peaches said, laughing. "You never know now days."

"All right, all right, all right!" Vendetta said, in her best Kevin Hart impression.

Peaches and Vendetta broke into uncontrollable laughter. For the first time in a long time, they were really able to laugh and get back to being themselves. Their laughter lasted only until they heard the first burst of automatic rifle fire.

"What the fuck?" Vendetta jumped up off of the sofa, and raced to the front window. She peered outside, and she could see Peaches' men running, pointing, and pulling weapons. "Something's going down, P! Stay in here! I'll be right back."

Vendetta pulled out the drawer of the credenza that Peaches had in her foyer. She removed a 9mm Glock from the drawer, cocked it, locked the bottom lock on Peaches' front door, and then raced outside.

Peaches raced to her kitchen, grabbed her iPad off of the wall, and then raced back into her family room, where she used the iPad to put the feed from her security cameras onto her big screen television. She could see chaos outside.

Vendetta raced to where Peaches' men were taking cover near the guardhouse at the entrance to her property. Someone with good sense, had broken out the AR-15 assault rifles and passed them out, while others had rallied themselves and formed a defensive perimeter to the West. She could hear a massive firefight taking place.

"What the fuck is going on?" Vendetta asked one of the guards running by with an assault rifle.

"The western perimeter has been breached!" the man shouted. "Two Hummers crashed through the wall, and dozens of men poured through the breach!"

A massive explosion went off to the East. They were both knocked to the ground. Vendetta peered up to see an enormous fireball rising up into the sky.

"Jesus!"

A massive siren went off, followed by flashing lights, and then a loud klaxon alarm. A second explosion rocked the ground, followed by another enormous fireball. It looked like something out of Iraq or Afghanistan.

A group of Peaches' men raced by, and Vendetta grabbed one. "What the fuck is going on?"

"They just breached the Eastern perimeter!" the man shouted. He was nearly in a panic. "They're everywhere! They're pouring over the walls like fucking roaches! Get the hell outta here!"

Vendetta ran into the guardhouse, grabbed the lone AR-15 from off of the wall, grabbed some full clips, and then raced off to the East to go and help.

Inside, Peaches worked her cameras. She could see them, all of them. There were dozens of them, all heavily armed, all dressed in black, with black balaclava mask covering their faces. They had crashed vehicles into the western wall that guarded her property, and blew a hole in the eastern wall. And now, they were climbing the fence and coming over the southern wall.

"Fuck this!" Peaches tossed the iPad onto the couch, raced into her master closet, and pulled out her baby. It was a Heckler & Koch G36C. But it was no ordinary G36, she had her's modified to fire .308 Winchester caliber rounds, or 7.62 X 51mm. It was like an AK-47 bullet on steroids.

Peaches pulled back the bolt on her G36, chambering a round. She raced out of her bedroom, to her great room, just in time to catch some of the attackers creeping around her swimming pool. She lifted her weapon and let loose.

The 7.62 X 51mm round tore through her walls and windows and reached out to her attackers. The massive bullets didn't just take off chunks of flesh, but took off entire limbs. One attacker lost an arm, another a leg, and a third lost his entire left side. The massive tumbling bullets put a hole where one attacker's chest used to be, while another hit home making sure that the last attacker would have to have a closed casket funeral. Peaches let her rounds fly with a vengeance, sending bodies falling into her swimming pool, quickly turning the water crimson red.

"C'mon, you muthafuckas!" Peaches screamed. "C'mon!"

Outside, Vendetta and five of Peaches' men made it to the East side of her estate. They took up positions behind water fountains, and quickly let loose on the men pouring in from the eastern breech.

"There's too many of them!" one of the bodyguards shouted.

Vendetta was in full agreement with him. They were pouring through the wall like ants. And these were just the ones coming through the eastern wall. The other bodyguard had told her that they were pouring through the wall like roaches on the West side as well. She hoped that Peaches had called the cops. They needed help, and they needed help *fast*. The best they could do is to try and hold them off for a little while, maybe kill enough of them to give them pause. Deep down, she knew that it was a false hope. They had came in numbers, and you don't come with these kind of numbers unless you're determined to get what you

289

came for. They were here tonight, to end the war with Peaches. They were here tonight, to kill everyone at the estate, including her.

Inside of the mansion, Peaches was holding her own. She was blowing limbs off of whatever came over the wall and into her backyard. She was even taking people out through the fence. Nothing could stop the force of the bullet that she was spitting out, it was just too powerful. And then, something equally powerful came her way. One of them managed to lob a flash bang grenade onto her back porch.

The power of the grenade shattered her back windows, and the percussion sent shock waves around her. The loud flash disoriented her enough to allow several men to scale the wall and take cover behind various statues and fountains in her backyard. They now had a foothold.

Peaches cleared her eyes, but the ringing in her ears still persisted. Fortunately for her, the grenade landed far enough away, that she was still coherent and able to put up a fight. She dusted the glass from off of her body, lifted her weapon, and started firing again. Although this time, she was taking fire back from the men who had managed to take cover in her yard. The fight was now three rifles against her one. And every time she took cover from one of their rifle blast, another man would scale the wall. Soon, the numbers against her would be too great. The rear perimeter of her yard had fallen.

Outside, Vendetta began to slowly pull back from her first position. They were closing in on them from all sides. She could see that the guys defending the West side of the estate were fairing no better. They were defending a smaller and smaller area, and soon, their perimeter would encompass the only main residence. She hoped that Peaches was okay. Her answer came soon enough.

Peaches fired and fired, and was giving as good as she was getting. The numbers against her were piling up, but it didn't matter. She was going to fight it out until help arrived. She still heard plenty of gunfire outside, which told her that her men were still fighting, and that gave her hope. She was hoping that Vendetta was okay. And then, a massive explosion ripped through her house, knocking her off of her feet. Dust and debris flew through the room, and a fireball rolled over her head. She turned and peered down the hall in the direction from which the explosion came. Her furniture was strewn all over the place, and her home was now on fire. She could feel a breeze coming from down the hall, and soon, she caught her first glimpse of one of her attackers. They had blown a hole in a wall on the West side of her home. They were now inside.

Peaches rose, and took off running. She caught two rounds and fell. She rolled over and fired back, killing the guy who had just shot her.

"Get up, bitch!" Peaches screamed. She used the butt of her rifle to help herself stand. And then she quickly took cover in a half bath in the gallery. She was bleeding bad. So much of her blood had ran down her leg that her completely soaked PJs made a sloshing sound whenever she moved. The bullets had ripped through her side.

Outside, Vendetta saw the massive explosion rip through the air, and saw chunks of the mansion fly up into the evening sky. That told her enough. The mansion had been breached. They had lost the battle. Tears rolled down her cheeks.

Vendetta didn't know what her next steps should be. She was now running low on ammo, and all she had were two more clips for the assault rifle, and a full clip in the handgun she had taken from the desk inside. She needed to get to the house. She needed to get to her friend. If this was it, and if they were going to die, then they were going to die together. Vendetta turned toward the men she had fighting with her. She knew that they were pretty much out of ammo as well.

"Cover me," she told them. They peered at one another, each understanding what she was about to do. All of them knew that they were going to die, and all of them understood that she was about to go on a suicide mission by running into that mansion. They respected her for it. They knew that she wanted to die fighting with her sister. The men nodded.

Vendetta turned to run, and that was when the percussion grenade went off. It threw her ten feet into the air, and twenty feet from where she had been crouched down. The bright lights from the grenade was the last thing she saw.

Inside, Peaches was sweating and bleeding profusely. She too, was now low on ammo, and masked men were pouring into her mansion. If they breached the master bedroom wall, then it was all over but the shouting. She had to get to her master bedroom. She had to get to the master bedroom closet. She could feel the blood running out of her, she could feel herself growing thirsty, and she was growing more and more tired with each passing second. Soon, she would pass out from blood loss. It was now or never.

Peaches lifted her rifle, and let loose a barrage of gunfire down the hall and into her living area. The massive rounds from her rifle went through walls and furniture like a hot knife through butter. She decimated men, wood, drywall, and furniture all at the same time. She could hear screaming. It was her opportunity.

Peaches ran with all that she had left in her, into her master bedroom, and then into her walk-in closet. The smoke from the burning fires covered her escape, but soon, the men would realize that she was no longer there. She had but a few moments before she was discovered. Peaches pulled out the fake wall that made up her shoe shelves, and punched the code into the steel wall behind it. She practically fell into the safe room, and was barely able to hit the button that would close the fake shoe rack on the outside, once again concealing the room.

Peaches crawled to where her first aid kit was, and pulled it off of the shelf, spilling all of its contents. The last thing she remembered were the voices screaming frantically on the other side of the wall, trying to figure out where she went. The cameras in the safe room showed the men tearing her home apart searching for her. A smile ran across her face as she watched with pleasure.

"Fuck you," she said weakly. She would be content to die inside of the safe room. Just so long as those muthafuckas on the other side of that wall didn't have the pleasure of killing her, or knowing what happened to her.

"Fuck you," she repeated softly. And then Peaches closed her eyes.

*****

The bouncing and jostling woke her. She was weak. Too weak to remain conscious. She could feel muscles, strong arms. She was being carried. She could feel the rise and fall of the steps as he carried her. She could hear the crunching of glass, smell the sweet scent of smoldering flames and burnt wood. One eye opened, and then briefly another. She took in her scene in quick glimpses. Like watching old photos. They were glimpses of a place she knew. They were glimpses of what was left of her home.

With each of his steps, he brought pain to her. Her wounds still burned like they were fresh. But the pain was what kept bringing her back to consciousness. How long she had been out, she had no idea. All she knew, was that they had her. They, had somehow found her. She saw men. Black men. Dark suited men. Heavily armed, serious looking, dangerous. They had her, and yet, she was still alive. Why? She did not know. To torture her perhaps? But why so gentle. No, these were different. There was something different about these men. She was slow to put her finger on it, but she knew for certain that they weren't her men. Who?

Peaches was carried out of her destroyed home, into the night air. She was thirsty. She needed water. Something, anything to drink. She was weak, she wanted to sleep. Her eyes were growing heavy again, despite her pain. She felt the comforting peck of soft lips against her forehead, and slowly began to recognize the scent of one whom she knew. And then, she recognize the comforting whisper of his confident voice telling her that she was going to be all right.

Peaches shifted her head and used all her strength to peer into the face of the man carrying her. She could barely muster his name before she once again passed out.

"Darius..."

Thank you for reading this incredible tale, and please stay tuned for the continuation of Peaches Story; The Takeover. Also, I would greatly appreciate it, if you would stop by Amazon and leave a review. Please spread the word to your friends and family!

You can join me on Facebook. I have several pages, so if you find one that's full, you can usually find another and add me as a friend. Also, like my Facebook page at Caleb_The_Hit_Factory_Alexander. And don't forget to follow me on Twitter for updates on the continuation of the series.

Stop by my website at; **www.GoldenInkMedia.com**
You can join my mailing list there.

Coming Soon;
Deadly Reigns V
Baby Baller
Peaches Story; The Takeover 2 (Parts 4,5, &6 on e-book)
Deadly Reigns; Chi-Chi's Story
Deadly Reigns; MiAsia's Story
Boyfriend #2,; Tameka's Revenge

And don't forget to check out;

Boyfriend #2
Belly of the Beast
Eastside
Two Thin Dimes
Deadly Reigns IV

CPSIA information can be obtained at www.ICGtesting.com
Printed in the USA
BVOW05s0914240116

434044BV00001B/120/P